Praise for the Natalie McMasters Mysteries

Stripper! A Natalie McMasters Novel (2018)

***** – Extremely well written. The plot was very entertaining and the characters were well developed and likeable. Told from the first-person perspective of Natalie McMasters – the book is a real page turner. Great read! – Amazon review

***** – Excellent crime/mystery story, kept me turning the pages. Burns has created a fascinating lead character--Nattie McMasters. She's young, sexy and courageous. – Amazon review

Revenge! A Natalie McMasters Mystery (2018)

***** – A fast-paced story, Intriguing true-to-life characters with an explosive ending. Looking forward to the next book! – Amazon review

***** – This was an unexpected gem. I was fully gripped from page one to the last word as the pace was fast without much down time. Natalie was the type of character I appreciate, with dimension. While hard, and often crass, there is also a vulnerability to her that makes her more than the average cardboard sassy heroine. – Amazon review

Trafficked! A Natalie McMasters Mystery (2019)

***** – Bluntly put, this ain't your average mystery book. It's gritty, raw, and "human" in the worst way possible. And I enjoyed it every dark minute of it! – Amazon review

**** – There was blood, whipping, love making, sewer stench, a tour of Manhattan and Kosher food, honor, despair, and a healthy dollop of deceit and mystery solving. Burns is a good writer and is on to something good with his Natalie McMasters Mysteries. Amazon review

Venom! A Natalie McMasters Mystery (2020)

***** – Venom is a twisty page-turner with non-stop action and an ending you won't soon forget. Thomas Burns is adept with character and setting description. Natalie McMasters will steal your heart! .Amazon Review

***** – I have loved this exciting series from the start and this installment did not disappoint! Full of suspense and emotion Venom showed even more character development and showed a vulnerable side to them all. I was immersed in the story and invested in the outcome. Amazon Review

Sniper! A Natalie McMasters Mystery (2020)

***** – Thomas A. Burns, Jr. has written another page turner. It seems there is never a good place to put the book aside to pick it up later. SNIPER! is an emotionally charged adrenaline rush right up to the last page. .Amazon Review

***** – This was a fabulous read! I have rarely read a book this edgy and cutting, best have some Jack Daniels to chase it. With themes ripped from today's headlines, SNIPER is a tour de force ride with a troubled young woman and her unusual family and social circle. Nattie is forceful, opinionated, and quick to give in to impulses - whether to take down a bad guy, bolster a loved one or have sex. SNIPER's plot is a fast-paced collision of gun control, 2nd amendment (plus 1st and 4th amendment) rights, political correctness, mob violence, PTSD, addiction (of all kinds) and parental rights. Yet these themes move the plot, which speaks to the author's skill. Amazon Review

Killers!

A Natalie McMasters Mystery

2 June, 2022

~~Thomas A. Burns, Jr.~~

To Kate:
Please enjoy, and stay in touch.

Published by Tekrighter LLC 2021

Dedication

I think it's particularly appropriate to dedicate this book to my family, since that's what it's all about.

Either kill me or take me as I am, because I'll be damned if I ever change.

The Marquis de Sade

Prologue

Blue lights strobe and electronic alarms howl like a banshee, sending agonizing lances through my forehead. Masked, scrub-clad men vainly attempt to keep the hallway clear. Dodging an overweight rent-a-cop, I fight my way to room 302, where my friend and mentor Rebecca Feiner lies. I'm too late! The doorway is jammed with hospital workers. I push my way through the throng—Rebecca is surrounded by a crash team frantically working on her. A doctor steps aside. She's not moving! The doctor shakes his head.

OMG! Rebecca's eyes are two bloody pits! He got to her! The motherfucker got to her! And it's all my fault...

Killers!

Chapter 1

Daddy used to say to me, "When it's raining, God's crying. What did you do to make God sad, Nattie?"

My name is Natalie McMasters. I'm twenty-two (today is my birthday!), short and blonde (OK, it's bleached), a pre-law student at State and a former private detective trainee at my Uncle Amos's 3M Detective Agency. And I'm standing in a soaking rain at my best friend's funeral (which is getting to be a habit) wondering WTF I did to bring it all about.

Dr. Rebecca Feiner was my therapist, my friend, and in many ways, my surrogate mother. She helped me discover who I am, got me over a buncha Catholic baggage and comfortable in my own skin, when I discovered I liked girls as much as guys. And she helped me through the crisis when I fell in love with my best friend while married to my wife. But like others in my life, she paid a price for her friendship with me. Last year, she became the victim of a vicious sexual assault perpetrated by an asshole who wanted revenge on me. That ultimately drove her back into a sick relationship with a former zaddy, a serial killer dubbed the Marquis by the news media, named for the Marquis de Sade, because of the way he tortured his vics before killing them. He vowed vengeance on me too, because he blamed me for snatching his wig. Did he murder Rebecca as a part of that revenge?

The WOAT is that today is my birthday. Last year on my birthday, a stan of mine burned my Uncle Amos' house to the ground. Now this shit happens!

Rebecca had no fam, so I decided to bury her in College Cemetery, a historical graveyard affiliated with State University in Capital City. I checked to see if there was room—I thought it would be an appropriate final resting place since she so loved counseling State students. Turned out that she had a plot there bought and paid for. State said they could provide a funeral service for a small fee, and as I did not know Rebecca's religious leanings (if she even had any), I agreed to that, too. By a happy coincidence, the Unitarian minister they engaged was the same dude who married me and my husband Danny—the Reverend Reilly.

Danny is here in his Marine uniform, as is his partner at the 3M Detective Agency, Leon Kidd, a tall, strapping black man who could be mistaken for a retired NFL player. Danny and Rebecca dated for a while, and Leon was instrumental in rescuing her from the predator who assaulted her last year.

My wife Lupe, our eight-year old son Eduardo, and my mom are also here, and about a dozen others have also come to pay their respects; some of Rebecca's colleagues from the Psych department, and students whom she was counseling. My Uncle Amos, the founder of 3M, sent his regrets—after all, he is in a wheelchair and didn't know Rebecca all that well anyhow. But I've noticed that he's been keeping his distance since Danny, Lupe and I decided to become a throuple. That just frosts his Southern Baptist ass.

Rebecca's shiny, dark wood casket is closed and sitting on a brass-railed platform above the open grave, protected from the elements by a canopy. There's room for the Reverend to stand underneath, but the rest of us have to be out in the rain. The air is what Uncle Amos would call pee warm, but no umbrellas or waterproof garments can truly keep the chill out of our souls. I can't help but remember that the last words Rebecca and I had before she was shot were in anger. I don't think for a minute that either of us really meant it, but the time for apologies is gone forever.

Reverend Reilly clears his throat as a signal for attention. When we're all looking at him, he begins, "At this hour, let us remember our beloved Rebecca, a beautiful and gracious lady who loved us all and gave of herself, to give us the strength to live our lives fully. She helped us cope with the adversities of life and allowed us to dwell in God's light, which shines on an imperfect world. She is not here now to help us with perhaps our greatest challenge—our struggle against the forces of despair and hatred that threaten to overwhelm us, because of the cruel and unjust manner in which she was taken from us. But remember that she is not truly gone—we carry her still with us in our minds and hearts. Let the courage and love she displayed in her life evoke our own, and let it strengthen us in the face of the evil which threatens to consume us. I speak not of the one who so cruelly and suddenly took her life; rather, I mean the anger, dejection and thoughts of revenge in the face of this perceived injustice that will poison our souls, causing us to overlook the beauty and dignity of Rebecca's life as well as our own lives, and ultimately drive us into a darkness from which

3

there may be no return. Let us call upon Rebecca's beautiful soul to strengthen us, and remind us of the deeper path of life, the path that leads us into the light of love, not into the darkness of hatred. Remember what Rebecca would want for us, and pursue that noble goal in her memory. So let it be, amen, amen!"

"Amen!" we all respond.

The reverend beckons me forward. "Ms. Natalie McMasters has agreed to deliver the eulogy."

I've been dreading this. I refused when the reverend first asked me—I mean, I knew that talking about Rebecca would make me cry, and I'm so not into showing emotion in public. Over the last few days, I tried several times to write something down, but I couldn't even. Finally, I realized that I'd just have to wing it. We'll just see what comes out.

"Thanks, Reverend Reilly, for your beautiful prayer. I'm sure that we all realize that what you said is true. It's so what Rebecca would want for us..." My words begin to choke me. WTF am I saying? "No!" I blurt. "That's a total crock! It's true that Rebecca was a beautiful person who wanted to help others live better lives, but just look at what it got her! I, for one, welcome the anger and hatred that her murder has caused to burn in me, to focus me on what's really important—finding her killer and bringing him down!"

"Nattie!" Danny hollers, shaking his head.

"STFU, Danny! You know it's facts! Why the hell did you join the Marine Corps if not to fight evil and right wrongs? That goes for you too, Leon. And Lupe, you know better than anyone else what happens when we let bad people do whatever the fuck they want." Did I just say *fuck* at a funeral service? "I'm going to take a vow right now, and I'd like all of you to join me. I'm going to hunt down this Marquis, however long it takes me, and make that shitheel pay for what he did to my friend! If you people don't want to help me, fine! I'll do it myself." A sudden rush of energy drains out of me like air escaping from a punctured tire, shutting off my voice. Everyone's standing there slack-jawed, looking at me like I've just peed on the casket.

After a moment, Lupe says, "Nattie's right. I do know what bad people will do to you if you let them. I tried to hide from them, but I could not. I think we should all help her do this thing."

Another beat, and Danny says, "I think so too. We can't let him get away with this." A rumble arises from the crowd, but I see more approval on faces than disfavor.

Words cannot describe the emotions that fill me, seeing this support from my fam. I have never loved them as much as now. I'm not naive enough to believe that this feeling will last, though.

Poor Reverend Reilly's face tells me he knows that his service has been totally carjacked and his lofty ideals stomped on. "I'm afraid I can't agree with you all," he says, "but it's ultimately your decision. I think there's nothing else I can do here." He walks off into the rain.

My eyes track the reverend as he wends his way among the scattered gravestones, making for the gravel road where the cars are parked. I notice a figure standing between two of the vehicles, observing our gathering. It's a man wearing dark hoodie against the rain. He's relatively short and broad; his form is eerily familiar.

I suddenly know who it must be... "It's him!" I holler. "The Marquis! He's here!"

I take off like a bat out of hell, and Danny follows. It doesn't take long before he's abreast, then ahead of me. Our stan dashes across the road and vaults the low stone wall on the other side, artfully dodging among the tomb stones.

Try as I will, there's no way I can keep up with a Marine. Danny reaches the road five yards ahead of me, hurdling the wall without stopping, pursuing the Marquis (it has to be him!) into the graveyard on the other side. As I clamber over the wall, Danny is now a good 50 feet away. Damn it! It's begun raining harder, and I've totally lost sight of the Marquis! I have to struggle now, just to keep Danny in sight. He's making for a group of trees about fifty yards ahead in the center of the cemetery—the Marquis must have gone in there. Shit! I'll lose both of them for sure in those woods! Of course, Danny goes in. I have no choice—I just keep running towards the spot where I last saw him, hoping to pick up his trail again.

Reaching the trees, I hear crashing ahead, followed by shouts. Small limbs whip across my face, lighting my skin on fire as I push through the brush; I have to slow my pace to avoid going down because I'm sliding on the damp leaves, vines snatching at my feet. Up ahead, it's a little brighter. I run into a small clearing where Danny is on the ground, his hand on his throat, struggling to rise. WTF happened?

There's crashing in the woods ahead of me, but the deadening effect of the thick brush makes it impossible to know exactly where. Conflicting choices tear at me—I want to continue chasing the Marquis, but Danny is down, fighting for breath. Has that motherfucker seriously hurt him? Danny's face is red and bruised, his mouth agape, his breath a rattling wheeze. I reach down and offer him a hand up, but he waves me off.

"Let me...get...my wind," he croaks.

It's a couple of minutes before he can speak coherently. By that time, the crashing in the brush has subsided—the Marquis is long gone.

"WTF happened?" I ask Danny.

"Fucker turned on me and put me down with some serious MMA moves," Danny says, still trying to catch his breath. "I've never seen anything like it before. It's not his fault that he didn't crush my windpipe."

A chill runs through me. Danny is one of the best hand-to-hand fighters I've ever seen, and this guy almost seriously injured him. Am I biting off more than I can chew?

"Was it him?" I ask. "The Marquis?"

"I think so," Danny replies. "I only caught a glimpse of his face under the hoodie, so I can't be totally sure." A beat. "C'mon, we need to get back and report this. He can't have gone far—maybe the cops can pick up his trail."

A cold ball grows in my stomach. I don't want the cops to pick the motherfucker up! I want his sorry ass all to myself. But I follow Danny back to where the others are waiting.

Lupe is totally ratchet when we get there. She doesn't know which one of us to hug first. She opts for Danny, prolly because he still looks like death warmed over. I'll forgive her, this once.

After we've settled down, we head to the cars. Me and Lupe came in my Jeep, and Danny drove himself in his pickup. As we near the Jeep, a campus police car approaches and stops. Two unis get out. One of them, a woman, looks at me and says, "Natalie McMasters?"

"That's me. Can I help you?" I don't like the way they're approaching, separating slightly to cut off escape.

At five feet away, the woman officer says, "I'm Officer Menendez and my partner is Officer Griffin. We'd like you come with us to headquarters."

"What for?" Danny says.

"Don't interfere, sir," Griffin says.

I've had some trouble with the campus rent-a-cops about carrying recently (campus is a gun-free zone), which is why I have my revolver locked in the console of my Jeep. "Look, Ma'am, I'm not carrying..." I tell her.

"It's not that. Your name has come up in connection with a recent break-in," Menendez says.

"What break-in?"

"At the Counseling Center. The office of the late Dr. Rebecca Feiner."

Yeet! A break-in at Rebecca's office? "I don't know anything about that."

"Nevertheless, Detective Sykes would like to talk to you."

I turn and point to the awning with Rebecca's casket underneath. "Hey lady, I've just buried one of my best friends. And I've told you I don't know anything. Give me a break here."

"Sorry. We've been told to bring you in. And don't call me lady. My name is Officer Menendez.

Danny pipes up again. "Is she being detained?"

Menendez looks daggers at him. "Sir, you were told to stay out of this."

"Am I being detained?" I ask her.

"Do you want to be?"

"Am I being detained?"

Her face hardens—she knows she's licked. "No."

"Fine. I'm going home to grieve now. Tell Detective Sykes I'll be in to talk to him on Monday."

"Detective Sykes is a woman, Ms. McMasters."

"Good. I'm glad to see women getting ahead in this sorry-ass world. Tell her I'll see her Monday."

After the two cops have gone, Danny says, "Nattie, are you sure this is a good idea? If they had probable cause, they'd have arrested you."

"I didn't do anything, sweetie," I tell him, "but I'd like to know what the hell is happening. Isn't it way sus that somebody broke into Rebecca's office? And why the fuck do they want to talk to me about it?"

"Cops usually don't answer questions from persons of interest."

Killers!

"This one will if she wants to get anything out of me."

Chapter 2

I spend the rest of the weekend exactly how I told Officer Menendez I was going to—grieving, with some help from a few boilermakers, and reminiscing about the good times I had with Rebecca. But I can't help dwelling on why the Marquis killed her. Was it to hurt me? Or was he pissed because he thought she rejected him? And why was Rebecca so salty with me the last time I saw her? She actually turned me into the cops for carrying on campus, which could have gotten me expelled and thrown in jail. I know it was illegal, but I didn't think she'd ever do something like that to me.

Monday morning, I drive over to campus and, leaving my revolver locked in the Jeep again, I go to police HQ in the basement of the Administration Building. The place is lit by dingy, flickering fluorescents and smells like a locker room. I tell the dude behind the desk that I'm here to see Detective Sykes.

"Your name?"

"Natalie McMasters."

He picks up a phone, punches a button, waits a sec. "Detective Sykes? A Natalie McMasters to see you." A beat. "OK, I'll tell her." To me: "You can go on back. She'll meet you."

I follow the corridor into the bowels of the building. It reminds me of being in the subway; the walls are tiled with small, yellowing rectangular tiles and the body odors get stronger the further I go. How the fuck do people even work in a place like this?

A cute, willowy brunette in a stripey business suit and a frilly blouse approaches. She's barely thirty and looks like a female executive instead of a cop. "Natalie McMasters? Julia Sykes. Come on back."

I expect the classic interrogation room with a metal table that has handcuff loops and chairs on both sides, but instead she leads me into a cramped windowless office, mostly filled by a gray metal desk. She's done a few things to make the place homey—framed pictures on the desk next to her PC turned with their backs to me, and an orange and blue State banner

9

hanging on the back wall. I smell canned flowers too; apparently, she doesn't like *eau de gymnasium* either.

"Sit," she says, waving me to a plastic cafeteria chair in front of her desk. "I apologize for the furniture. We're kinda at the bottom of the University budget around here. Can I get you a soda or anything"

I'm still wary; never trust a cop who's trying to be nice. "I didn't even know that the campus police had detectives."

"I know, right? But they don't have detectives. They got me." She hesitates, then goes on. "A lot of people call us rent-a-cops or worse, but they don't realize that we have to police the equivalent of a small city with just a third of the force that the Capital City police has. And we even have a greater jurisdiction than the city cops. We're county officers, not just campus." Another beat. "So your name has come up in connection with a break-in at Rebecca Feiner's office. I'd like to ask you a few questions about that. I understand that she was your campus counselor. By the way, I'm sorry for your loss."

"Thanks. But I don't know anything about a break-in. First I heard of it was when your officers told me. How did my name come up?"

She hesitates, then her face tells me she's made a decision. "I'm going to level with you. We had an anonymous tip that you were involved."

Seriously? "So you sent cops out to haul me in from my best friend's funeral based on an anonymous tip?"

She's got her chin propped up in a cupped hand and she's smiling at me. I can't help notice that she's totally cute. "I'm the lone detective her, and I've got a lot of cases on my plate," she says, "so I have to investigate each one as efficiently as I can. I'm sorry about the bad timing. But you're here, now. So, can you think of anyone you've pissed off who would want to get you in trouble with us?"

Can I! "I hope you know who killed Rebecca. The Marquis. He and I have a history." I go on to give her the short version of what happened at the relationship clinic last spring, and about the Marquis' threat against me. "I still have the note he sent me, if you'd like to come by the house and see it."

"I would," she says.

"So what did they take from her office?" I ask her.

She removes the hand from her chin and sits back in her chair. "I'm going to be honest with you. Her PC was totally wiped. And we could find no patient file for you. So one possibility was that if you did it, you didn't want the info she had about you to get out. But we did check your phone, and found out it was nowhere near the Counseling Center at the time of the break-in." She smiles. "Of course, a smart cookie like you could have always left it home."

"It was home because that's where I was," I tell her. "But it's totally true about the file. Would you want your shrink's info about you made public?" I think of something else. "You should also know that I've had some trouble with *SOS* recently." *SOS* is the campus newspaper, *The State of State*. "A reporter there, Betsy Kiefer, has it in for me. She thinks I'm responsible for her sister's death."

"Were you?"

"No. The Capital City cops were. You can ask them."

"I'll do that too," she says, making a note on her phone. "Frankly, all the publicity you've had lately convinced us you should be looked into, especially given that anonymous tip." She picks up a small sheaf of papers and taps it on her desk to even it out. "But now that we've talked, I'm pretty sure you had nothing to do with this."

Duh! "Facts," I say. "Can I go home now? I'm still grieving, you know."

"Sure. I'll call you if there's anything else." As I turn to go out the door, she adds, "You can expect a visit from the FBI too, you know."

I turn back to her. She's got an impish expression on her face that's totally sexy. I briefly wonder if she likes girls and is coming on to me. "The FBI?"

"Uh-huh. We've got word they're coming to town and will likely take over the case since we're probably dealing with the Marquis. That's another reason I wanted to get moving on this break-in. I'd love to find that sucker before they do and stick it to them."

He's evaded the feds for two decades, I think. I doubt that he's gonna wait around for you to catch him, sweetie. I head out the door.

A couple of days later, I'm alone at our townhouse. Danny and Lupe are at work. I'm supposed to be in class this morning, but I totally can't summon up the energy to go. After all that's happened in the last few weeks, college seems more and more irrelevant.

The townhouse was trashed in a riot a few weeks ago and most of our shit was stolen or destroyed. Management has been dragging their feet about doing repairs, even though the lease says it's their responsibility. But cleaning up the mess after invasions by both the rioters and SWAT is our problem. Since Danny and Lupe are working, I guess that's my job.

I've got me a bucket and brush and I'm trying to scrub scuff marks off the hardwood floors and the walls when the doorbell rings. Shit. I look like just what you'd expect when a girl's cleaning up—I'm wearing a headband, a too small t-shirt knotted under my boobs and my nastiest pair of distressed jeans. I so totally don't want anyone but fam to see me. But I go to the door and squint through the peephole. WTF? A postlady? Who personally delivers mail anymore?

I open the door. The hot blast of air nearly takes my breath away.

The postlady looks totally on fleek in her powder blue golf shirt and steel gray shorts. How can she look so cool in this heat? "Natalie McMasters?", she asks.

"That's me."

"I have a registered letter for you. Sign here." She hands me an envelope with a green sticker on the front. I sign in the space required, print my name. She tears off the sticker and keeps it. Handing me the envelope, she tells me, "You have a nice day."

"You too." The return address is Holly and Bloom, the company that manages the townhouse complex. Oh good, maybe it's a check to use to fix the place up. I tear it open, take out the letter, and start reading.

WTF! They're not renewing our lease? We have to be out in a week?

I storm in to the townhouse complex office and tell the girl behind the desk, a twentysomething who with a short black butch and huge glasses whom I've dealt with before, that I want to talk to the manager.

"He's not here," she says, not even bothering to look away from her monitor.

I wave the letter between her face and the screen. That gets me some eye contact. "What do you know about this?" I ask her.

Looking at me like something on her shoe, she takes the letter and scans it quickly. "They're not renewing your lease," she says, tossing it back on her desk.

No shit, Sherlock. "Why not?"

She's staring at her monitor again. "I'm sure I don't know."

"Well, I'd like to find out."

"So call the main office."

That's the way it's gonna be, right? I've got to get out of here before I bang 30s on this bitch.

Back in the townhouse, I call the number on the letterhead.

A male voice answers. "Holly and Bloom Property Management."

"Hi, this is Natalie McMasters. I just got a letter from y'all that our lease has been canceled. I thought we had about six months left. What's going on?"

"Let me transfer you to Mr. Schwartz." Elevator music fills my ear and I wait some more, getting more and more ratchet by the second.

Schwartz comes on the line, and I tell him what I told the other guy. "What's your address?" he asks. I give it to him. "Hold, please." The sappy music comes on again. Now I'm way beyond ratchet.

A couple of endless minutes later, Schwartz is back. "I've looked up your account, Ms. McMasters, and I'm sorry to tell you that the letter is accurate. You've been canceled and given a week to vacate."

"How can you even do that?"

"I'd like to point out that I did not do that, Ms. McMasters, Holly and Bloom Property Management did." Whatever. "There's a clause in the lease that you signed that Holly and Bloom may void it at any time if it is determined that your occupation of the property might compromise the safety of the other residents of the complex. Several of your neighbors have indicated that they fear for their safety because of recent incidents at your address."

"That's a crock! We didn't ask a bunch of looters to break in and trash the place!"

"Hmmm. There's a note in your folder about a TV interview that you gave that some considered inflammatory, as well as allegations of unlawful cohabitation occurring on the property."

"Inflammatory! What about my first amendment rights? And who I live with is none of your fucking business..."

"We're not Congress, Ms. McMasters, we're just a property management company concerned for the safety of our residents. And who lives and what happens in our properties is most definitely our business. I'm afraid the order stands. You must be out in a week."

Killers!

We go back and forth a couple more times, but he doesn't budge. Finally, I holler, "I'm calling my lawyer!"

"That's certainly your right, Ms. McMasters. Have a nice day." He kills the call.

I call my attorney Gary McDougall, who tells me that these days, many leases contain language allowing management companies to evict residents who turn their properties into stash houses, meth labs or the like. "You can try to get a judge to issue an injunction, but given the recent lawlessness in the wake of the shootings, I seriously doubt we can get the case heard in a week," Gary tells me. "I think your time and money would be better spent finding another place to live."

Fucking A! Uncle Amos says that it's always better to give folks bad news on a full stomach, so instead of calling them at work, I decide to wait until after dinner to tell Lupe and Danny.

My phone dings and I check the screen. *Tai Chi, one hour.*

I recently took up Tai Chi to learn to defend myself. At 5'1" and 95 lbs, I need all the help I can get. But with Rebecca's death, it's become way much more. My *sifu*, Ye-ye, has become my new counselor. He's just the dude I need to talk to right now.

I grab my Tai-chi clothes and my green sash, jump in the Jeep and drive to his place on Green Lake, about ten miles out of the city. Part of the lake is in a state park and the rest on private land. Ye-ye has built his tiny house on the lakeshore. He's also constructed a pavilion that he uses for training; a peaked, sheet metal roof supported by wooden pillars, enclosing a rectangular area about 20' by 40', with an unobstructed view of the lake. I find him stripped to the waist, working in his vegetable garden in the broiling sun. Dude must be over eighty, but his body is that of a much younger man, every muscle clearly defined.

"You're early," he says as I approach. "Wassamattah?"

Time was I didn't want to tell him my troubles, but I'm totally over that now. "I haven't even told Danny and Lupe yet," I finish. "I don't even know if we can find a new place to live that fast."

"Don't worry," Ye-ye says. "We Chinese have lots of experience being told to move on a moment's notice. These things usually work themselves out. You can stay here until you find a place."

"I doubt your little house would hold four of us."

14

He waves at the lawn in front of the pavilion. "You can camp in the field."

"I don't know..."

"Why don't you ask Danny and Lupe to come here for dinner tonight? I haven't even met them yet. I'll make you a Chinese meal and we can talk about it. Meanwhile, let's do the form. That will get your mind off your troubles."

I text Danny and Lupe to call when they can, then go change for the form.

A Tai-chi form is a series of postures simulating a fight with imaginary opponents, meant to build muscle memory so the movements just emerge when you get into an actual fight. Ye-ye's form is called Wudangshan 108 and takes nearly an hour to do. It requires so much concentration to perform the complex series of postures that there's literally no room in my mind for anything else. We begin with a series of breathing exercises that he calls *qi-gong*, which are meant to build chi, that mysterious internal force from which Tai Chi derives its power, then we go into the form itself. I don't have it memorized, so I just follow his lead. Each time I do this, I learn something else about it. By the time we're through, I'm as limp as a dishrag, but Ye-ye looks like he could go on for the rest of the afternoon. But a feeling of peace and inner rightness suffuses me, and I've almost forgotten that I have a week to find another place to live. Almost.

Lupe calls a little later.

"Is Danny there?"

"Yes"

"Put me on speaker."

Without telling them about the eviction notice, I manage to convince them to come to Green Lake Pavilion for dinner. After hanging up, I tell Ye-ye and he says, "Wait here," disappearing inside his tiny house. He returns holding a fishing pole and tackle box. He points to the lake. "Go catch dinner," he says.

Lupe and Danny arrive separately around six that evening. I managed to pull half a dozen small bass and as many sunfish from the lake, while Ye-ye harvested a mess of greens from his garden. That and a pot of rice will feed the five of us. We're sitting in a circle in the pavilion, enjoying my catch, while I tell them about the letter from Holly and Bloom.

15

Killers!

"How can they do this?" Lupe explodes. "This is America! You cannot just throw someone out of their home!"

"I'm afraid they can," Danny says. "Look people, I'm sure that business about the riot is just smoke to cover up the real reason they want us out. We knew when we entered into our family arrangement that some people would take exception to it, and it's kinda become public knowledge since Nattie's been on TV so much lately..."

"Hey, don't blame me..."

He makes me talk to the hand. "I'm not blaming you, Nattie. When I agreed to this marriage, I never intended to keep it a secret, but I knew there would be ramifications. One of those is that Eddie has to live with your mom and another is that my relationship with Amos has tanked. Now there's this. But I still love you and Lupe. We'll work this out."

I have tears in my eyes and I see that Lupe does too.

Ye-ye says, "Maybe after dinner, all of you would like to try a little Tai Chi Chuan? It's excellent for getting your mind off of discouraging things."

Danny says, "I've always thought that Tai Chi was great exercise for old folks, but not much as a self-defense technique. That's why I encouraged Nattie to take Krav Maga instead."

"Krav Maga is a hard style—really not much good unless you are big and strong," replies Ye-ye. "Strength does not matter for Tai Chi Chuan."

"Strength always matters," says Danny. "At least it does if both combatants have equal training."

"Strength no matter," Ye-ye repeats. "Someone stronger than me could never defeat me unless they were a better Tai Chi player." To Danny: "You think the stronger person always wins?"

"I think they have a huge advantage." replies Danny.

"Do you think you are stronger than me?" asks Ye-ye.

Danny looks at Ye-ye's slight form. "Probably."

Yeet! I think I see where this is going.

"Would you care for a little match?"

Danny smiles. "I wouldn't want to hurt you. And I don't think I could hold myself back against a trained opponent."

Ye-ye returns Danny's grin. "Let me worry about that. You want to try?"

I remember what this little old man did to four younger, stronger opponents who attacked me while ago. "That might not be such a good idea, Danny."

Now Danny looks insulted. "Seriously? You think he can take me?"

"You haven't seen him fight. I have."

Danny looks at Ye-ye. "You're on," he says. Oh brother. Now I can smell the testosterone!

We clear away the bamboo mats and get the dinner dishes out of the pavilion. Ye-ye says to me and Lupe, "Stand outside, please. Pavilion now for Tai Chi players only."

We do as he asks. Danny strips off his t-shirt, displaying his well-developed shoulders and six-pack. Ye-ye does the same, and Danny's eyes widen as he sees that the old man's muscles rival his own. Thing is though, Danny has fifty pounds on him, easy.

As, the two face off in the center of the pavilion, Danny asks, "What are the rules here?"

Ye-ye smiles. "We don't need no stinking rules. Do anything you want."

"How will we know who wins?"

"You will know."

Danny takes a boxer's stance, his hands raised in front of his face. Ye-ye stands easily in *wuji-bu*, his feet shoulder width apart, arms hanging at his sides. As Danny dances forward, Ye-ye steps out with his right foot into a broad stance, his legs spread far apart. I know that this is called is *ma-bu, or* horse stance, because it looks like he's astride a horse. He begins rotating his hands in front of him in a mesmerizing fashion, one hand moving up while the other moves downwards—a move from the form called cloud hands.

"Tricks," says Danny, as he steps in and flicks his open right hand at Ye-ye's face. I can tell that the blow, though lightning-fast, has no power behind it; Danny is trying not to hurt the old man. Big mistake.

Ye-ye's left hand, rising in the rhythm of the movement, grasps Danny's wrist and jerks the Marine towards him. Danny, suddenly off balance, stumbles forward and Ye-ye steps into him, sliding his left foot behind Danny's leg, rotating his hips to deliver a forearm strike to the collarbone. Danny goes over backwards and I wince at the thud as he hits the floor. Ye-

ye steps back into *wuji-bu* and bows his head slightly, the shadow of a grin on his face.

Danny gets to his feet, his pride hurt more than anything else. "Okay then," he says. "Round one to you. Best two out of three?"

Ye-ye clasps both hands in front of him, and raises them in a Taoist salute. "Whenever you're ready."

Now that Danny knows the mettle of his opponent, his face hardens with determination. Ye-ye goes back into cloud hands, waiting. Danny suddenly dives for Ye-ye's waist, intending I guess to grapple the old man and take him to the floor. But Ye-ye again steps into him, his rotating hands suddenly shooting straight out to land on both of Danny's shoulders in a hard push that lifts the two-hundred pound Marine off his feet, sending him sailing backwards. Luckily, Danny knows how to fall, so he rolls and springs to his feet, now some ten feet away from the old man. He immediately charges, hoping to catch his opponent off guard, but this time, Ye-ye dodges and slips behind him, grabbing him around the waist and sweeping his feet from under him with a kick, before depositing him on the floor once more. The old man follows up with a kick that stops just a hairsbreadth in front of Danny's Adam's apple.

Danny's looking up at Ye-ye, his face as white as a fish's belly. As Ye-ye extends a hand to help him up, Danny says in a disbelieving voice, "That's exactly what he did to me."

"What who did to you?" I ask.

"The Marquis."

Chapter 3

The four of us are sitting in a circle in the pavilion again, sipping steaming tea from small round cups.

"Who is this Marquis?" asks Ye-ye.

"His real name is Leonard Ashworth," I answer. "He's a serial killer that the FBI has been hunting for two decades. He murdered my friend Rebecca and he's promised to come after me too."

"And you think he knows Tai Chi Chuan?" Ye-ye asks Danny.

"That move you got me with was the same one he used the other day, right down to the throat kick," says Danny. "I only just got a hand up to block the kick, or I'd be in the hospital or dead right now."

"Tai Chi Chuan is pretty small world," says Ye-ye. "What does this guy look like?"

"He's short for a dude," I answer. "About five-six. In his forties, I think. He's kind of a pretty boy. He's got a broad upper body, golden hair and blue eyes. He was wearing a full beard when I saw him last. Speaks with an old-timey Southern accent. Not country; like in *Gone with the Wind*."

An uneasy expression crosses Ye-ye's face.

"Do you think you know him?" I ask.

"Dunno. Why are you looking for him?"

"I told you. He killed my friend."

"Better leave that to the police."

"They sure as hell haven't done much of a job so far." I tell him.

"If we can figure out where he is, we can tell the cops," says Danny. "Let them take it from there."

Fuck no! But I don't say it.

"If this guy is any good at Tai Chi Chuan, he could be really dangerous," says Ye-ye.

"Tell me about it," says Danny.

"Will you look into him?" I ask.

"I will see what I can do," Ye-ye says. "But if I do find him, you must promise not to mess with him. Tell the cops where he is."

"I promise." Not!

Killers!

Danny clears his throat so we all look at him. "Time to change the subject. Because we were all involved in a very sad duty on Saturday, we forgot something very important."

Oh shit!

He smiles. "It was Nattie's birthday. I propose that we have a little celebration now." He gets up and goes to his truck, removing a large cardboard carton from the back, which he carries over to the pavilion. He begins taking things out and laying them on the floor. A large, white bakery box, some paper plates, napkins and plastic forks, a box of candles and two packages wrapped in bright paper and ribbons. Before long, he's lighting twenty-two candles on a cake. When he's done, he says, "Ok, y'all. One, two, three... Happy birthday to you..."

I can feel my face burning, as I blow out the candles. I'm so glad he remembered!

Danny picks up one of the presents and hands it to me. The weight tells me what it is, but I act surprised when I tear off the paper to find a gray plastic pistol case. I flip up the catches and remove the small black handgun from the Styrofoam.

"It's the new Sig P365, to replace the one you lost a while ago," Danny says.

I admire the sleek little pistol, turning it from side to side, until I see something wrong. "It doesn't have any sights!" I say.

Danny smiles as he takes the pistol from me, and points out small aperture on the rear of the gun. "Look there."

I take the gun back and sight out over the lake. A bright green dot illuminates the small orifice.

"It's the SAS model, and it's snag-free," says Danny. "It has no exterior sights."

"Then how do you aim it?"

"It's just point and shoot. Put the green dot in the center of mass. It's also a night sight, tritium-enhanced so it works even in total darkness." His eyes are shining and his tone tells me how much he loves this little gun. "We'll go to the range tomorrow and you can try it out."

Lupe rises and moves over by Danny to pick up the other package, about five inches long and an inch wide, and hands it to me. This is unusual—she usually gets me clothes, and this looks more like it would hold a fountain pen. I tear off the wrapping and find a black box labeled with a red bird's claw in a circle and the brand name *Microtech.* I open it, removing an owner's manual, and see it contains a slender, black pocket knife with a thumb slide. I look questioningly at my wife. "Danny helped me pick it out," she says. Of course, he did.

I take it out of the box and try to push the slide forward. It's hard. Suddenly, a wicked, three-and-a-half inch, double-edged blade shoots out the end of the handle with a *Snick!* It's serrated on the bottom half way down to do even more damage when pulled out of a wound. I stupidly run my finger along the blade and a thin red line appears like magic. "Ouch!" I holler, dropping the knife and sticking the hurt finger in my mouth. This thing's like a razor!

Ye-ye makes a hissing sound.

"What?" I ask him as I retrieve my present. "You don't like weapons?" I push the slide again and the blade smoothly retracts back into the handle.

"I like weapons just fine," he answers. "I have a beautiful 17th century *dao* from the Song dynasty that my *sifu* gave to me. I will show it to you sometime. But the problem with weapons is that they give a false sense of power. A weapon is only as good as the one who wields it."

"I've always considered weapons, or even fighting, as a last resort," I tell him. "But if I have to fight, I want to be prepared."

His expression softens. "Good attitude," he says. "Just remember though, if this Marquis knows Tai Chi Chuan, he will take your weapon away and turn it on you."

A red sun turns the lake crimson, and we stay to enjoy it until it sinks from sight. As we're getting ready to pile into our respective cars to go home, Danny says to Ye-ye, "Maybe we could get together sometime and you could show me some more of that Tai Chi."

"Can always use new student," the old one says. "Lupe, you are welcome to train with us too."

She surprises me when she answers, "Maybe I will."

It's still early when we get back to the townhouse. We drove in a caravan, so we're all getting out of our cars at the same time, when the sky lights up like it's daytime. Thunder crashes, then the heavens open up and rain pours in sheets like it can do only in the South. By the time we get the front door unlocked and we're inside, we're totally drenched. I'd left the cooling system on when I went out, so I feel my skin chill and my nipples harden.

"I've got to get out of these wet clothes and into the shower!" I announce.

"Why should you go first?" asks Lupe. She holds a fist above an open hand, offering a bout of rock, paper scissors.

"Our shower is big enough for three, you know," Danny says.

It sure is. That's one of the things I'll miss about this place.

We all go into Lupe's bedroom, where the huge master bathroom is, shedding clothes as we go. When we decided to become a throuple, we agreed to let sex be spontaneous and to rely on each other to speak up if anyone felt jealous or unloved. That's worked just fine so far. By the time we get into the bathroom, we're all naked. Danny slides the glass door open and cuts on the shower, and my shivers begin to subside as steam fills the room. "Not too hot," I tell him.

The three of us get into the stall and Lupe closes the door, then Danny grabs the soap on a rope that's hanging from the shower head, working up a rich white lather before running the soap between and over my titties. Lupe pushes in next to me, telling Danny, "You can do me, too."

Danny has always been very attentive to Lupe's wishes when we make love. She's an avowed lesbian, although she does enjoy penetration when I do it with my fingers or toys. The two of us have recently talked about her going further with Danny. As a former stripper, she's done countless lap dances with guys, but the only penetration she's ever experienced with men has been rape. Danny knows this, so he has been very careful never to touch her there unless he knows she wants it, and to back off if she shows any signs of distress. And while Lupe will tell you that she's not really turned on by guys, I know that she has come to love Danny very much.

Danny rubs his soapy hands all over both of us girls, paying lots of attention to our titties (just like a guy!) before making circles on our bellies, then snaking his hands between our legs. I feel Lupe stiffen, so I pull her back against the shower wall and put my arms around her neck saying, "Bae, it's okay," before planting my mouth on hers and twirling my tongue inside. She loosens up and begins to kiss me back, and I spread my legs a little to give Danny more access. Lupe begins to make little moans as Danny gives her the same treatment, and I pop my mouth off of hers and lower my head to suck and bite at her large chocolate nipples. I do so love both of these people and I desperately want this experience to be a good one for her. I back off a little so Danny's hand slides out from between my legs, then I lower my hand to help him pleasure Lupe. Her breath begins coming in short puffs, then she stiffens as she comes. Danny takes her by the shoulders and gently lowers her to the shower floor so she doesn't fall as her legs give way. After coming to herself, she reaches up to fondle Danny. Looking at me, she says, "Come here and help me, *Cariño*."

I kneel down alongside her as she stokes Danny's length before offering it to me. She plays with his undercarriage as I slowly service him orally—the pressure of his hands on my shoulders tells me he's rapidly approaching his own climax.

Lupe says, "Share him with me," pushing her face against mine so he pops out of my mouth, and she begins running her lips along the length of him. I join her, and our mouths meet as he thrusts his hips back and forth, enjoying the experience. The warm shower cascades down over all of us, so his warm juices are instantly washed away when he explodes.

The shower is getting colder, so I know it's time to get out. We dry each other off and adjourn to Lupe's big bed, leaving the towels on the floor for morning. Lupe pushes Danny down on his back, then says to me, "Help me get him ready for you." She starts massaging him with one hand while pushing my face toward him with the other. I take him in my mouth, and it doesn't take much of that before he's ready again. I begin to mount him face-to-face, but Lupe says, "No, do it the other way. I want to see." So I get on backwards, then lean back on my arms while she sits in front of us, playing with herself while she watches us. Soon I begin to feel my own release growing, so I close my eyes to enjoy it. Suddenly I feel yet another sensation down there—Lupe's tongue. It's just too much, and I holler and nearly pass out when I explode.

Later, as we're lying in bed with Danny in the middle, cuddling the two of us in his strong arms, I think how mean and petty some people can be, labeling what the three of us have as sinful, dirty, or wrong. What it is, is love, and love can never be any of those things. Love is love, y'all.

***

Killers!

After his guests have left, Ye-ye busies himself cleaning up. He carries the dishes down to the lake to wash them, then leaves them out where the sun will dry them in the morning. He gives the pavilion one last sweeping, to respect the space. He looks to the sky as clouds obscure the thin crescent moon and darkness descends, mirroring the darkness in his soul. A moisture-laden breeze blowing off the lake heralds a storm—a moment later, a fanfare of thunder and a flash of lightning announce its arrival. The old man sinks into a lotus position in the center of the pavilion to await its passing. The sky opens and a cascade of BBs begins bouncing off the tin roof.

Ye-ye understands how small the world of Tai Chi Chuan in America really is. Even in a country so large, serious practitioners have at least heard of the others, if they are not directly acquainted. From Nattie and Danny's description of this Marquis, Ye-ye wonders whether the killer might be one of his former students, Larry Tyson. Tyson was the only student with whom Ye-ye eventually refused to train, because the man had a definite mean streak and continually misused the Art.

Could the man who nearly put Danny Merkel in the hospital be Tyson, the infamous Marquis, a serial killer responsible for two dozen murders or more? Ye-ye isn't sure, but it does bear looking into. And if it comes down to a contest between the old man and his former protege, Ye-ye isn't entirely sure who would win.

Despite his uncertainty, Ye-ye smiles. He had all but given up hope of reestablishing himself as *sifu* of his own school. He had resigned himself to a solitary existence, exploring the subtleties of the form here in his own little corner of the world, while he waited for death to take him on his next great adventure. He only accepted the gig at the failing downtown dojo because the owner, a karate master and an old friend, had implored him; besides, the rent was cheap. Then Natalie McMasters walked in with a request to study Krav Maga, and he had convinced her to try Tai Chi Chuan instead. As they played that first night, Ye-ye noticed that Nattie had a very strong *chi*, wild and untamed, as was to be expected from a novice, but holding great promise.

The storm is intense, but brief. As the rattling above comes to an end, Ye-ye's eyes light upon the now still surface of the water and he's reminded of a passage from the *Tao Te Ching*—*Fire distances itself from its nemesis, the*

Lake. Ye-ye knows that he is the fire. Is the serenity of the lake seducing him from his true purpose; training Natalie to her full potential? It seems now that he's gained two more students. Is the Mother of All Things trying to tell him that he still has unrealized purpose, which will emerge in the person of Natalie McMasters? Only time will tell...

Chapter 4

Despite our lovemaking last night, the mood in the townhouse is gloomy the next morning. Lupe's breakfast tacos and her *café de olla* are bitter on my tongue. This place has been my home for a while now, and I've finally gotten comfortable here, especially since Lupe and Danny have moved in. I'm totally salty that we're being tossed out on the street, just because some totally unwoke mofos don't like our lifestyle, which is absolutely none of their business, by the way. Lupe and Danny have to leave for work soon, so it looks like it's gonna fall to me to get on the 'net and gin up some places for us to check out for new digs.

My phone lights up and starts playing Burna Boy's *Anybody*—my ringtone for an unknown caller. I pick up.

A female voice says, "Is this Natalie McMasters?"

"Yes."

"Hold for Mr. Talbott..."

Who? The phone goes dead for a sec, then a deep male voice with a strong southern accent is in my ear, "Ms. McMasters? Beauregard Talbott here. How are you this fine day?"

"Gucci. Who are you?"

"Ms. McMasters, I'm an attorney who is the trustee of the estate of Dr. Rebecca Feiner. I'm pleased to inform you that you have been designated as the beneficiary of a trust she set up, and I wonder if you could come to a short meeting heah today so we can discuss yoah bequest."

Rebecca left me something in her will? "I guess..."

"Would 11:30 be all right?"

"Today? I guess so."

"Fine. We're Willy, Talbott and Hightower, at 1600 MLK Plaza. See y'all in a little while." He kills the call.

I remember that firm. Jedidiah Hightower totally ripped me a new one last year at that office. But this guy Talbott sounds valid.

I get ready to go, packing my new P365 in a pocket holster and my knife in the other pocket. It's going to be a hot one today, so I decide to wear shorts and leave my backup revolver and ankle holster home.

26

At 11:30 on the dot, a secretary conducts me into Beauregard Talbott's office. She looks like she could model for magazine covers—this firm obviously spares no expense on window dressing. It's lucky I left early—I had to go back to the car to lock up my Sig because I encountered a giant *No guns* sign on the front door of the building. But at least I've got my knife.

Beauregard Talbott is an overweight fiftysomething with graying brown hair, dressed in a light blue pinstripe suit, white shirt and paisley tie, sporting a gold Rolex. He rises as I enter the office and extends a hand, which I take—it feels like one of those fish I caught at Ye-ye's yesterday.

"That will be all, Pris," he says to the eye-candy. Waving toward an armchair upholstered in blue leather in front of his desk, he says, "Take a seat, Ms. McMasters. May I call you Natalie?"

I prefer, Nattie, but that's only for friends. But there's no need to be an asshole, either. "Sure," I tell him.

"So I guess y'all and Dr. Feiner were pretty close," he says. "You took care of her funeral expenses." A beat. "I'm sorry for yoah loss."

I hate it when people say they're sorry for my loss. They don't mean it. "Thank you."

He opens a manila folder in front of him—for show, prolly. He should damn well know what's in there. "Well Natalie, I'm pleased to inform y'all, that while Dr. Feiner made a number of small bequests to various institutions and causes that were dear to her heart, she has placed the bulk of her estate in trust for you."

WTF?

"That includes her home, Hyacinth House, the contents, with the exception of her personal patient files, and the grounds. There is also cash and securities that comes to...", he picks up a piece of paper from the folder and scrutinizes it, "...four hundred and eighty seven thousand, six hundred and ninety two dollars and eleven cents."

I don't believe what I just heard. "Four hundred and eighty seven thousand, six hundred and ninety two dollars and eleven cents?"

"That's right, as of nine o'clock this morning. The bulk of the monies are in stocks and bonds, so the value fluctuates. The value of the house and grounds is somewhere around two million five. Do y'all have your own financial manager?"

"No..."

27

Killers!

"That's all right. The account is currently being managed by the Newberry Group, and they're the most reputable financial firm in the city. They'll take good care of y'all."

This can't be happening! Not again! I had a very dear friend pass a couple of years ago, who left me everything and added me to the lease for the townhouse we're in now. I've gone through most of that money since, but now this happens just when I need it. "Didn't Rebecca have any family?" I ask Talbott.

"No. She was an orphan. It's my understanding that she was her parents' sole heir." He gives me a little time to take a breath, then goes on, "Now I know that it's going to take y'all some time to get used to this. But all that's required today is to sign some papers."

A thought occurs. "You say she left me her house?"

"And the furnishings and grounds."

"When would it be possible to move in?"

"Well, Dr. Feiner owned the house free and clear, so there's no mortgage to assume. And since she set this up as a trust, there's no probate. So, I guess y'all could move in whenever you wanted to."

I may identify as an atheist, but I'm starting to get a way strong belief in my guardian angel.

After returning home from the lawyer's office, I'm as ratchet as a cat in a room full of rocking chairs until Danny and Lupe get home. When Lupe gets in, she goes immediately to the kitchen to start dinner.

"Let's order out tonight," I say. "Pizza OK?"

"How come? I thought we were trying to save money."

"Not tonight, Bae," I smile as I realize that we don't have to save money anymore. "I want to have a family meeting after Danny gets home."

"Why? Is something wrong?"

I smile to put her at ease. "Just the opposite. I have some great news."

Lupe hates secrets, and she tries to get it out of me, but I resist. Finally, Danny comes in. Lupe says immediately, "Nattie wants a family meeting!"

Danny looks puzzled, but he agrees. "Let me order the pizzas first," I say, just to watch Lupe squirm. After that's done and we're all sitting in the great room, I tell them my news.

"Holy shit!" says Danny.

"We can move in this weekend," I say.

28

"OMG, Nattie," says Lupe. "I did not know that Rebecca felt that way about you."

I think of the last time I spoke to Rebecca, when she tried to have me arrested for carrying a gun on campus. "I didn't either," I reply. Knowing that she did makes it all the harder for me to accept her untimely death. The Marquis will pay for this!

***

It's Saturday night, just after sunset. Lupe, Danny, Eduardo, and me are sitting in the contemporary living room at Hyacinth House, all silver, black metal and glass, watching a half moon rise outside the floor-to-ceiling windows. It's not far from the townhouse, so we didn't have a lot of trouble moving in, especially since a lot of our stuff was stolen in the aftermath of the riot last month. The sprawling, glass-walled A-frame house, nestled in a spacious clearing in a pine forest, overlooks a landscaped circular driveway, and has two, single-story grey brick annexes on either side. The outside windows are mirrored so you can't see inside. Right inside the entryway, a circular staircase with an elevator in a a glass tube alongside gives access to the second floor—Rebecca also used to see patients here, and some of them were infirm. A matching detached garage has space for two cars, but we're all parked in the driveway because we're using the garage to store our stuff until we can figure out what to keep. The living room, dining room and kitchen comprise the rest of the first floor, with bedrooms in the wings and upstairs. The house is sparsely furnished, so there'll be plenty of room for our stuff. It still smells of the hyacinths that Rebecca was so fond of—their sweet scent brings tears to my eyes. God, I miss her! I totally hope that I'll be able to live here comfortably because of the many associations, both good and bad, that I have with this place.

Eduardo, our eight-year old, is Lupe's son, but right now he's being supervised by my Mom because CPS doesn't consider our fam "moral" enough to have a child in our home. The property has a guest cottage about 50 yards from Hyacinth House in a grove of trees. I convinced Mom to move in there; she was living in our old family home in Fayetteville, but that's a two-hour drive from here. Now we can visit with Eduardo whenever we

Killers!

want, and still adhere to the CPS restrictions of not living under the same roof.

We're waiting for Leon Kidd and Mom to arrive, ostensibly for an impromptu housewarming. Mom was gonna try and get Uncle Amos to come tonight—I need to discuss something with him, and it's not how to arrange the furniture. I had a way hard time getting Uncle, a fundie Baptist, to accept my marriage to Lupe, but he finally came around. But when Danny joined the fam, Uncle just couldn't get his head around a throuple. It's been way rough for Danny working with him, and I've heard little from him since the ceremony that united the three of us.

A high-pitched buzzing sounds throughout the house—an alarm at the entrance to the gravel driveway, letting us know that someone's on their way in. Danny and I go outside to meet them, while Lupe heads to the kitchen to bring out the platter of Mexican snacks she's prepared.

Leon's vintage Caddy is pulling up in front of the steps. God, I hope Uncle is with them!

The rear door opens, and Mom gets out. She goes to the passenger door, opens it, and I see Uncle's hunched form inside. I don't want to know what she said or did to get him here—I'm just glad he came.

The driver's door opens and Leon exits the Caddy. He's dressed in a green silk shirt with palm trees on it over a pair of tan Dockers. He opens the trunk and gets out Uncle's wheelchair while Danny trots down to help Mom extract him from the Caddy. He's going to be in a helluva mood—the old Marine hates people fussing over him, reminding him that he's infirm. Once he's in his wheelchair, Danny and Leon pick it up by the arms and walk him up the stairs so he doesn't have to go all the way around to the ramp. Eduardo has already opened the front door and gone back inside, so I lead the way to the living room where he's attacking the snack plate despite Lupe's remonstrances. We get settled, and Mom gets her brother a plate of food and a beer from a tub of ice. The rest of us fuel up, too.

"Nattie, I'm mighty sorry that you've lost your friend, but I'm happy to see that you have such a fine place to live now," says Uncle. "She must have really set store by you." He's studiously avoiding looking at Lupe or Danny. Pretending they're not there isn't gonna make them go away, you old bigot.

"I think she did, Uncle. I only wish I'd known it while she was alive."

"Life is too short to be livin' with regrets, Nattie."

I decided to take the bull by the horns. "I know it, Uncle. That's why Lupe, Danny and me decided to live together as a family. We'd love to have you be a part of it."

He just looks at me with a stone face, saying nothing. *If you don't have anything nice to say...* I follow up with, "And I've decided to track down the son of a bitch who killed Rebecca." That got his attention.

"And jes' how you aimin' to do that, girl?"

"With lots of help from my Uncle, the great detective."

One thing about a Southerner, he just hates to say the word no. It's rude, and he'll go to just about any lengths to avoid it.

Uncle skillfully dodges the n-word. "That don't sound like it's gonna keep the lights on in the office, Nattie."

"I know it, Uncle, and that's why I wouldn't dream of asking you to do it for free. I've come into some money along with this house, so I'd like to hire 3M to help me with this." I know he won't take money from me, because I'm family, but I'm hoping to shame him into helping. "I'll need Danny full-time, and you and Leon to use your resources at the office to get me information when I need it." Private investigators have access to databases and software not available to the general public.

Danny says, "If it would help you out, I'd be glad to take a leave of absence and forego my salary, Amos."

Now Uncle has a look on his face like he's eaten a big wedge of cheese with no Ex-lax in the house. In desperation, he looks at Leon. "What do you think about this, Cap'n?"

Kidd's sour expression reveals how much he hates the nickname Uncle's saddled him with. "I think it would be just about impossible for Nattie to do this on her own, Amos, even with Danny's help. And this scumbag has threatened her life, you know. What he's done to Rebecca certainly shows that the threat is serious."

"Well, bidness has been slow lately, so I guess I could spare Danny if'n he don't draw no salary. And Nattie, you know that you have access to the office facilities any time you want 'em."

"I wasn't sure that was still true, but thank you," I say. "But does that mean that you and Leon will help us?"

"I don't know that I can. We have our insurance work to pay the bills, and that doesn't leave much time for much else."

Killers!

"I'll help," says Leon. Yeet! You could cut the tension in here with a knife.

"Off the books?" asks Uncle, meaning Leon won't get paid for his time, either.

"If I have to." Now Leon sounds mad as a wet cat too. It was never my intention to drive a wedge between Uncle and his partners, but if he's going to take this attitude because he doesn't like our lifestyle, screw him!

The driveway buzzer sounds again. A chill runs down my spine—I'm not expecting anyone else.

"'Scuse me, y'all," I say as I get up and head for the front door. Once out of sight of the group, I draw my new Sig from its holster, holding it behind my back pointed at the floor. The humidity takes my breath away as I open the door and go out onto the front deck, squinting against the headlights coming around the circular driveway. Fear rises into my chest from my belly. When the headlights turn so they're out of my eyes, I can make out a small red roadster rolling to a stop behind Leon's Caddy. Wait a sec, I know that car...

The headlights die, the driver's door opens and a woman gets out. She's almost as short as me and has steel gray hair framing a round grandmotherly face. She's wearing a white sleeveless top festooned with blue and yellow flowers over a pair of aquamarine shorts and strappy sandals. I recognize her instantly.

"M.B.! What the hell are you doing here?" I met Maribeth Woodrow earlier this year at Love In The Mountains, the relationship clinic I went to with Lupe and Danny, trying to mold the three of us into a fam. That's also where I first encountered the Marquis.

"Now ain't that a fine welcome for an old friend," she says, coming up onto the porch. After holstering the Sig, I hold out my hand to take hers, but she ignores it and sweeps me into a hug instead. She pushes back, still holding my shoulders, and says, "Land sakes, let me look at you, honeychile. You're as pretty as a cherry on an ice cream sundae, and twice as sweet." She steps back and sweeps an arm to indicate the house. "It looks like you're surely livin' in high cotton these days."

"What are you doing here?" I ask again, shaking my head. "How did you find me? We just moved in the other day." I realize that's a stupid statement just as soon as it's out of my mouth. M.B. is a retired FBI agent—she can damn well find anybody she wants to. Hmmm...

"I heard about what happened to your friend Dr. Feiner. I'm so, so sorry, Nattie." Indicating the house again, she says, "She shore must have loved you."

"Believe me, I was shocked." A thought occurs. "How's Chipper?"

Her face falls and I instantly wish I hadn't asked. "He's gone too, Shug. Heart attack, a couple o' months ago."

"I'm so sorry!"

"S'alright. It was fast! Never knew what hit him. I'm gettin' by. The Bureau has given me a part-time job under a new program to rehire retirees." Her eyes are moist. No, you're not getting by, I think.

"Well come inside and meet everybody."

M.B. knows Lupe and Danny from LITM, and Mom and Eduardo from the hospital where we both ended up later, but she hasn't met Uncle or Leon. She greets everyone like she's known them forever. Is that a twinkle I see in Uncle's eye as she bends down to take his hand?

After she's gotten herself a plate and a beer, I tell her the reason for this gathering. "Good," she approves. "Knowin' you, I reckoned you'd have somethin' like this in mind. I'd be proud to help ya if'n you'll have me." If I'll have her! Holy shit! This lady chased serial killers for the FBI for thirty years. The Marquis is still a thorn in her side—he killed her best friend and has gotten away with it, so far.

I look at Uncle. "Well, that should make you happy, Uncle. With the FBI on our side, we won't need anything from 3M after all."

"Now wait a cotton-pickin' minute, Nattie. I never said I wouldn't help you. I'd like to!"

Since when? He's staring at M.B. as he says it, and she rewards him with a smile. OMG, he's turning red! You old goat!

"You can never have too much help," M.B. says, "especially when you're dealing with somebody like the Marquis."

"When and where are you fixin' to start this foolishness, Nattie?" Uncle asks me.

Danny and me had talked about this earlier. "When we first met the Marquis, he was going by the name of Barrett Tybee, although his real name seems to be Leonard Ashworth. His alias suggests that he might have some connection to Tybee Island, Georgia. I did a quick Google, and found that there's only one person named Tybee living on the island now—an old man. Possibly he's a relative, but I don't think so. Anyway, there could be a connection on the island."

"Good a place to start as any," Uncle agrees. So now it seems he's on board.

"We ought to go and check out LITM, too." M.B. says. LITM is Love in the Mountains.

"Wasn't the house destroyed in the fire?" I ask her.

"Sure, but the Marquis obviously got away. Probably holed up in those tunnels underneath that you told me about. Might be some clues down there still."

"LITM is closer than Tybee Island," I say. "Maybe that should be our first stop."

"I think so too," says M.B.

Lupe sounds off. "What about me? What can I do?"

All of us look at her, unsure how to answer. Finally I say, "You stay here and go to your NA meetings." At my words, her lower lip protrudes and she looks at the floor.

"Hey, maybe you can help Amos and me with our research," says Kidd. "We'll find something for you to do."

She gives him a vague smile, but clearly, she's far from happy. Truth is, I don't want Lupe anywhere near this mess. I'd like to wrap her up and lock her away somewhere until we get the Marquis out of our lives. She's still fighting a heroin addiction that she got when she fell in with some bad people last year. She's doing way better now, but she totally doesn't need any more stress. Losing Rebecca was bad enough. I want to keep Lupe as far away from the darkness in my life as I can.

I change the subject. "Where are you staying?" I ask M.B.

"Nowheres, yet. I just got in."

"There's plenty of room here. We'd be pleased to have you."

"I'll jes' take you up on that," she says.

I bring M.B. up to date about my encounter with Detective Sykes. "Apparently the Marquis trashed Rebecca's campus office, stole her files and erased her computer. Who knows what we might have lost because of that?"

"This was Rebecca's house, right?" M.B. asks pointedly.

"Yes," I say, then her meaning becomes clear. "Holy shit!"

I'm a step ahead of M.B. when we get to the second floor where Rebecca's office is, with Danny just behind. We barrel into the office—Rebecca's Mac sits on her desk near the window. I slide into her black mesh desk chair and cut on the machine. In a minute, it boots up—to a dead black screen with a flickering white cursor in the top left corner. Shit! It's been wiped!

M.B. and I look at each other. "He was in this house!" we say simultaneously.

"Wait a sec," Danny says. "He could have hacked in from outside."

"But the computer was off," I say. "He couldn't hack a computer that wasn't turned on, could he?"

"Maybe..." M.B. begins.

"If he could do that, then why did he break into Rebecca's office on campus?" Danny asks.

"I dunno," I say. "Maybe the computer security is better on campus." A beat. "But that's beside the point. If he got in here, he has the code for our alarm system. We have to change it, right now!"

"Not necessarily," says M.B. "He could have jammed the alarm system so it couldn't send a signal to the security company's office when he got in. But the system itself should have an internal record if it was triggered."

"How could we find that out?" I ask.

"Call the alarm company," says Danny. "They can scan the system."

I run downstairs and get the phone number off the keypad by the door, come back to the office and call the company on the speakerphone on Rebecca's desk. They give me some shit at first. "If there was a break-in, we'd have informed you and called the police," the agent says.

"Just scan the system to be sure," I tell him. "I'll wait."

"Okay, but I'm telling you..."

"Just do it, dude."

A minute passes. Then, "Shit. I mean..."

"What?" I ask him.

"The system registered an alarm a week ago, on the 28th. But that alarm never registered in our office."

"What time was the alarm?"

Killers!

"10:30 am."

10:30? That was during Rebecca's funeral! "Are you sure?"

"Yes, ma'am. Look, we're very sorry the police were not notified, but the alarm never registered in our office," he says again. "We'll send a technician out in the morning to check your system to ensure this never happens again."

"Fine," I say, but I hardly hear him. I hang up the phone. Turning to Danny and M.B., I say, "It wasn't the Marquis. Danny, you were chasing him in the cemetery when the alarm registered."

"So he's got an accomplice," M.B. says.

I look back at the black screen on the computer again. Something's nagging at me. "Look, y'all. Rebecca was kinda old school when it came to computers. She used to take notes at our therapy sessions in a notebook. Maybe there's something else here that he didn't find."

"Let's take a look," says Danny.

Even though I think it will be useless because someone's already searched the office, I begin going through Rebecca's desk. The top drawer contains all the usual junk; pens, pencils, binder clips, push pins, a key... Holy shit! A key?

It's a flat brass key with deeply cut teeth and the name Donald embossed on the rounded top. A quick Google on my phone tells me that the Donald company makes all kinds of keys.

"It looks like a key to a safe-deposit box," M.B. says.

"But where?" asks Danny. "There's no bank name or number on it."

"A sensible security precaution should it be lost or stolen," M.B. says. "But it could be a key to any kind of lock box. It's a big house. Maybe she hid it here, in another room."

"I guess we've got a long night ahead of us," I say.

Turns out it's not such a long night after all, though. We go downstairs to get the rest of the squad to help us search the house for a safe or a lockbox, and it takes Eduardo just ten minutes to find it, in the pantry of all places. No wonder the burglar didn't see it; the pantry door opens inward and the safe is behind it on the bottom shelf, with a few jars of pickles stacked in front of it. It's only about a foot on a side, with an alphanumeric keypad and a keyhole on the front. Leave it to a little kid!

"The pantry is actually a great place to hide something like this," M.B. says. "A thief would go straight for the bedroom, never think to look there."

I try the key we found in in the safe door and guess what? It doesn't fit. Shit.

"So now we need to look for the combination," says M.B.

"I doubt that Rebecca would have written it down," I say. "And I don't think she'd use her birthday, phone number or other personal identifier."

"Then what would she use?" asks Danny.

M.B. answers. "Something she wouldn't forget." Duh.

I kneel down in front of the safe, staring at the keypad. It's like and old-timey telephone keypad, with both letters and a number on the same button so you could use a number or a word as the combo. I think a sec, then type:

H Y A C I N T H

CLICK!

Eduardo, who's watching me carefully, bursts into applause.

Inside are various pieces of jewelry, a roll of $100 bills secured with a rubber band and a white business-sized envelope addressed in cursive to Dr. Rebecca Feiner. There's no return address. The hackles on the back of my neck rise; that handwriting is eerily familiar. I feel a brief pang of guilt, then quash it as I take out a piece of paper, precisely creased into thirds. I unfold it and a check flutters out onto the pantry floor. The sense of *deja vu* is overwhelming.

May 21, 20___

My Dear Rebecca:

I hope this finds you well. Since you were so dissatisfied with the counseling you received at Love In The Mountains, I am refunding your entire payment for the sessions. Unlike you, I keep my word.

I want you to know that I am disappointed and angry that you canceled our engagement. You would have had a happy and fulfilling life as my submissive. However, I now hold you responsible for the loss of my business, my home, and the life of my sister, because it was you who

Killers!

brought that viper, Miss Natalie McMasters, into our bosom. There will be consequences.

Someday, I will call upon you. It may be next week, next month, next year, in five years or more. But rest assured that I will call upon you, and we shall have our reckoning. Let this check be a reminder that I am a man of my word. Until we meet again, I remain, faithfully yours,

Leonard Ashworth, aka Barrett Tybee

My bones have turned to ice. This is almost word for word the letter I received from the Marquis last May.

Chapter 5

From the Journal of Rebecca Feiner
May 28, 20___

I have been a nervous wreck ever since I received that letter from Barrett (Yes, I know now that it's not his real name, but it's how I first knew him, so I'll keep on calling him that.).

When I canceled our engagement, I had no idea that he was a monster. Now that I do know, I'm afraid. Terrified, actually. My recollections of our time together at Hopkins are hazy. I know that we had a deep relationship that was terribly flawed, but I'm having difficulty remembering the details. Strange that, because I do remember being very much in love with the man.

At other times when I have been fearful and uncertain about the best course of action, I have found journaling to be a means to calm my raging emotions and organize my thoughts, helping me to choose the best path forward. I hope it will serve me well again.

I am truly sorry that I got Natalie involved with this evil, evil man. Despite our unhealthy relationship, I thought that Barrett might really help get the throuple going, or convince the three that it wasn't meant to be. I was wrong about that. Natalie has become like a younger sister to me—I love her impulsiveness, her steadfast loyalty to those she loves, and yes, even her stubbornness, although it makes me want to slap her silly at times. Now I must do what I can to protect her from this madman, even if it costs me dearly. And I must somehow repay her for the danger and the misery I've brought into her life.

***

So, where to begin? Back at Hopkins I suppose, where Barrett and I first met when I was studying for my Ph.D. in Clinical Psychology. The course work was challenging, almost overwhelming. I certainly had no space for a relationship in my life, yet I couldn't help but notice him in class. It did not take more than a couple surreptitious glances on my part before he was sitting beside me. I was looking to the front, concentrating on the prof, when the scent of Old Spice and perspiration washed over me. I turned to see a stocky man with unkempt, shoulder-length, dirty blonde hair, a full beard and a radiant ivory smile that flashed white against his suntanned skin. Somehow, just looking at him made me feel like I was the only other person in the room with him. Notwithstanding the inappropriateness of the location, I felt an overpowering urge to smile back and a stirring in my belly.

The prof's gravelly voice invaded my reverie. "Ms. Feiner?

"Huh, what?"

"The Asch conformity experiments? You did do last night's assignment, didn't you? Explain them to the class, please."

My tongue felt like a swollen slug in my mouth as I rose and did a terrible job describing the classic psychological experiments. I glanced sideways at Barrett as I was babbling, and his expression of pure sympathy made me angry and comfortable all at once.

When class was over, I gathered my things, intending to leave without speaking to him. But his hand touched my wrist and a warm tingle suffused my entire body.

"Miss Rebecca, I feel as if I was responsible for your embarrassment earlier." His voice was low and melodious, warming me like a fine, sweet brandy. "I hope y'all will give me the chance to make it up to you by allowing me to take you to dinner this evening."

What could I say but yes? He brought me to a tony restaurant in the East Harbor. When we stepped inside, I took in the embossed crimson wallpaper, the dark wood paneling and the gold-rimmed service plates gleaming on white table cloths under a myriad of lights from brass chandeliers—the rich aromas of bread, meat and wine brought tears to my eyes. I was sure that, as a poor graduate student, he couldn't afford this place, but when I turned to him to demur, that disarming smile of his made me feel like I'd be desecrating something sacred. He ordered us a rich, curried lobster soup, an arugula salad with a bracingly sharp vinaigrette, succulent, juicy grilled loin lamb chops and for dessert, a decadent cheesecake resting in a pool of white chocolate mousse, with a salted caramel sauce on top. I don't remember all of the things we talked about, but I do remember that it felt like I had known him forever.

When dinner was done, if he had asked me back to his place for a night of love-making, I surely would have said yes, but like a true southern gentleman, he escorted me back to my flat instead. Standing in front of my door, my lips were throbbing for his kiss, but he merely took both of my hands in his huge furry paws and squeezed them gently. Looking deep into my eyes with his moist, pale blue ones, he said, "I had a wonderful time this evenin', Miss Rebecca. I surely do hope we can do this again very soon."

As he turned and walked to the stairwell, I had a powerful urge to call him back to me, but I resisted. Later, as I lay in bed vainly seeking sleep, I finally let my hand creep downwards, imagining what might have been as I brought myself to a shuddering climax.

I really had no idea...

***

I suppose the best path forward is to try to find out what happened to Barrett after LITM burned. If I do, I can always turn my information over the FBI. So to begin, what do I really know about the man who called himself Barrett Tybee?

He got his Ph.D. in Clinical Psych from Hopkins in 2007. He also practiced Tai Chi, getting up before the sun every morning to go out to the city park to do his kata and find others to play with. Because of his surname, I always suspected that he had some connection with Tybee Island in Georgia, but he was surprisingly reticent about revealing any details of his early life. Towards the end of our time at Hopkins, I became ill and had to be hospitalized. When I got out, Barrett was gone and had left no word. Naturally, I was saddened, but since he chose not to share his plans with me, I could do nothing but honor his wishes. That was the last I heard of him until he sent me a flyer about his program at LITM.

So how to track him down? I suppose I can start with the Tai Chi angle, get involved with the communities on social media. I remember we visited an old master who had a retreat somewhere in eastern Alabama. Maybe Barrett has kept up with him. Then, there's Barrett's other avocation...

Killers!

Chapter 6

A **moldy odor in the air portends rain. The evening sky is mottled** with purple bruises, and blood red sunlight seeping through open wounds, as Ye-ye's ancient truck judders down a dirt two-track winding through a towering hickory and red oak forest. He gives the old truck a little more gas and the clattering becomes truly scary; he tries to decide which is worse—reducing the 1937 Chevy into its component parts, or getting bogged down in a muddy morass if the sky opens up as it is wont to do in these parts. He opts for the potential mud instead of the actual shaking and slows the truck again.

Rounding a curve, he rattles beneath a traditional Chinese entry gate featuring a two-tiered hip roof with upturned eaves that used to be scarlet. Ye-ye helped his friend Li-Chin build that gate out of cinder blocks, which were then plastered over to provide a smooth surface that could be painted white; now it's stained with green mold and brown mud. A dangling sign displays the Hanzi characters for Wudang Mountain—Li-Chin had the temerity to name his retreat after the birthplace of Zhang Sanfeng, the creator of Tai Chi Chuan.

It was Li-Chin's dream to create a haven in America where Tai Chi players could gather to practice and pass on their Art. To that end he purchased this abandoned camp in the wilds of Alabama, which he renovated with his own hands and the help of friends. Although many considered the place primitive and uncomfortable, it was paradise to men such as Li-Chin and Ye-ye who had survived Mao's depredations in China. Forty years ago in June, Li-Chin held the first annual festival for Zhang's birthday—that year, only ten people showed up; Ye-ye was one of them. The festival eventually grew to hundreds each year, and serious Tai Chi players made the pilgrimage here for the privilege of studying with *Sifu* Li-Chin and his disciples. And it was here that Ye-ye first met Larry Tyson, who became his student.

As Li-Chin got older, attendance at the festival waned and he finally canceled it some years ago when it became too much for him to prepare for. However, Wudang Mountain still remained a popular retreat for Tai Chi players. Li-Chin never charged anything, but almost everyone who came left a *hongbao* containing anything from a few dollars to several hundred. Even though the camp was decidedly low tech (Li-Chin had neither a PC nor a phone), the stream of visitors enabled Li-Chin to keep his finger on the pulse of the Tai Chi community. If anyone had a clue to the present whereabouts of Larry Tyson, it would be Li-Chin.

Approaching the main lodge, a one-story ranch house sheathed with pine boards, nestled at the foot of the dark mountain that gives its name to this place, Ye-ye becomes worried. The house appears dark and deserted. A pickup nearly as decrepit as his own is parked outside, so Li-Chin is here. Shame fills Ye-ye as it sinks in that he hasn't visited his old friend in many years.

As he gets out of the truck and stretches muscles cramped by the long drive, Ye-ye notices an eerie silence—no birds chirp in the trees, no katydids sing in the meadow, no frogs drone in the lake. A sudden moist breeze rustles in the pines, bringing with it the odors of dead wood and decaying foliage, and the old man feels a sudden chill—like someone stepped on his grave. He trots up the three steps to the wraparound porch where he's spent many a night with Li-Chin discussing the Art, noting that most of the rocking chairs are gone, and the ones remaining have pieces missing. The boards creak as he approaches the closed front door, grabs the handle and depresses the latch. A slight funky sweetness from inside reaches his nose—it's the smell of death. He swings the door wide and enters a rustic living room furnished with homebuilt chairs, a sofa and low tables, dark masses growing from the floor preternaturally illuminated in the orange light of the sunset coming through the windows. He winds his way between them to the doorway on the far side that leads to the kitchen, passing the entrance to a dining room containing a large trestle table that would seat a dozen easily. The table, along with every other flat surface, is covered with papers; letters, flyers, newspapers and the like.

As Ye-ye nears the doorway to the kitchen, the decomp smell becomes ever stronger. The kitchen is darker than the living room because its windows face away from the setting sun, but Ye-ye can't help but notice the shadowy heap on the floor in front of the stove. He finds an oil lamp on a shelf and plucks a match from a wall dispenser to light it. His worst fear is visualized in the stark yellow light—it's Li-Chin, stone dead.

Killers!

Ye-ye pushes a stack of paper onto the floor, sets the lamp on a table and bends to examine his friend's corpse. Li-Chin is clad in a black robe and a pool of congealed blood covers the floor beneath it. He strokes Li-Chin's chest and his fingers come away red. He has to look very carefully at the black cloth to see the three small holes over the heart. It's obvious that the *sifu* was surprised by his attacker, or Ye-ye would expect to see another body besides Li-Chin's. The corpse is beginning to smell and bloat, so Ye-ye knows that it has been a few days since his friend was killed. He couldn't imagine why someone would have done this. Despite his martial expertise, Li-Chin was a sweet old man who had nothing but good will for anyone he met. He had little worth stealing and would likely have offered food and shelter to anyone seeking them.

Ye-ye sighs. He's aware of the duty that he owes his friend, so he'd best get on with it. He finds Li-Chin's bedchamber and locates a clean white robe in a drawer. As he removes it, he notices that it conceals a steel lockbox, which he ignores for the moment. He removes the robe and carries back into the kitchen, where he strips the bloody clothing from Li-Chin's body, then dresses the corpse in the robe. He carries Li-Chin into the dining room, where he lays him out on the trestle table after clearing it off. He rifles drawers until he finds some candles and candlesticks, fits two candles into the holders, and places them at the head of the table. Back in the kitchen again, after some searching he finds tea, rice, water, a bag of apples and eight bowls. The tea, rice and water each goes into its own bowl while he puts a single apple into each of the remaining five. He then arranges all of the bowls at the foot of the funeral table; the rice, tea and water in a line beneath Li-Chin's feet, and the five bowls of fruit in a circle under that. Lastly, he finds an incense burner on a shelf and some incense in a drawer. He places his oil lamp between the two candles and the incense burner in the center of the circle of bowls, then applies a match to all.

It's also customary to place small objects that the deceased was attached to in life on the funerary table, so Ye-ye returns to the bedroom to find something appropriate. He remembers the metal box in the drawer—that might be a suitable place to begin his search. A little padlock hangs from a hasp on the front, but is not locked; why should it be when Li-Chin was the only one in the house. Ye-ye opens the box to find a wad of cash and a small spiral notebook, which contains entries of amounts going into and coming out of the box. Obviously, Li-Chin did not trust banks, so he set up his own system. Ye-ye scans the recent entries, which are in Chinese, to see if he recognizes anything. He finds a disbursement of $2000 to a Xióng jīn several months ago and a chill runs up his spine. Xióng jīn was the Chinese name Ye-ye gave to his student Larry Tyson. The date is a few weeks after that on which Natalie told him that LITM burned.

It was well known in the Tai Chi community that Li-Chin could be generous if the cause was sufficient. Apparently, having lost much when his mansion was destroyed, the Marquis had sought out Li-Chin for help. Is that why Li-Chin has been killed? Was the Marquis here? *Or is he still here?*

A faint sound disturbs Ye-ye's musing—the creak of a board outside on the porch. He silently pads to the front door, hyper alert. Pressing his ear against the rough wood, he hears nothing but the wind. He places his thumb on the latch and depresses it slowly. Before he can open the door, splinters riddle his face as bullets tear through the wood...

Killers!

Chapter 7

Because my old Jeep is a two-seater, I decide that I need something bigger for our trip. I'm at the Jeep dealership by the airport first thing Monday morning, and an hour later I'm signing on the dotted line for a new, bright red Rubicon five-seater. It's definitely cost hella bread, but not knowing where this adventure will take us, I want to be sure we can go anywhere. Besides, thanks to Rebecca, the bread is no longer an object. When I pull it up in front of Hyacinth House, Danny is flabbergasted. "How much did you pay for that?" he asks. "Why didn't you take me with you—I could have gotten you a better deal!" Sure you could, I think, but I want to get us out of town today.

OTOH, Lupe thinks it's wonderful. "Ohhh! It's beautiful! When can I drive it, *Cariño*?"

"After we get back, we'll take it out for some four-wheeling," I tell her.

"What do you mean, 'After we get back'? Who is we? Where are you going?"

When we talked it over yesterday, me, Danny and M.B. decided that the first stop in our investigation would be Greypeak, Georgia, where LITM, Barrett Tybee's former relationship retreat, is located. We knew that the fire destroyed a lot of it, but it was the last place we saw the Marquis. He must have survived by retreating into the tunnels that honeycombed the mountain under the house. Hopefully, we can find a clue to his present whereabouts there.

"I told you last night." Sometimes she conveniently forgets. "Me, Danny and M.B. are going to LITM, to look for clues to the Marquis' whereabouts. You have to stay here if you want to keep your job. And Eduardo needs his Mama." Her lower lip begins to pout. "I'll call you every day and let you know where we are and what we're up to."

Her expression doesn't change, but she says, "Okay, but you be sure you call. I am going to worry until you are home." She will, too.

It's already in the high eighties as we leave the city, but the temperature and the humidity drop steadily as we enter the mountains. It's nice to be able to hang an arm out of an open window for a change as we ride along.

We arrive in Greypeak by early afternoon. It's a sleepy mountain town in Phillyaw County in the northeast corner of Georgia. It's been over six months since I was here, and if I had it my way, I wouldn't have ever come back. Too many bad associations. The town looks even more run down. A few brown leaves cling for dear life to spindly trees on a grubby, yellowing lawn in the town square park, giving the whole place a distinct air of deterioration. The Methodist Church with its three-story attached office building and free-standing steeple is still on the corner, but water stains on the concrete and a few broken windows makes it look like a decaying public works project. The A-shaped sidewalk sign that announced the nightly NA meetings is gone, and I don't think it's because the drug epidemic in Greypeak is over. We pass a decrepit Piggly Wiggly, a few dilapidated Victorian houses, and that mainstay of southern towns, the dollar store, to reach the Greypeak Rexall drug store on the next corner. I know there's a coffee shop inside, probably still in business, not because it's the best food in town, but the only food.

"Anybody hungry?" I ask.

"I could eat," says Danny. Stupid question. A Marine can always eat.

"Whatever you want," says M.B.

This town is as dead as a pile of rats that gnawed on a box of arsenic, so there's plenty of curbside parking. I swing into a space.

Greypeak Drugs occupies a Depression era red brick building with an orange and blue Rexall sign perilously hanging from the second story. After we get out of the Jeep, M.B. takes out her cell phone and begins taking pictures of the buildings and the park across the street. I lead the way to the plate glass door of the drugstore, opaque with ancient grime, and push it open. M.B. snaps another couple of pix as we enter. A bell dings as the odors of burnt coffee and old food slap us in the face. The coffee shop is right inside, consisting of a counter flanked by a row of round, blue-upholstered stools with Formica-topped tables scattered about, surrounded by straight-back chairs covered in orange vinyl. The place is totally deserted and the flickering yellow fluorescent bulbs overhead evoke a sense of destitution.

A short flight of stairs leads to an upper level in the rear. We head that way, M.B. still taking pix. WTF! She's worse than a tourist, and there's even nothing tourist worthy here. "What's with all the pix?" I ask her.

47

Killers!

"When you're investigating, you document everything," she says You never know what might be important later." Right.

In the back of the drugstore, we find wooden display cases with curved glass tops on either side and a white-topped counter at the rear with a burned-out neon Rexall sign above it. A fiftysomething balding dude in a white coat with his name on the pocket is standing in front of a shelf half-filled with packs of cigarettes. More shelves holding prescription meds are behind. Yeet! Sickness and health, all in one place.

I remember this dude from last time. "Hi, Ernie."

He squints at me over a pair of clunky glasses with tape on the plastic frame. "Do I know you, Miss?"

"We met when I was here about four months ago."

"Hell, I cain't remember four hours ago. What can I do for you?"

"Do you serve lunch anymore?"

"Not a hot lunch. Cook quit 'cuz I couldn't pay her. We got packaged sammiches, Co-cola and such in the cooler up front."

I'm totally no foodie, but I shudder at the thought of a plastic-wrapped cardboard sandwich chock full of chemicals and all the roach parts you can eat. "There's no other place to eat around here?"

"Y'all can get takeout at the Piggly Wiggly, but they don't have much different than we do. Y'all'll have to go all the way to Carron if'n y'all want a restaurant."

I hesitate, then, "What's happened here, anyway? Greypeak's like a ghost town compared to when I was here before."

"What happened was Dr. Barrett's place on Rattlesnake Mountain burned down. His bidness brought a buncha rich folks to town. Now that he's gone, so are they. And so are a lotta jobs."

I suspect that many of those jobs were in the meth industry. But a pang of guilt still sticks in my chest. I was at least indirectly responsible for that fire.

"Sandwiches, chips and cokes will be fine, Nattie," says Danny. "We can eat 'em in the park across the street so we don't get the new Jeep dirty."

"Go up front and pick out what you want, and I'll be right down to ring you up," Ernie says.

***

48

Thomas A. Burns, Jr.

After a lunch that tasted like Greypeak looks, we hop back in the Jeep for the short drive to Rattlesnake Mountain. On the right, the Tabernacle of the Holy Spirit, a snake-handling church housed in a decaying white clapboard building with a cross above the door, still looks to be a going concern. Rattlesnake Mountain looms ahead—the lower two-thirds is forested, but the top is sooty black and brown from the fire that nearly cost all of us our lives. A gravel two-track that runs up the mountain comes up on the left, and I take it. The road is way rough, but I drop the Rubicon into four-wheel and we cruise on up through a forest of maple, oak and pine, snaking back and forth through the trees almost like we're on a highway. Suddenly the trees on my side vanish, giving me a spectacular view of the surrounding countryside as we effortlessly climb a thirty-five percent grade. The fire damage begins near the top—apparently the fire did not jump down the steep slope. In another hundred yards or so, the road twists onto a broad, level plateau that looks like the surface of the moon hit with a blowtorch. It smells like the day after a barbecue and is covered with innumerable pieces of charcoal—the remains of a huge, five-story hotel that used to look out over the valley. I begin itching all over as I spot the melted corpse of an ancient hearse. Behind the hotel site are stubby charred tree stumps no more than a foot tall, and beyond that, the blackened remains of a once fine stone mansion looms. This formerly opulent house was the home of Barrett Tybee.

"You don't have to stick to the road anymore," says Danny, back-seat driving from the front.

I toss him a glare as I shift into low and drive directly toward the house. The Rubicon bounces and sways as it makes its way among the rocks and burned stumps before the ride abruptly smooths out as we hit the paved driveway. As we approach the house, I can see that our trip up here was wasted—no way we're going to be able to get inside. Stone doesn't burn, but the wooden skeleton that supported the stone totally did, allowing the upper floors of the palatial mansion to collapse into the basement, leaving nothing but a pile of rocks. I assume the Marquis sought shelter below after we left him and his butler Stoney here when we escaped the fire by helicopter.

Danny plays Captain Obvious. "We can't go in there." Duh!

49

Killers!

"We may not have to," M.B. says. "Look, Tybee got out of there somehow, and I'm sure he didn't wiggle through the cracks in that pile of rubble and stroll down the mountain. So there's gotta be another way in. Where is it?"

On my previous visit here, I learned that the house and grounds were originally designed by the Olmstead Brothers for the infamous Georgia moonshiner Junior Earl Melton. In addition to throwing totally lit soirees for customers from all over Georgia, Junior Earl also ran his liquor business from his mansion, including production and delivery. "I think I might know," I say, and I turn the Jeep around and head for the south side of the mountain. "There was an old road here leading to a path that went down the back," I tell them. "Why build a road and a path unless it goes somewhere important?"

In a couple minutes we arrive at a boulder that juts out over the bluff with a fine view of the valley beyond. Nearby is a steep, rocky path that winds its way downward.

"I can't drive down that," I say.

"The Rubicon might could make it," Danny says, "but you shouldn't unless you've got a lot of four-wheeling under your belt. Let's go back to the highway and see if we can get around the mountain, find the bottom of this trail and see what's there. If we can't, we'll come back here and I'll drive."

"Sounds like a plan," M.B. says.

I turn us around. As we reach the center of the clearing where the hotel used to be, a brown-and-white car with a blue light bar on the roof tops the rise.

"We have company," I say unnecessarily.

The blues flash and the siren bleats, warning us to stop. I pull up so the Rubicon's bumper is five feet from the police car, and the engine cuts out when I apply the brakes. The cop car's door opens and an officer gets out, dressed in a perfectly creased brown uniform complete with a leather Sam Browne belt holding a large, holstered automatic. A shoulder patch reads Phillyaw County Sheriff. I recognize the short, stout dark-haired woman that I've met before. How can this be? I start to get out of the Jeep.

The sheriff's hand goes to her sidearm. "Stay in the car, Miss." Then her eyes fix on my face. "Natalie McMasters!" she snarls. "What the hell are you doing back here?"

I just can't help myself. "What the hell are you doing out of prison?"

Her face would boil eggs. "No thanks to you, a jury of my peers found me not guilty."

I don't believe it! "Bullshit! How could you not know your deputies were dealing meth?"

For a minute I think she's gonna draw that gun. I want to reach for mine, but I don't have a death wish—I know to keep my hands in sight when an armed LEO stops me.

"I don't need to explain myself to you, McMasters," she says. "You jest fire up that fancy Jeep and get yerself the hell off this mountain. It's dangerous here since the fire."

"It was dangerous here before the fire," I say. Sheriff Francine Sawyer was the officer in charge of investigating a series of murders that happened while we were here before. Everybody calls her Sheriff Frank–the joke was her daddy wanted a boy. She was also a sub in the Marquis's kinky sex cult, along with Rebecca. No wonder she never found a perp for the killings in which her BF was complicit. I knew she had been arrested in the aftermath of the fire, and I thought her conviction, on drug charges at least, would be easy peasy. But never underestimate the power of corruption in a small southern town. I have no wish to get involved with her now, and explain why we're all armed. I fire up the Jeep again, throwing it into reverse so I can back up and get around her. After we pass, she turns the cop car around and follows us down the mountain. At the bottom, I have a decision to make—go right to Greypeak, or left out of the county. I opt for left, thinking that she'll want to go back to her office in town, but she swings her car behind us.

"Gonna make sure we follow orders," I say. "Looks like we're in for a little ride."

Sure enough, she dogs our heels until we pass a highway sign that says *Leaving Phillyaw County—Y'all come back!* Looking in my mirror, I see that she's stopped, watching us until we crest a hill. Once the cruiser is out of sight, I pull off the road.

Killers!

"Now what?" I say to my squad. "Who knows how long she'll sit there to see if we turn around?"

"I can't see it being more than five or ten minutes," Danny says. "Besides, she can't legally keep us out of the county."

"No, but she can follow us everywhere and generally be a pain in the ass," I say. I mess with the buttons on the Jeep's navigation system to see if there is another way back. I can't find one, at least not without driving for hours. We wait twenty minutes just to be sure she's gone, then turn around. The sheriff's car is nowhere to be seen. I scan the roadside carefully, looking for a dirt road that goes where we want to, and I spot an area on the right that looks less heavily grown than the surrounding woods, just after we pass the turnoff for Rattlesnake Mountain. I put the Jeep into four-wheel drive again and inch into the brush. The Rubicon has an iron grille guard on the front that will hopefully keep our radiator from being punctured by whipping branches. The brush gets even lighter, and then we're on a two-track with woods on either side.

"Looks like this road has been maintained," M.B. says from the back seat. She's right. The undergrowth on the roadside has been trimmed back and I see a pothole that has been filled with gravel. The dash compass tells me that the road runs south around the base of Rattlesnake Mountain, then swings west around the side of the mountain away from the highway. "Hope we don't run into any company back here," M.B. says. Suddenly I'm glad that my Sig is in the console.

The road takes another turn, to the north this time, and the bulk of Rattlesnake Mountain looms over us. "Better stop here," says Danny. "I'll do a recon on foot."

"What do you mean, you will," I clap back. "Why don't we all go?"

"Because if there's a troop of unfriendlies up there, one person is a lot less likely to be noticed," Danny says.

M.B. takes Danny's side. "Y'all know he's right."

"Yeet! Can't fight two against one. Go on Danny."

Danny draws his .45, gives me a mock salute and goes off into the bush, silent as death.

So now M.B. and I have nothing to do but wait. It's mid-afternoon and not a breeze is moving. The woods smell of flowers and decay. Sweat runs down the back of my neck into my shirt, making me squirm. We could jump into the Jeep and fire up the AC, but then we might not hear Danny if he calls for help. I look at M.B.—she's as cool as an iced watermelon at a summer picnic—she must have done shit like this a million times in the FBI. I stifle the impulse to complain; can't let her think I ain't got her nerve.

Two sharp cracks split the air, coming from the direction where Danny disappeared. Gunfire! OMG! I yank the driver's door open, grab my Sig from the console and take off running after my husband.

Chapter 8

From the Journal of Rebecca Feiner
July 1, 20___

The clinical psych program at Hopkins had proven to be very demanding indeed. The hours were brutal; up before six in the morning and rarely in bed before midnight. The volume of reading and course work was impossible for one person to keep up with, so most of the students had formed pairs or study groups to distribute the effort. Naturally, Barrett and I decided to work together. I suppose it was also natural that we became lovers.

***

About a month after our meeting, we were in bed at my place after a protracted study session. We had sex even though I really didn't want to—Barrett said he'd never be able to go to sleep after such intense mental activity if we didn't. Our love-making was awkward; Barrett's foreplay was perfunctory and rough, so I just pulled him on top of me and encouraged him to get it over with. I didn't orgasm, and I don't think that he did, either. Stress will do that.

Afterwards, we were lying there, me with my head on his outstretched arm, gazing into his pale blue eyes, while he carelessly ruffled my hair with his other hand. "What's the matter darlin'?" he said.

"It's not you," I reassured him. "It's me. I've just had so much to deal with lately. I don't think I'll be ready for Gruder's exam on Wednesday and I'm falling further and further behind in my other classes, even with your help."

"I can help y'all with all of that, if you'll let me."

"We're already studying together. It's not helping much."

"I didn't mean with the studying. It's your attitude, darlin'. You need to find a way to let go."

"I can't let go. This is too important to me."

"Sure you can, love." He paused. "I can show you how, if y'all'll allow me to."

Now I'm intrigued. "How?"

"Evah done role play?"

"What do you mean?"

54

"Like when we were kids. Play pretend. Do a scene."

A frisson of apprehension ran up my leg. "What kind of scene?"

"Oh, one where y'all're not in charge of everything..."

"What do you mean?"

He was quiet a moment. Then, "How about the student and the professor?"

"What?"

"I'm your professor. Y'all're failin' my class. You need an A to get into med school. And you'll do just about anythin' to get it.

I felt a smile coming on as I got where he was going. "I'll do anything," I said breathily, drawing out the last word in a fake southern accent.

Barrett's boyish face split in a wide grin and his azure eyes were shining. My heart just melted. "Anythin', huh?" He jumped out of bed, pulled on his boxers and his jeans, threw his shirt over his shoulders and began to button it. "Get dressed and meet me in my office in five minutes," he said in a stern tone, then left the room.

So I had a pretty good idea of what was about to happen, but I was intrigued nevertheless. I sat up on the side of the bed and reached for my underwear, then reconsidered, putting on just my jeans and a blouse. I went into the hall, then down to Barrett's study. The door was closed. I put my hand on the knob, thought a sec, then removed it and knocked.

His voice was muffled. "Come in."

He was sitting at his desk, glasses perched on the end of his nose, reading a book. He didn't look up when I entered.

"Professor?"

"Office hours are ovah, Miss Feiner," he said.

I put just a bit of a whine into my tone. "I know it. But I just had to see you, sir."

He put his book down and regarded me with a look of distaste. He picked up a folder, took out a sheet of paper and studied it. He said, "Lookin' at the last paper you turned in, I can imagine why. Evah considered a career as a convenience store clerk?"

Even though I knew this was a game, that comment stung. "I'm sorry, sir," I said. "I know it was bad. But I have so much work..."

"Bullshit. Y'all're sloppy, lazy and inefficient, Miss Feiner."

My stomach was hollow. "I know, Professor. But I just have to get into to med school. Please. I'll do anything..."

Killers!

He just sat and stared, his eyes boring into me, not a trace of a smile, or lust in his eyes. Then he said, "Perhaps what y'all need, young lady, is a good spanking. It may help y'all remember yoah responsibilities."

A spanking? He's got to be kidding? His expression was unwavering. No, he wasn't kidding. Now I was truly getting scared.

"Come ovah heah."

I hesitated, then moved slowly toward him. Maybe you had better put a stop to this, Rebecca, I thought. But I kept going, drawn like a moth to a flame.

"Take down your jeans," he said when I stood in front of him.

It was make or break time. I could end this right here. My hands fell to the snap; I hesitated, then undid it and slid down my jeans. Barrett's eyebrows went up when he saw I' wasn't wearing panties. He slid forward in his chair, and motioned. "Get ovah my knees," he said.

I complied. "Don't hurt me," I whined. My little girl voice wasn't faked.

He seized both of my wrists in one large paw and held my hands behind my back. He kneaded my butt cheeks with the other hand until I relaxed them, despite myself.

CRACK!

Oh my God! That hurt! Barrett began to knead my cheeks again, periodically sliding his finger between them. The pain faded, replaced by a warm tingling.

CRACK!

I yiped again, wiggling on his lap to free my hands to grab my hurt. I might as well be trying to escape from handcuffs.

"Pipe down, Miss Feiner, y'all'll wake the neighbors," he said, massaging my ass once more.

"But you're hurting me..."

"A spanking is supposed to hurt, you ninny," he said. He spread my legs a little with his hand, began stroking my sex, slipped a finger inside, removed it.

CRACK!

That time I gritted my teeth so as not to cry out.

Maybe he sensed my acquiescence, because the slaps began to rain down fast and furious. One landed squarely on my genitals and I cried out again. The pain was like nothing I had ever felt and I was worried about bruising. Suddenly he pushed me off his lap onto the floor and stood up. He slid down his jeans and his boxers and he popped out, rampant. He reached down and grabbed my hair, pulled me up and thrust himself in my face. "Y'all know what to do!" he snarled. He put both hands

56

on my head as I serviced him, thrusting deeply, heedless of my gagging. His hands fell to my shoulders, then he picked me up and laid me face down on the desk, spreading my legs wide with his feet. A sharp bolt of pain as he entered me; he grabbed my long hair and began thrusting savagely. My butt was burning and an acute pain lanced through my back each time his loins slapped my rear, but as he continued, I felt the beginnings of an orgasm in my belly. What's wrong with me? His thumb pressed on my other orifice—oh no, not there, please! The thumb stayed in place, circling, but thank God he didn't go any further. The fire in my abdomen continued to build, then suddenly he was shouting, bucking like a madman. My insides convulsed, and I cried out too, ecstasy washing away the pain.

Later, back in bed, I lay curled up in his arms, my head on his chest, a dull burning throbbing in my butt. He had insisted that I take some ibuprofen before we laid down. It was helping.

"You hurt me!" I said accusingly.

"Had to be done," he replied. "Tho' next time, we really should use safe words and set some hard and soft limits."

"Safe words? Limits? What do you mean?"

"Y'all could have said stop, you know. You didn't.

"I thought I did."

"I heard a lot of caterwauling, but not that word."

I think he's right. I didn't tell him to stop. "What are safe words?" I ask again.

"Most people use green, yellow and red. Green means 'Keep on doin' what you're doin', honey. Yellow means "I don't think I like this'. Red means 'Stop that right now!' "

"And limits?"

"A hard limit is something y'all never want to do. If I know something's a hard limit, I'll never try it. A soft limit is something you're not sure about, but might be willing to try. Anal sex is a good example; it can be a hard or a soft limit. If we're exploring a soft limit, that's where the safe words come in."

"Sounds like you're pretty experienced with this," I say.

"Ah like to dominate," he says. "It's my way of getting all the bad juju out of my system."

"At my expense?"

"Not at all. Haven't y'all figured out yet that the sub has all the power? If I want our relationship to continue, I have no choice but to honor your limits and pay attention to the safe words. On the other hand, submitting yourself to me could free

Killers!

you in ways you've never dreamed possible. Y'all're a control freak, Miss Rebecca. In this clinical psych program, y'all've found something you can't control, and it's eatin' you alive. You're incredibly intelligent, but you're findin' that it takes more than intelligence to be successful in this program. You must immerse yourself in it in a way where y'all must give up control, and right now, you just can't manage that. Submitting yourself to me will teach you how to let go in other areas of your life."

As strange as it may seem, his words made sense. I had been fighting the program ever since I started it—maybe it was time to let go. "Okay," I said, "But my first hard limit is that you never spank me like that again. It really hurt! And no anal sex, either."

He smiled deferentially. "Why don't you draw up a list of your hard and soft limits on paper, and we can discuss them before we do our next scene. Then you can learn to trust that I won't do anything you're not comfortable with."

"Okay." I snuggled into the fur on his chest, inhaling his maleness. A curious sense of peace and contentment came over me as I contemplated putting myself in this man's hands, wholly and unreservedly. Of course, I did not know then what I do now...

***

If I'm going to find Barrett again, I'm convinced it will be through his involvement in the world of BDSM. There are many websites where one can find partners—surely he's got to be on some of them. I'm sure he's too canny to post pictures, but I think I know him well enough to recognize him from an online profile. At least it's a place to start.

Chapter 9

As the door bursts open, Ye-ye glides backwards effortlessly. A **short man** with stringy black hair and a ragged beard, dressed in tattered old clothes like a street person, is framed in the doorway, holding an ugly black pistol.

Sun-tzu said, If the enemy is in superior strength, evade him.

Ye-ye spins and dives into the dining room where Li-Chin lies.

The gunman pursues the old Chinaman, only to encounter an object flying towards his face as he enters the dining room. He has only enough time to bring an arm up to prevent it from hitting him in the head. The vase shatters into shards, but it is eggshell porcelain and has not enough weight to dislodge the gun from his hand. Nevertheless, the gunman goes down in case there's another missile following. His gun spits tongues of flame in the direction from which the vase came. But no one is there.

The gunman rises and carefully enters the kitchen, which also appears empty. A cold draft smelling of night-blooming flowers draws his attention to the closed screen door. The sun has fully set, so he can see dark masses of brush in the back yard undulating in the wind. He crosses the kitchen on cat feet, ducking down as he pushes the screen door outward, wary of more objects directed at his head, searching for any motion in the darkness. Nothing. He straightens up and steps out on the back porch, looking right and left. Unfortunately for him, since he's just left an empty room, he fails to look behind him.

Ye-ye soundlessly launches himself from the slanted roof, chopping down at his gun hand, breaking the attacker's wrist. The gunman wheels just in time to take a stiff hand to the diaphragm that takes every bit of the breath from his body. The fight is over before it starts.

Grabbing the guy by his collar, Ye-ye hauls him to his feet. Slight and short, the thug is hardly larger than a middle-schooler, but the *sifu* is wary since he has no idea what skills the man may possess. He knows that the blow he struck would incapacitate anyone for at least a few minutes, but that's little time to find something in Li-Chin's rambling house to tie the fellow up with. Back inside, Ye-ye pulls the man's shirt off his shoulders and downward, pinning his arms against his sides. The fellow cries out in pain as his broken wrist is jerked in the process. Ye-ye does not feel sorry for him.

Ye-ye hustles the attacker back into the kitchen and shoves him onto a chair. "If you try to run," the *sifu* warns, "I will catch you and break something else." The man glares at him sullenly, subdued but by no means cowed. Ye-ye begins rifling drawers to find something to secure him with, and gives a satisfied grunt when he comes up with a bag of zip ties of various sizes. He binds the prisoner's hands and ankles, then carries him into the living room and throws him on the couch.

The old man considers his options.Li-Chin has no phone, so calling the law is out of the question. Ye-ye could just leave him here and inform the police about Li-Chin's murder when he's safely away, but that might make the gunman look more a victim than a murderer; who knows what story he would tell, or how it would be received. It seems there's nothing for it but to carry the guy to the police himself, bringing the gun along so its bullets can be matched to the ones that killed Li-Chin. *All things are difficult before they are easy,* Ye-ye thinks, then begins preparing for the journey.

Two hours later, the *sifu* is occupying a holding cell in nearby Baynesville, Alabama, along with an assortment of drunks, hookers and other lowlifes. His attacker is doubtlessly more comfortable in his hospital bed on pain meds, where he was sent for treatment of his broken wrist. The deputy that Ye-ye spoke to was properly apologetic, but he told the *sifu* that he had no choice but to lock him up since a murder had apparently occurred. Someone would have to go to Wudang Mountain to sort out what had actually happened. Ye-ye found an unoccupied area of concrete floor to stretch out on, since the deputy had told him that the preliminary investigation would likely not be completed until the next day. He was given a greasy sandwich and a cup of coffee the color of branch water for breakfast, neither of which he would touch. One of the erstwhile drunks in the cell with him was more than happy to have a second breakfast.

Since thankfully, lunch had not yet arrived, Ye-ye figures it's before noon when the deputy comes for him, conducts him through a squad room smelling of burnt coffee and old clothes, filled with men and women at desks who pay not the slightest attention to him, and ushers him into an office where a heavyset white guy in a black and tan uniform sits behind a desk surrounded by piles of file folders and papers. He does not rise to greet his visitor, but acknowledges Ye-ye with a nod.

"Come in, come in, Mr. ahh..." he glances a sheet of paper, "...Shēn-Yu. That's a Chinese name, right? Please sit down."

Ye-ye says, "Yes, sir." as he sits in a wooden armchair in front of the desk. He notices a placard facing him that reads, Sheriff W. H. Silas.

"I guess the county owes you some congratulations, Mr. Yu," the sheriff says. "Do you know who it was that you brought into us last night?"

"Doubtless he is man who murdered my friend Li-Chin."

"I think you're right," the sheriff agrees. "His fingerprints came back from AFIS. His name is Ricardo Cruz, and he's wanted for a string of murders across the southeast going back ten years."

Ye-ye sits silently, showing no outward surprise at the sheriff's words.

"We searched the property and found his car parked in the woods. 'Pears he rented it at the Savannah airport. You got any idee why a wanted serial killer would drive all the way from Savannah just to kill an old Chinaman in Alabama?"

"No sir," Ye-ye responds truthfully.

The sheriff scowls. Obviously, that's not what he wanted to hear. "You want to tell me why you drove all the way here to see Li-Chin?"

"No sir," Ye-ye says again.

"Now look, this is a murder investigation..."

"And you have murderer. Why you need anything else from me?"

The sheriff scowls. "It was you that laid old Chin out of the dining room table." It's not a question. "Didn't it occur to you that you were destroying evidence?"

"No sir. My only concern was preparing my friend's soul for its final journey."

"I could arrest you right now for interferin' with an investigation," the Sheriff threatens.

"If you must, you must," Ye-ye responds.

The sheriff's frown deepens. That's not what he expected to hear, either. Damn all furriners, anyway! He makes a decision. "You'll have to fill out some paperwork. You can write English?"

"Yes, sir."

Killers!

"We'll need you back here in a few months to testify at the trial. We can extradite you and charge you if you don't show, unnerstand?

"Yes, sir."

"Get on outta here," the Sheriff growls.

Ye-ye reflects that a few hours in jail and an hour of paperwork is a small price to pay for freedom. He is anxious to get to Savannah as quickly as possible.

Chapter 10

I'm charging down that dirt road for all I'm worth, M.B.'s shouts for me to stop ringing in my ears. I ignore her—my husband's in trouble!

The woods are lighter up ahead and the odors of rotten fruit, woodsmoke and motor oil hang in the air. I burst out into a grassy clearing where the steep, rocky side of Rattlesnake Mountain, bearded with gnarled brush and stunted trees, rears up about fifty feet in front of me. I scan the area, looking for Danny. A cave mouth about 10 feet wide opens on the far side of the clearing, remnants of an old railroad track exiting onto the red clay clearing floor. A stone arch has been built inside the opening to buttress the top and keep it from collapsing, but some missing stones indicate that it might no longer serve that purpose. A rocky trail, the one coming from the overlook above, I assume, winds down to the right of the entrance. Rattlesnake Mountain itself rises straight up above the cave for nearly a hundred feet before sloping inward the rest of the way to the top.

No sign of my man. I call out, "Danny! Where are you?"

I hear a snapping sound as something whizzes past my head, followed by a sharp CRACK! I hit the ground and start crab-walking backwards towards the safety of the woods. More bullets kick up puffs of dirt ten feet in front of me and a flying shard stings my cheek. Where the fuck are those shots coming from?

I crawl behind a bush, which provides poor cover at best, and survey the mountainside. A couple more shots ring out, thankfully not coming close. This time I spy wisps of dust to the left of the cave opening, about twenty-five feet up. Staring harder, I can make out a couple of dark spaces in the rock about eighteen inches wide and a foot high, very difficult to see from where I am because of the scrub brush growing on the mountainside.

There's rustling behind me, and M.B. sidles up next to me on her belly, with a full-sized semiautomatic in her hand.

"You idiot!" she whispers. "Do you think you're bulletproof?"

Killers!

I ignore the shade she's throwing me and point out the openings on the mountainside. "The shots are coming from there."

"Since he's not dead on the ground, Danny must be in the cave," M.B. says. I wince at the thought. "Cover me—I'll try to get in there and help him."

"I want to go!"

"No way, darlin'. I expect I've been in a few more gunfights than you have."

Unfortunately, she's right. "What do you want me to do?"

"Just empty your magazine up there where they're shootin' from. You're not tryin' to hit anyone, just get 'em to keep their heads down until I can get out of their line of fire. Then stay here until me or Danny calls you. Better yet, get even further back in the woods so they can't target you."

She's right again. I hate it! "Okay," I tell her.

"Ready? One, two, now!" Bending low, M.B. runs right to get close to the mountainside where the shooters can no longer see her. I let loose a fusillade of bullets toward the murder holes. The guys inside must've seen my muzzle flashes, because when I stop, a couple more bullets clip the branches above my head. Shit!

CRUMP! The ground shakes and flame and white smoke streams from the holes on the mountainside. Seconds later, a column of smoke shoots straight up some fifty feet into the sky. WTF? That was an explosion and Danny is in there! I get to my knees as M.B. disappears into the cave. I hit the button to drop my mag, replacing it with the one on my belt, then pointing the Sig downward, I follow M.B.

Inside, the cave opens up into a large chamber maybe twenty feet at the highest point. The only light is coming in from outside, but I can see the silhouettes of a couple of trucks ahead of me. I call out again. "Danny!"

From somewhere in front of me, a muffled voice. "Here!" Thank God! He's OK! I see a glow from the direction of the voice, indicating an entrance to another chamber. "Stay put, Nattie. Let me see if I can get some lights on."

The light ahead disappears, so I wait, unwilling to venture further into the darkness. A sweet solvent smell makes my eyes tear and my pulse beats loudly in my ears. Abruptly, a motor begins to growl, then the rear cave entrance blazes white. Still holding my pistol towards the floor, my finger off the trigger like Danny taught me, I run inside a large cave with strings of incandescent bulbs strung from poles around the perimeter. The cavern is huge, maybe fifty feet across and thirty high, with several vehicles in various stages of deconstruction scattered about, surrounded by metal tool chests on wheels and squat wooden shelves holding even more tools. A rickety wooden staircase against one wall rises to a landing in front of a cave mouth some twenty feet up. Danny and M.B. are standing in the back next to a large black generator connected to a bank of compressed gas tanks. The faint smell of smoke is mingled with the scents of gasoline and motor oil, which makes me uneasy.

I trot toward Danny and M.B. "What happened?", I ask.

"Damifino," says Danny. "I was just getting ready to go upstairs to see if I could find the guys who were shooting at me outside, when the ground shook and pebbles from the ceiling started raining down on my head."

"There was some kind of explosion up there," I say. "That stopped the shooting."

"Maybe it put the shooters out of commission," Danny says, "but I'll still have to go up and clear the area. It's never a good idea to leave an enemy on your six. You two wait here."

"Now just a minute..." I begin.

"Nattie," Danny uses his patient tone, which I hate. "We don't know what's up there. If I have to bail in a hurry it will be great if there's no one else in the way. Besides, you and M.B. can watch my six."

Why is everybody but me always on fleek today? "Okay," I agree. Danny mounts the stairs and disappears into the passageway at the top.

I resist the urge to begin counting while we wait. Purely to kill time, I say to M.B., "This is a strange place for a car repair business."

"Looks more like a chop shop to me," she says. She's obviously in no mood for a convo.

We wait some more. What's it been now, five minutes? It shouldn't take Danny that long to get up to the room where the shots came from. Just when I'm ready to go after him, the sound of retching comes from above, and Danny pops out of the passageway, looking as green as a dude who ate a week-old sausage. He stands on the landing sucking in a great lungfull of air, before carefully making his way down the stairs.

"What's wrong?" I ask him.

Killers!

"Oh man! I thought I was gonna pass out! They must've had a meth lab or something up there. The whole place is a mess, filled with noxious fumes, and there's two bodies. Their guns must have triggered the explosion."

Deja vu! A meth lab explosion the last time we were here was responsible for the fire on the mountaintop. "Why would someone put a lab up there?"

"Because there's a big shaft to the outside in the roof of the chamber," Danny says. That explains the column of smoke I saw.

"So what now?" I ask.

"Do what we came here for," says M.B. "That's a dead end up there?" she asks Danny. He nods. "Then let's explore down here to see if we can find a way to the passages under the mansion. The Marquis had to get out of there somehow."

Danny points to the exit on the wall opposite the stairs. "Let's try that way."

Chapter 11

From the Journal of Rebecca Feiner
July 8, 20___

Images whirl through my head. Nude and bent nearly double over a vaulting horse, a CRACK! splits the air as a whip lashes across my butt and upper thighs, sending fire coursing along my nerves.

Suddenly it's me wielding the whip, on a helpless woman bound before me. Her screams ring loudly in my ears as the tendrils lash her breasts, and vivid crimson lines spring into life.

My eyes snap open. In bed, in my room, chilled but sweating, my breath comes in ragged puffs as my heart pounds wildly in my ears. It was a dream! That epiphany does nothing to remove the overwhelming sense of dread that lies cold as a gravestone in my belly. Hope is ephemeral. Dread is forever.

I shouldn't be surprised that I'm experiencing night terrors. I've been spending a lot of time on the Internet lately, making profiles on BDSM websites for prospective partners to see and looking at plenty of seedy pictures. I used my training as a psychologist to profile Barrett, to aid in specifying preferences that would draw him to me. I've not provided any pictures of me yet, but I'm afraid I'm going to have to if I want people to interact with me. I thought I had put my attraction to the lifestyle behind me, but that was proven a lie when I met Barrett again at LITM and fell right back into the old, toxic ways. I'm hopeful that I'm on the right track to finding him again on these websites, but my search has rapidly become an obsession—I feel the old yearning again, making it difficult to stick to my goals.

Done safely, BDSM can be a healthy outlet for negative emotions and add spice to one's sex life, but it can be downright dangerous if done badly, or with someone you don't know and trust. And it's powerfully addictive. The key to a good experience has always been to trust your partner. My downfall was that I thought I could trust mine.

***
67

Killers!

Back in Baltimore, I did some research after the spanking session with Barrett, and drew up a list of so-called hard limits. It included no painful spanking, cutting, burning, electricity, scarring, choking, force feeding; no gags, hard paddles, whips, or canes; no anal sex or defecation/urination play.

"That doesn't leave a man much to play around with, does it?" was his response after he read it.

"What? Dress up is OK, so is mild spanking, oral sex and restraints, within reason."

"What's within reason?" he asked.

"That's what the safe words are for."

He smiled. "You're learning."

That night, he started the session by insisting that I drink a hot cup of herb tea. "It will relax you," he said.

"What's in it?"

"GABA. It occurs naturally during the fermentation of this kind of oolong."

GABA is gamma aminobutyric acid, which functions as a neurotransmitter, blocking specific nerve signals and decreasing nervous system activity. It attaches to receptors in the brain and produces a calming effect, quelling anxiety, stress, and fear. It's found in several other fermented products, like miso, tempeh and kombucha.

Later, Barrett's got me tied face down on his brass bed, paddling my butt with a two-sided paddle—the soft side warming me up, and every once in a while, the hard side providing a satisfying sting, which he immediately soothed with strokes from the cushioned side again. My head felt like it was stuffed with cotton—I'd no idea that GABA was so potent

He gave me a particularly hard smack with the hard side of the paddle and I yelped, "Yellow!"

"Sorry, darlin'." The pillowy side stroked my butt and upper thighs some more and the pain ebbed.

Finally, he stopped paddling me and began messaging my buttocks and rubbing his hardness against me. I pushed back against it, but every time he withdrew, making me want him all the more. Suddenly, a brief flash of pain and he was inside, beginning slow, rhythmic thrusts. Faster and faster, he grabbed my hips, then let go, and began hitting me with the soft paddle again. The strokes came quicker, harder, then a CRACK!, and a sharp sting.

"Yellow, yellow!"

He obediently ceased paddling and slowed down his thrusts.

"Green," I sighed, sinking back into the soft GABA fog in my brain.

After a while he sped up again, and began slapping my ass with his hand. It hurt some, but I didn't want to keep yellowing him, so I gritted my teeth and endured it. His slaps increased in frequency and force and tears filled my eyes. But I didn't say the safe word, and I didn't know why.

Abruptly he stopped hitting me and pulled out; he must have been on the verge of climax and trying to prolong his pleasure. His hands fell to my hips again, and I suddenly felt the head against my other orifice, stroking, wetting, probing, nudging inside!

Searing pain filled my world...

"Red! red!"

Chapter 12

The ancient truck cruises down the right lane of the interstate at a fast fifty mph, windows all the way down, warm air swirling throughout the cab. During the trip from Alabama the hot weather had broken, so Ye-ye is fairly comfortable without AC. Even this close to Savannah, the highway is rural with mixed forest on either side; scrawny pines rear above stunted hardwoods, straining for precious sunlight. The usual detritus from passing motorists—cans, bottles, fast-food wrappers—litters the planted brown-green divider in the road center; a blatant manifestation of the disrespect that Americans display for their planet.

General James Oglethorpe founded the city of Savannah in 1733 and it later became the capital of the British colony of Georgia. Though not strictly on the coast, it grew to become an important seaport in the 1800s and was spared destruction by Union General William T. Sherman on his March to the Sea. The city lies on the Savannah River, which connects it with the Atlantic Ocean, and it is currently the largest port in Georgia. Lying in the low country, it consists of swampy lands, salt marshes and barrier islands. Ye-ye first came here in 1980. After fleeing Maoist China, he became associated with the dancer Sophia Delza at her Carnegie Hall academy in New York City. Eventually dissatisfied with her emphasis on Tai Chi Chuan as a form of dance and exercise, ignoring its martial roots, he decided to strike out on his own. Delza graciously offered to introduce him to some of her colleagues at the newly opened Savannah College of Art and Design, where he might recruit an initial pool of students for his own school. Business was slow at first, but Ye-ye had learned to live on air and water in China, so after teaching in church basements and parking lots for a few years, he was finally able to afford a modest storefront. Not long afterwards, Larry Tyson entered his life.

While almost anyone can learn the basics of Tai Chi Chuan, only a very few have the innate talent to master the ancient art. Larry Tyson was the student that every *sifu* dreams of. The young man astounded his master by learning all 108 postures in the form in a little less than six months, and he could them forwards and backwards after only a year, starting anywhere

Ye-ye asked. At that point he was ready to study the real art of Tai Chi Chuan.

After two more years, Ye-ye considered Tyson nearly his equal, at least as far as physical proficiency was concerned. But Tai Chi Chuan is at least as much spiritual as physical, and in that aspect, Ye-ye was beginning to think that something was fundamentally wrong with Tyson. Little things at first; a wicked gleam in an eye, or a blow delivered with excessive energy while sparring. Eventually, Ye-ye began to notice the bad *chi* emanating from his student. His offers to help correct it were gratefully accepted, but they never seemed to help; in fact, the man's *chi* degraded to the point where Ye-ye became truly troubled. He knew that the personal power granted by mastery of *Tai Chi Chuan* could be seductive, leading to bullying or worse, and while he seldom saw such tendencies in Tyson during training, he suspected that his student was misusing the art outside of class. Finally, when Tyson delivered a particularly humiliating defeat to another student during push hands, Ye-ye told him if he ever did it again, he must leave the school. Tyson said, "As you wish, *sifu.*" and never came back.

Not long afterwards, a disillusioned Ye-ye left Savannah to become an itinerant teacher again, traveling to various Tai Chi schools around the country, bartering instruction for room and board. He wasn't at all sure that guilt about the loss of his best student didn't have a lot to do with his decision.

Nearing Savannah, more buildings appear on the roadside, none of which were here when Ye-ye left 20 years ago; car dealerships, office buildings, fast food joints, big box stores, and new construction all compete for space. Ye-ye wonders again exactly what he's going to accomplish here. He has no idea if Tyson is still in the area or where to look for him. Still, was it a coincidence that Roberto Cruz came from Savannah to Alabama to kill Li-Chin?

Ye-ye decides to drive by his former storefront on Broad St, now MLK Boulevard. He will be immensely surprised if a Tai Chi Chuan school still occupies it, but it's a place to start. The highway rises onto an overpass, and Ye-ye takes the left onto Veteran's Parkway almost automatically. The highway descends into the city streets, becoming MLK Boulevard, a broad thoroughfare with a central median, lined with a mixture of historic and new buildings.

Killers!

A flash of a Chinese characters on the roadside catches his eye. The storefront dojo still there! Now it's called the Saltgrass Martial Arts Studio. Heedless of traffic, he makes a U-turn in the middle of MLK as horns blare, pulling up in front of the streetside windows. Along with Chinese calligraphy, posters for Karate, aikido, and kung-fu (the hard version of Tai Chi Chuan) decorate the glass. Ye-ye knows that these days, many schools teach more than one style of martial arts for economic reasons.

The studio behind the plate glass windows is dark; not surprising since it's midafternoon. Ye-ye realizes he's had nothing to eat today except a handful of rice left over from last night's dinner and a couple of sips of water. To save money, he normally prepares his own food on the road, but he abruptly decides to celebrate his return to Savannah with one of his favorite meals, which he's sure he can find cheap. Turning onto Broughton Street, he scans the establishments on either side until he sees a hole-in-the-wall seafood place advertising a low country boil. For ten dollars and change he gets a half pound of shrimp boiled with potatoes, sausage and corn; enough for at least two meals. He takes his time peeling the crustaceans and indulging in another guilty pleasure; iced tea so sweet it would make your teeth hurt. Afterwards he drives back to the Tai Chi studio and parks in front, intending to get a little sleep in the driver's seat until the place opens for the evening.

It's 7 pm before the inside lights come on; the teacher must have entered the building though a rear door. An old couple loiters on the sidewalk outside. The door opens and they go in, soon to be followed by two more people; another older woman and a young man wearing the traditional Chinese outfit consisting of a baggy white coat with braided buttons and equally roomy pants. The ages of the first two students indicate to Ye-ye that this is a Tai Chi Chuan class, and he decides to let it begin before going inside.

Through the plate glass window, Ye-ye can see that the class is being led by a short woman with closely shorn dark hair, clad in black Chinese garb. She begins the class with an incantation followed by a *qigong* routine. Ye-ye enters and takes a seat in a plastic chair along the back wall. It's a typical dojo with mirrored walls on three sides and a white and black Yin-yang flag hung high above the mirror in front. A small wooden stand next to his chair holds a potted bamboo, three blue/white porcelain statues of ancient,

72

stooped Chinamen, which represent the Tai Chi masters Chang San-feng, Wang Tsung-yueh and Wu Yu-hsiang, and a framed photograph which he cannot see because its back is to him. However, he knows it would be a picture of the *sifu* of this school, and possibly his master or some of his colleagues.

The teacher seems competent, although Ye-ye can spot some areas in which she needs correction. On the other hand, the students are mediocre. The young instructor acknowledges his presence with a glance but does not interrupt her class, which is normal practice. The exercise runs for about 15 minutes, after which the teacher gives the students a break and approaches Ye-ye.

"*Nǐ hǎo, gǔ yī,*" she says, giving him a two-handed Tai Chi salute. "My name is Vivian. May I help you?"

"*Nǐ hǎo,* Vivian. I'm just watching. Your form is very good."

She looks puzzled. "*Xiè xiè.* You look familiar, sir. Have we met? At a competition or a workshop, perhaps?"

"I don't think so," Ye-ye answers.

"What is your name?"

"You can call me Ye-ye."

She smiles. "OK, but you're not my grandfather."

Ye-ye returns her smile. "Your Chinese is very good."

"Thank you. *Sifu* taught me."

"Who is your *sifu*?"

Her eyes flit to the photograph on the little table. She picks it up, looks at it and her eyes widen. She looks at Ye-ye, back to the photo, then shows it to him. It's a picture of himself and Larry Tyson, taken some twenty years ago here in this room.

"You are Sifu Shēn-Yu! You taught Sifu Xióng jīn!"

Ye-ye nods, rises and clasps both hands in the Tai Chi salute. Vivian returns it.

"I would be honored if you would lead the class in the form," she says

"Of course. How much of it would you like to do?"

"They are all beginners," Vivian says. "Grasp sparrow's tail and single whip? Then we can work with them individually."

Killers!

Ye-ye again gives Vivian the double-handed salute. She returns it, then moves to stand beneath the Tai Chi flag.

"Class! I have a wonderful treat for you this evening. I would like to introduce *Sifu* Shēn-Yu, who is a lineage holder of our form and the teacher of *Sifu* Xióng jīn, our master. He has graciously consented to lead us this evening, and then give us corrections one on one." She nods to Ye-ye, who moves to the front of the class as Vivian takes a place with the students.

Ye-ye stands with feet together, solemnly surveying the group, then intones, "*Yù bèi,*" as he bends his knees slightly, rotating his hips and stepping out with his left foot to assume the *wújí bù* stance; feet shoulder width apart, knees slightly bent. "*Yù bèi shì,*" he says, bending his knees again so as to use his entire body to raise his arms chest high, rotating his hips to draw them back, dropping them to his waist again before pivoting left into *gōngbù*, his left foot extended, right foot back. He then flawlessly executes four of the eight basic energies of Tai Chi Chuan in succession; *peng, liu, ji,* and *an,* watching the students out of the corner of his eye. He's pleased to see that Vivian's movements, while not perfect, are sufficiently refined for a teacher. The students however, have far to go. He takes pride in the knowledge that Nattie, who has been studying with him only a few weeks, can do these moves nearly as well as Vivian does. He finishes the series with a posture unique to Tai Chi Chuan, single whip, his left arm fully extended with his right arm cocked at the elbow at shoulder height, hand curled into a bird's beak. To finish, he gracefully transitions back into his beginning stance. The class is silent when they're done, subliminally aware that an extraordinary event has just occurred.

Ye-ye works with each of the students in turn for the next 30 minutes or so, having them demonstrate the postures that they've learned and correcting serious and small imperfections. He does not correct Vivian, as it would be unseemly to correct the teacher in front of her class. When they're done, Vivian closes the session with the incantation that expresses the central principle of Tai Chi Chuan; "*Shǒu è bāguà, jiǎo tàwǔxíng*"—"The hands pass through the eight gates, the feet walk the five elements". The students pack their things and depart, leaving Ye-ye and Vivian alone in the dojo.

"Would you like me to correct your form?" he asks.

"I would be honored, *Sifu.*"

For the next forty-five minutes, Ye-ye watches as Vivian goes through the form. Larry has taught her well—she would place highly in many competitions. He tries to pick out generalities rather than specifics to correct so as not to overwhelm her. When he's finished, she salutes him again, saying, "Much thanks, *Sifu.* I shall remember this night always."

Ye-ye sighs inwardly. Now it is time to come to the real reason he is here. "I am looking for your *sifu*," he says. "You can put me in touch with him?"

"Of course," she says, and his heart sinks. If Xióng jīn is indeed the Marquis, Ye-ye must get Vivian and the other students away from him, but he is not sure how. It would be much better for them if they never found out what kind of monster their revered teacher is.

Vivian removes her cell phone from her bag and pushes some buttons. "Here is his number..."

Ye-ye holds his hand out for the phone. "May I?"

"Of course."

Ye-ye touches the number on the screen and the phone shifts to calling mode. He holds it to his ear, listening to the ring sounds, dreading an answer.

"Hello Vivian." says a familiar voice.

"We must talk, Larry," Ye-ye says.

"Ah, *Sifu*! Ah've been waitin' to heah from you. Why don't y'all come and see me?"

"Where do I go?"

"Vivian will bring you."

Killers!

Chapter 13

Danny leads the way. The passageway is about ten feet wide, high enough so the brawny Marine doesn't have to bend over. The ceiling is shored up with timbers every ten feet or so, and two parallel iron rails run down the center. It's unlit, but the flashlights on our cell phones are enough to keep us from stumbling over the railway ties or stepping in a hole.

"What is this place?" I ask rhetorically.

"I'll bet it's an old confederate lead mine," M.B. says. Bullets were always scarce during the war, so mines were developed all over the South."

After travelling through the passageway for a couple minutes, it broadens out into a chamber with a metal staircase at the opposite end, leading to a hole in the ceiling. "That staircase is totally not from the Civil War," I say.

"There probably used to be one made of wood," says Danny, pointing at some rotting boards laying nearby. "Somebody's been maintaining this place."

The stairs take us to another tunnel that slopes gently upwards. By now, the chemical smells have been replaced by the odors of mold and earth. It's cold and damp in here, and a shiver runs through me. An image of tons of earth looming over me comes into my mind, and my breathing grows short. Stop it, Nattie!

Again, the passage opens into a chamber. I spot a rotting wooden platform on the floor, old ropes dangling from the ceiling around it. I see a dark hole about fifteen feet up. Looks like a large dumbwaiter—I saw similar ones in the tunnels below the mansion when I was there.

"Here's a ladder," Danny says, shining his light on it. It's two red nylon straps with thin, silver metal rungs between them, and it vanishes into the overhead hole, extending out of the range of the cell phone lights. Danny holsters his pistol, turns off his light and puts his phone in his pocket—he can't climb with anything in his hands. "I'll clear the area when I get up there, then y'all can come up," he says. I hope I can do this. I've always had a slight case of claustrophobia, and climbing a ladder in pitch darkness is not high on my list of fun activities.

Danny's only been gone a couple of minutes when I hear a muffled "Clear!" from above.

"You go, Nattie," M.B. says. "I'll follow when you're up."

The ladder sways precariously as I mount it, and I'm soon in darkness. I suck in a deep breath and continue climbing, trying not to think about the distance to the ground or what might be in this pit along with me. But it's only a minute or so before I see a glow above—Danny's light. As I get to the top, he reaches down and puts his hands on my upper arms, hauling me out of the hole onto a solid surface. He's propped his phone against a wall, and the light reveals a stone floor and walls. There's a faint odor of wood smoke, and something else—a smell you never forget once you've encountered it. Death!

We call out to M.B. and wait for her to ascend; Danny gives her a hand up too. He aims the light on his phone forward and leads the way along a stony, upward-sloping passageway just wide enough for one person at a time. "Y'all leave your lights off and follow mine," Danny says. "I have no idea how long we'll be in here."

After about fifty feet, the passageway ends at a blank wall.

"WTF? Something isn't right," I say. "If Barrett got out this way, there must be a way forward."

"Secret entrances?" scoffs Danny. "Really?"

"Don't forget who built this place, Danny." It was Junior Earl Melton, the prohibition-era moonshiner, who made fools of the local cops and the feds by running an illegal business under their noses. "I found secret panels in the mansion when we were here before."

The wall ahead is earth, with protruding stones. A large boulder about two feet across sticks out of the wall a good twelve inches at knee height. I grab it, pushing, pulling, trying to get it move. It just sits there like, well... like a rock.

Danny touches my shoulder to move me out of the way. "You need a Marine for this job," he says. After a minute, he stands up. "That rock isn't gonna move."

M.B. sidles up between me and Danny. "Maybe what you need is a little old lady," she says. She kneels in front of the boulder, poking and prodding

Killers!

it with long, sensitive fingers. "Ah!" she says as she turns a small protuberance on the stone's face. The back side of the rock separates from the wall, allowing it to swing outward. Inside is a cement tunnel, obviously man-made, sloping upward. M.B. looks at me. "After you."

"Na-ahh! Danny, you see if there's any spiders in there."

Danny obediently shines his phonelight inside. "Looks clean to me. I'm going in." He turns off the light, plunging us into blackness. "Can't hold a phone in there, but it should be OK if I go slowly." I hear him scrambling on the stone, then the sound gets fainter. I assume he's inside.

M.B. says, "Nattie? You OK?" She knows what happened to me the last time I was here.

Shit! No fucking way I want to crawl into that hole, even with Danny ahead of me. I tell her, "Maybe you better go first in case I have to bail out of there in a hurry." She doesn't argue.

In a minute, I feel rather than see her absence. I stand there shaking. Shit shit, shit shit, shit shit, shit. All right, goddamn it! I'm going! Getting down on hands and knees, I feel around for the sides of the tunnel, then scramble forward. I have to hold myself back from moving forward at top speed, just to get it over with. I hear movement in front of me, then M.B.'s voice, "Y'all coming, Nattie?"

"I'm here." My breaths are coming more quickly as I crawl forward, forcing myself to slow them down to avoid hyperventilating. It seems like I've been in here forever, though I know it's only been a few minutes.

Oh no! I'm losing the battle, exhaling much too quickly. Lightheadedness signals fast-approaching hyperventilation. All of a sudden, bright light fills the tunnel and I squint at the glare.

"I'm at the end." Danny's voice ahead is faint. He must be shining his light down the tunnel. "Keep on coming, y'all."

Now that I can see, the rest of the crawl is a snap. Another door lies open at the end of the tunnel and Danny helps me out so I can stand upright. We're in a familiar stone corridor; I've been here before! We're in the Marquis' lair, under the ruins of his mansion!

Chapter 14

From the Journal of Rebecca Feiner
July 14, 20___

I've been searching multiple BDSM websites for traces of Barrett Tybee for about six days now, but no luck so far. Based on my profile of him, I've been refining my own profile on the various sites to minimize the number of inquiries and ensure that most of those I do get are serious.

It's been hard. I felt dirty and disgusting when I finally broke things off at Hopkins. Those last days are still hazy—I've got a gut feeling that something really bad happened, and I've just blotted it out. I despaired that I'd never be able to find a satisfactory, traditional relationship again. Tormented by vague, darkly erotic dreams, from which I woke shivering and sick to my stomach, I was afraid to seek therapy, because I feared that I couldn't bring myself to tell someone about all the things that I'd done. Time is a great healer, though. I finally got my degree and moved away from Baltimore. The dreams became less frequent and less intense. While I never did get into another committed relationship, I found that I was able to start dating again, and even to enjoy an occasional tryst as long as I knew that it only had to go as far as I wanted it to.

I've felt myself sinking back into the old ways since I've been cruising the BDSM websites. Unwilling to use an actual photo of myself for my profile, I've purchased several alluring pictures of women that match Barrett's type on a stock photo site. Of course, some men are looking for just anyone to have sex with, and they'll respond no matter what I look like or what my profile says, but these guys are pretty easy to weed out. Some of them are truly heartbreaking, though, lonely souls who have no idea how to relate to a woman. They mistakenly think that BDSM will lead to an endless stream of women for sex. Then there are people of both sexes who are in existing toxic relationships, looking for a change. As a psychologist, I want to tell them that if they can't handle a traditional relationship, they most certainly won't be able to cope with the complications of a BDSM relationship. Finally, there are tons of men who just send me pictures of their genitalia.

Why do guys send women dick pics? I suspect for most it's a transactional expectation, meaning that they hope to get similar pictures from the women in return. Men are obsessed with genitalia, while women tend to consider the whole person. Many males exhibit mating strategies typified by a certain amount of brass and audaciousness; for them, negative attention is often better than none at all. For some, rejection is the main source of titillation; for others, it's exactly what they fear. Too often, men assume their idea of an appropriate message to a woman will be considered so by the recipient as well. Here are three examples of messages that I received, each accompanied by a dick pic:

I'll whip your butt till it's bright cherry red (I don't think so!).

I want to tie you to my bed and eat your pussy and ass (now that's more like it!)

How would you like me to put clothespins on your tits and give you electric shocks? (Umm, no...)

Because many men and women who engage in BDSM are in the closet, BDSM friend finder sites have been plagued by malware that can track users or trash their computers. Extortion attempts are rife, too. Here's a typical extortion email that I found in my inbox soon after my profiles became active.

Hello slut!

You'll be interested to know that I hacked your webcam and caught your last masturbation session on video. I'm sure your family and friends will be delighted to see it after I send it out to all of your contacts. But don't worry. If that thought distresses you, just reply to this email. Then go to the website I will send you and buy $10,000 worth of bitcoin for delivery to an address I will give you. I promise that I will send you my only copy of your video and not bother you any further.

Because I know that this news will be distressing, I am giving you 24 hours to compose your response. After that, the world is going to see you for the slut you are.

This guy must be a real computer genius to take a video on a computer with no webcam...

This is getting me nowhere! I'm no closer to finding Barrett than when I started, and I feel infinitely worse about myself. A perverse longing for the crack of a whip against my flesh grows inside me; that frisson of pain that's like a drug coursing through me, leading to an orgasm so intense that I literally pass out at the end of it. And something in my head is fighting to get out—it haunts my dreams, a dark play on a blacked-out stage, full of screams, anger and fear.

Suddenly, my computer pings. I have installed a security program to detect malware and other intrusions. Because I'm worried about Barrett finding out I'm hunting him, the software will sound an alarm if someone tries to track my IP address. I studied up on IP tracking when I determined which software to purchase. While IP trackers don't necessarily identify the system owner, many give the latitude and longitude of the computer to the person who's tracking the IP address. Which means, if this is Barrett, he'll know it's me.

I have always been a proponent of strict gun control. I think that the general availability of guns in the U.S. is a disgrace, and responsible for the fact that we lead the world in gun violence. But I'm also horribly afraid. No one can protect me from Barrett if he comes for me. For Nattie, it's simple. If anyone tries to hurt her, she just shoots them. It's disgusting that, at her tender age, she's killed half a dozen people—at least that's all she's told me about. Nevertheless, I'm ashamed to admit that I've been looking at pistols on the Internet.

What am I becoming?

Chapter 15

We emerge into a stone corridor. Danny's light dances in the heavy air, illuminating a hanging, dusty mist foul with the sweet smells of chemicals and death. The Marquis and his evil sister were operating a meth lab in here that blew up—I seem to have a habit of being around when that shit happens. My chest tightens, and M.B. starts coughing.

"C'mon, people!" Danny wheezes. "Let's clear this area so we can boogie on out of here."

"It might help if we leave that door open," I tell Danny. I can feel a cool breeze on my face from below. I notice that on this side, there's a facade on the door that perfectly matches the walls—you'd never notice it if it was closed.

Danny leads the way down the corridor, largely intact because it's lined with stone set in concrete. Some of the light fixtures on the ceiling are still intact, but they are not working, of course. We step gingerly over the remnants of a wooden door on the right. That was where the meth lab was, and the chamber beyond is now inaccessible, littered with dirt and debris brought down by the blast. A passage branches off to the left and the one we're in continues onward, ending at a set of stairs blocked by rubble from the fire that raged above ground. I know from before that there are two more rooms down the passage, and I shudder at the memory of what I found in one of them.

"Lessdoodis," Danny says. We move down the hallway and he uses his left hand to open one of the doors, his .45 in his right. He steps inside and I can see his light glinting off metal bars at the back of the room. I shudder again. This is where I found one of the Marquis's eyeless vics.

Danny plays his light around the chamber. "Clear," he says, stepping back outside and closing the door. We turn to the other door, behind us, which M.B. is covering with her pistol. I know what used to be in here, too, and I'm not keen on seeing it again, but there's no help for it.

Danny eases the door open and the funk of decomp rushes out, not overpowering, but totally there. Danny shines the light inside and says, "Oh, my God." He steps in, and I follow.

The chamber walls are festooned with assorted knives, spears, pincers, spiked clamps, thumbscrews and shackles. A black mass occupies a waist-high metal table in the center of the room—Danny's light reveals dark brown, leathery skin, curly black hair, bones and teeth. It's a man's body, fastened to the table with leather straps on his wrists and ankles—I know in an instant who this must be.

The last time I saw Barrett Tybee, the Marquis, he was accompanied by his African-American butler, Stoney, who agreed to remain behind with his boss because the helicopter that evacced the rest of us from the inferno could carry no more people. Despite myself, my gaze is drawn to that terrible table like an animal to a trap, to see the horror that the Marquis has wrought.

Stoney's corpse is partially decomposed, white bones poking out of dryish skin. The light reveals movement on the surface; ugh!, bugs!; ants and beetles that will slowly reduce the body to a skeleton. White teeth protrude from the skull in a grisly smile. Enough of the face is left to tell that the eyes have been removed.

"What kind of monster could do this to a faithful friend?" I ask.

M.B. answers in a lecturing tone. "A psychopath. At Quantico, we've known for years that the Marquis is a sexual sadist. He probably learned the behavior as a child—some kids are driven by a compulsion to find out what's inside of things, whether it be a toy, Daddy's watch or the family pet. During adolescence, the Marquis likely discovered that he became sexually aroused when he was doing surgery; now, he may not be able to have a satisfactory orgasm at all without it. He probably stretches out his operations over several days, beginning with the eyes and other external amputations before ripping inside of his victim in an orgy of violence. He really has no sense of friend or enemy: to him, people are just things to be used for his sexual gratification."

The coldness of M.B.'s lecture is repelling; maybe that's her way of distancing herself from something too terrible to think about closely. Poor Stoney has been here for a while, possibly since the day of the fire. And there's no sign that anyone has lived down here; Barrett must have left soon after he finished with his butler.

But where did he go? We've searched about everywhere down here. I know there's a shaft that leads to a tunnel to the ruins of the mansion, but it's likely not worth checking out—to do so would be very difficult and there's no place there for someone to live. And we've seen earlier that the burned-out mansion is uninhabitable.

"Let's just get out of here," I say. "We've struck out."

We head back into the tunnel towards the chop shop, closing the door behind us to keep the noxious fumes out. My head begins to clear as we work our way downwards, but I don't really feel much better. We still have no idea where Barrett may have gone after he left here. As we exit the cave, the sky is turning rosy; it will be dark soon. A light rain is falling, moistening our clothes as we trudge along the two-track to the Jeep. It's still warm and steamy, though.

"I'll be glad to get out of here," I say to no one in particular, trying to blot the horrors of the cave from my mind.

"Looks like that's not going to happen right away," M.B. replies, pointing ahead.

I look up and see the sheriff's car parked behind the Jeep, blocking us in. The lady herself is using the rear of the Jeep for cover, her service weapon is trained on us.

"Y'all come up real slow now," she says. "Keep your hands where I can see 'em. I even think you're going for a gun, or that you're going to run, I'll drop you."

I should be scared, but I'm not; I'm just mad AF. Too many goddamn guns have been pointed at me today.

"All of you, get down on your knees, then lay down on the ground face first," Frank continues.

This may not be the smartest thing I've ever done. "Fuck you. No." Her eyes widen and her face hardens.

"Nattie..." Danny says.

"Last chance, McMasters. Get down now, or I'll shoot."

"If you're going to shoot us, you'll do it whether we do what you say or not. You can't afford to arrest us, you know. As soon as we get to a courtroom, we'll tell everybody what's been going on out here. Then you can explain that meth lab and chop shop in your backyard. Oh, I'll bet you didn't even know they were there, right? Just like you didn't know before that your deputies were selling drugs. Or you can just put that fucking gun up and let us leave. I for one won't be back to bother you anymore. I've had enough of this fucking place."

Watching her face is like watching a dog think. After a minute, she points her weapon skyward, decocks the hammer, then holsters it. "OK," she says. "Y'all climb into that fancy Jeep and get the hell out of my county. Don't come back, neither."

"Don't worry about it," I tell her.

She gets into the police car and backs down the two-track, leaving us room to drive out. I decide to go down to the mine entrance where I can turn around, so I don't have to back all the way to the highway.

"You took a big chance there, Nattie," Danny says.

"I don't think so," I reply. "The last thing she wants to attract attention to what's going on here. I expect she's paid people to look the other way from her small-time meth operation, but I don't think it's enough to get them to overlook three murders."

Danny claps back, "But what about the people here who are being hurt by the drugs she's selling? I don't know if I can just let that slide."

"You won't have to," says M.B. "I know a guy in DEA who'll just love to hear about it. She'll get what's coming to her."

I hate to think it, but I don't really care.

***

Sheriff Frank sits behind the wheel of her cruiser, watching the red jeep roll past. She picks up a sat phone from the seat beside her and brings up the speed dial menu.

A voice murmurs in the earpiece.

"You were right," she says. "They just left."

More buzzing in her ear.

"I don't know what they found. They blew up the lab, though. I think that I'm going to need somewhere to hole up now."

The voice on the phone speaks again.

"OK, sweetheart," says the Sheriff. "See you real soon."

Killers!

***

Later that evening, Danny and I are in bed in the Super 8, miles from Greypeak. We're both naked, but given the day's events, sex is not high on our to do list. I'm happy just to press my body against his, basking in his warmth with my head lying on his chest.

"I'm bummed," I tell him. "I totally thought we'd find some clue about Barrett's present whereabouts here. Now we're back to square one."

"You'd better get prepared for the possibility that we may never find him, Nattie. After all, the Marquis has been ducking the FBI for over twenty years."

"But..." My phone on the nightstand begins playing Shawn Mendes and Camila Cabello's Señorita—Lupe's ringtone! I grab it and hit the button. "Hey, Bae. Wassup?"

"*Cariño*, how are you?"

"Good. You're on speaker, sweetie. Danny's here."

"Hey, Danny."

"Hey, Lupe."

"What you been up to?" I ask her.

"Getting ready to go to a meeting in a little while," she says. "Do you know when you're coming home?"

Shit, girl, we just left. "Not really." I give her a recap of the day's events, leaving out the gruesome parts—Lupe worries. "We really didn't find out anything new here. We're just talking about what to do next." There's something in her tone that I don't like. "Are you OK, Bae?"

Suddenly, she's crying! "No, I am not okay. I miss you. I feel useless. I am afraid for you and Danny, and I want to help."

"You are helping, Lupe," says Danny. "Holding down the homefront, taking care of Eddie..."

"Bullshit! Judy is doing that! I get to see him maybe an hour or two after school. The rest of the time I teach fat old women how to dance on a pole, or hang around with a bunch of addicts. I am worthless!"

I'm suddenly totally ratchet. I've had a way shitty day. I got shot at, crawled around in a filthy hole, dealt with decomposing corpses, and she's bitching about a bad hair day at work? "Lupe! Get a grip! You're not

86

worthless. You're doing exactly what you're supposed to. Taking care of yourself, staying out a harm's way so I don't have to worry about you too. We'll be back as soon as we can, and hopefully we'll have found the Marquis and sicced the feds on him. Meantime, I need you to be strong. OK?" There's silence on the line. "OK?" I say again.

"OK," she says hesitantly.

"Go to your meetings, and don't do anything stupid. It's a totally big help if I know that I don't have to worry about you and Eduardo."

"OK," she says again, resignation in her tone. I think she means it, this time.

"Well see you soon," I say, then I hit the button and the phone goes dark.

Danny is quiet for a minute, then says, "Don't you think you were a little hard on her, Nattie?"

I want to tell him to fuck off too, but instead I clap back, "Not really. Lupe's had it rough ever since she got addicted. And she's always been a worrier. I think the best thing for her is to stay out of this."

He pulls me closer. "Don't you think you need to ask her what she wants?"

"You know what she'll say, Danny. To be with us. But what can she do but be in the way?"

He doesn't answer, but I can sense his disapproval. Fine. Be that way.

Finally he asks, "So what do you think we should do next?"

"What we talked about. When we first met the Marquis, he called himself Barrett Tybee. Maybe he did that because he has an association with Tybee Island, here in Georgia. I think that should be our next stop. M.B. agrees with me."

"Tybee Island it is, then," he says.

I feel something growing stiff against my leg. I look at his face, see his smile. I push on his chest, and he takes the hint and rolls over on his back. I climb onto him and slide down to take his hardness inside. His hands come up to grip my hips, and I start a slow, rocking motion.

Tomorrow just has to be a better day, I think. Then I give myself over to my lover.

Killers!

Chapter 16

Ye-ye closes Vivian's phone and hands it back to her. "Your *sifu* says that you will bring me to him."

Vivian nods. She reaches behind the counter and retrieves a large purse which she places on top of it. Opening it, she comes out with a black and yellow object that has a rounded front and a pistol grip. A stun gun!

"Why you need that if you know Tai Chi Chuan?" Ye-ye asks.

She smiles apologetically. "The neighborhood around here is not so great at night. Would you believe we've actually had people come in off the street to rob us during class? I didn't want to take a chance that one of the students would get hurt in a physical altercation, so I got this."

Ye-ye nods sadly. It is that kind of a world.

Vivian kills the lights, they go outside and she locks the doors. A three-quarter moon illuminates the street nearly as brightly as daylight, and a cool breeze blows in from the river, wafting the salty scent of the marsh beyond into the city. Ye-ye opens the passenger door of his truck, waits until Vivian gets in before closing it, then he goes around to get behind the wheel.

At Vivian's direction, he drives west out of the city, turning south on I-95.

"How far do we have to go?" Ye-ye asks.

"It's about two hours," Vivian answers. Ye-ye settles in for a long drive.

Vivian is quiet, which suits Ye-ye—he is a man of few words. He doubts that the young woman realizes that her *sifu* is a serial killer, and he's not going to tell her. No loyal student would believe such a thing without proof, and Ye-ye has none.

The interstate is traffic-free at this hour, so the time passes quickly. They exit the highway not far from the Florida border and turn east, traveling on a series of smaller and smaller roads. Just the kind of place where a criminal would go to bury himself, thinks Ye-ye. Finally, they're driving along a tree-lined, single-lane asphalt road with glimpses of a silvery river on the right, shimmering in the moonlight. The air is still and

88

humid, smelling of fish and decaying vegetation. The truck judders as the road abruptly changes from pavement to dirt, and Ye-ye taps the brake to slow the old pickup. Ramshackle wooden buildings and decaying trailers emerge from the trees on the left like skeletons rearing up from the grave, and the truck's yellow headlights pick out a weather-beaten sign on the riverbank—*Tilghman's Landing–General Store & Vacation Cabins*. Not a place that I would choose to spend a vacation, Ye-ye thinks.

"We're here," Vivian says unnecessarily.

The general store is an unpainted, two-story wooden building with a semicircular packed dirt yard in front. Floodlights on the eaves of its roofed porch illuminate a couple of antique Pure gas pumps that were formerly green and white. Ye-ye barely notices the lights glowing inside, behind two large, filthy windows covered with a metal grille of black triangular mesh. He stops the truck next to the gas pumps, then kills the engine. Opening the door, he gets out. Vivian follows.

As Ye-ye and Vivian approach the porch, the screen door squeals on rusty hinges and three men come outside; two white, one Negro. Ye-ye recognizes his former student Larry Tyson; a short, stocky bear of a man in his forties, dressed in cut-off jeans and a t-shirt, his short legs ridged with muscles and tendons. He's clean-shaven and a light blond peachfuzz covers his head. Upon seeing the visitors, his face lights up with an amazing, perfectly white smile beneath piercing blue eyes. His companions are older and taller, both six footers, wearing dirty jeans and t-shirts with big bellies bouncing beneath, but they somehow seem smaller in the presence of their leader.

Vivian greets them. "*Nimen hao, Sifu*, Trevon, Lucas". The men nod.

Ye-ye addresses his former student. "It has been a long time, Larry."

"Yes it has, *Sifu*," he responds. "Why do you not call me by my Chinese name?"

"I am not sure if you are worthy of it any longer," Ye-ye replies.

"You wound me *Sifu*. Tell me, what brings you here?"

"I think you know."

"I'm sure I don't."

All right, let's play your game, Ye-ye thinks. "We have a friend in common—Natalie McMasters."

Killers!

"Ah, dear Nattie. How is she? Has her ridiculous three-way marriage imploded yet?"

"No, it's doing quite well, I think. Which I assume you already know.

"I'm surprised to hear it."

"She seems to think you want to hurt her." Ye-ye continues.

"Hurt her? I tried to help her."

"She says you are not what you seem. You threatened her."

Ye-ye eyes the two other men, who have moved right and left, and are now flanking him. Vivian has retreated back against Ye-ye's pickup.

Larry Tyson approaches within six feet of Ye-ye. "And what does Natalie say about me?" he asks.

"That you are a murderer. That is why I don't call you by your Chinese name."

"So that is what you think, too?

"That is what I came to find out," the old man says. A beat. "I'm sorry to tell you that someone has killed our old friend Li-Chin."

"You think it was me?"

"No, I captured the man who did it, and turned him over to the police. But I wonder if he did it for you."

"Why would I want to hurt *Li-Chin*?"

"Possibly because he knew where you were." A brief flicker on Tyson's features tells Ye-ye that he may have hit the mark.

"I am sorry to hear that Li-Chin is no longer with us. He has done much for the Art." Tyson raises his arms in a push hands posture. "Would you care to play, *Sifu?*"

Tyson steps forward. Ye-ye does the same, and each man touches his hands to his opponent's wrists, each one's eyes boring into the other's.

Chapter 17

From the Journal of Rebecca Feiner
July 20, 20___

Another week has gone by, and I'm no closer to finding Barrett. It's become obvious that I need a different plan. But what?

Besides BDSM, Barrett's other passion is Tai Chi. I find it ironic that he could be involved in two things that were so disparate; the same man who could play push hands in the park with old people on Sunday morning could also gleefully wield a paddle on my naked ass. I suppose that is part of the complexity of the man that attracted me to him.

One time while we were at Hopkins, we took a trip to a farm in Alabama, where Tai Chi players from all over the east coast had gathered. Barrett did most of the driving, so while I remember it was in Alabama, I'm hazy about exactly where. It was like an Asian Woodstock—people camping, cooking outdoors, organizing impromptu Tai Chi classes and demonstrations and yes, a considerable amount of sex going on in those tents, not always between people who had traveled there together.

A few minutes on the Internet search brings up a page for a Wudang Mountain, near Cedar Bluff, Alabama. I'm sure that's the place! I hit F12 to open the developer tools and type some script to tell me when the web page was last updated. Hmmpf. Ten years ago. I remember that the guy who owned the place was pretty old. Who knows if he's even still alive?

Further investigation of the Wudang Mountain page reveals no phone number, email address or contact information – it's just a bunch of pictures from the Tai Chi festivals. A Google search for Wundang Mountain, Alabama, still gives no contact info.

I think a minute, then go to the Cedar Bluff webpage, and find a phone number for the Chamber of Commerce and call them. It rings for a while before someone finally picks up.

"Cedar Bluff town hall, Regina speakin'. How can we help you today?"

"My name is Rebecca Feiner. I'm a, er... writer, and I'm working on a story about Tai Chi. I remember going to a gathering of Tai Chi people near

Killers!

Cedar Bluff about fifteen years ago. I was wondering if you knew anything about that. Is it still going on?"

"Mercy, no, that festival stopped years ago. Shame it was, too. Brought a lot of bidness into town while it lasted."

"Do you remember who ran it? Where it was?"

"I don't remember the old fella's name, but he's Chinese. I think he's still around. Barry over at the Piggly Wiggly would likely know."

"Have you got a phone number for Barry?"

She gives it to me, and after a little more conversation about when my and where my article will come out, I get her off the line. A quick call to the Piggly Wiggly gets me in touch with Barry, who tells me that the Chinese gentleman in question is called Li-Chin, and that he still comes in for supplies every couple of weeks.

"He ain't got no phone, not even a bank account. Pays me cash for his groceries."

"Do you know where he lives?"

"Homesteads out at the old Morgan place on County Road 700." He gives me directions. I thank him and kill the call, then find the place on Google Maps.

Looks like I'm taking a road trip to Alabama.

It will take the best part of two days to get there, and I'll be traveling alone. I remember the alert that I got, telling me that someone had tracked my IP. Suddenly, I know what I must do.

That afternoon, I find myself someplace I thought I would never be. In a gun shop. Predictably, there's a group of fiftysomething white rednecks hanging out in the back who act as if the place is their second home, but a young black couple and three unaccompanied women, two Caucasian and one Asian, are also shopping. I shiver inwardly at the thought that these instruments of death have become so commonplace in America.

The clerks are both white guys in their twenties. When it's my turn, one wearing a name tag that says he's Andy asks if he can help me. When I tell him I'm looking for a handgun, he says, "You know you have to have a permit from the Sheriff, or a CCH, to buy one, right?"

"Yes I do know. I applied for one last week and I have it here." I had to give my fingerprints so they could run a background check. I take the permit out of my wallet and show him.

He asks me a bunch of questions about why I want a gun, how much experience with firearms I have, and what kind I'm looking for. I tell him I'm not sure. He replies, "Based on what you've told me, I'm going to suggest you get a revolver. They're simple to use and maintain and fun to shoot." He reaches into the display case and brings out two, one chrome, and one black. Either would fit in the palm of my hand.

"These are both chambered in .357 magnum, but to start with, you can shoot .38 specials, which are cheaper and have a lot less recoil. You do know that you can't carry concealed without a permit, right? But open carry is legal in this state, so as long as the gun can be seen, you'll be all right."

I look down at both guns, almost afraid to touch them. What am I doing? I come close to just walking out, but then I remember Barrett's letter. *...rest assured that I will call upon you, and we shall have our reckoning*, it said.

"I'll take the silver one," I tell him.

Killers!

Chapter 18

We get up early Tuesday morning, 7 am. The Super 8 advertises a free breakfast, but I don't have much hope it will be any good. Prepackaged pastries and dishwater coffee I don't need. But Danny just has to check it out, so I go with him. I'm pleasantly surprised to find a buffet with biscuits, gravy, scrambled eggs, sausage and bacon. Danny and I load up paper plates to the breaking point, while the ever-practical M.B. gets yogurt and cereal.

Unlike our cheerful mood when we left home, we're now subdued. I didn't realize how much we were counting on finding a clue to the Marquis's whereabouts in the ruins of LITM. This trip to Tybee Island seems like a long shot at best, but I don't have a clue about what else to do.

We roll out in the Jeep at 9 am—Tybee Island is a 6 hour drive, mostly on two-lane roads that should have light traffic. The cool mountains gradually give way to warmer lowlands with mixed coniferous and hardwood forests and open fields. It's warm enough to keep the windows open but not so hot to require the AC—it would be a pleasant ride except for the uncertainty that hangs in the air like smog.

Convo in the car is *très* sporadic. Danny, riding shotgun, is reading a Georgia tourism book, periodically enlightening us with interesting facts about the Peach state (like that it's called the Peach state—yawn!). After a while, he starts seriously getting on my nerves. M.B. has got the right idea, snoozing in the back. Asleep or awake, I'm totally happy to have her and her extensive FBI experience tracking serial killers on this trip.

We stop for gas and a bag of burgers halfway there. As we're leaving the drive through, I notice a pea green VW microbus parked in the lot. Looks like a real hold over from the 70s. I'd be totally embarrassed to drive something like that.

Munching a burger, I ask the squad, "Anybody got a plan for when we get to Tybee Island?"

"We need to look for serial-killer related things," says Danny.

"Duh! I'm sure if there was a bunch of murders there, M.B. would already know about it. Right?"

"Of course," M.B. replies. "But Danny's right. We're not looking for a string of killings *per se*; we already know there aren't any. But we are looking for evidence of the things that breed a serial killer, or other evidence of his presence."

"Like?"

"There's a concept known as the homicidal triad..." M.B. begins.

"I know about that," I interrupt. "It came up in another case. Bed wetting, fire-starting, cruelty to animals."

"Barrett Tybee looks to be in his forties," M.B. continues. "He probably started acting out in his teens. So we are looking for crimes in the early 90s—maybe a rash of animal killings, mutilations, or fires, or a series of other violent incidents that don't rise to murder. Physical and sexual abuse during childhood is also huge pre-disposer. We can look for evidence of that, too."

"But doesn't that kind of stuff happen almost everywhere?" Danny asks.

"Unfortunately, yes. But if we can find evidence of cases egregious enough, it might provide a clue to the Marquis."

"That could be difficult," says Danny. "Those things get pretty well hidden in small communities like this one."

"He said his name was Leonard Ashworth."

"And we'll certainly check out that name," M.B. says.

"He would be a psychopath, right?" I ask.

"The more exact diagnosis is anti-social personality disorder, or ASPD–people who may have exhibited socially irresponsible behavior, a disregard for the rights of others, have difficulty with showing remorse or empathy and recurring problems with the law. People with ASPD tend to be skilled actors whose manipulate people for personal gain. He might also lack deep emotional connections, have a superficial charm about him, be very aggressive, and get very angry sometimes."

"That's a great description of Barrett Tybee," I say.

"And many of these guys have sexual issues; they can't get off without violence."

I hesitate for a sec, then think, *she's dead, it won't matter.* I tell them about finding Rebecca and Barrett in a BDSM sex scene with two other women while we were at LITM.

Killers!

"Wow," M.B. says. "If I'd known about that then, I'd have been sure he was the Marquis."

"But how do we find out about all of these things?" I ask.

"What we really need is to find a busybody who was around during that time," Danny says. "A real gossip who knew everybody's business."

"That's right," says M.B. "We just need to start knocking on doors, talking to people. Someone will turn up."

I'm glad she's so optimistic.

It's getting on about three o'clock. We pass through the outskirts of Savannah, crossing the river into the salt marshes beyond. A steady east wind blows in from the sea, carrying a salty, grassy odor. The landscape—lime green swaths of swamp grass interspersed with vibrant silver pools—is beautiful and serene.

"I wish we were here on vacation instead of on this awful mission," I say. "Maybe we can come back someday when this is all over."

A sign comes up on the left—a turnoff for Fort Pulaski.

Danny reads from his guidebook: "Fort Pulaski was bombarded by the Union in 1862 and the commander surrendered it the next day. It eventually became an important bastion for the capture of Savannah by the Union Army."

"So what?" I say.

"Hey, it's our history."

"Like I said, so what?"

M.B. intervenes to forestall an argument. "We need to find a place to stay." We didn't book ahead because we didn't know when or even if we'd even be here.

Danny speaks up. "The guide says peak tourist season is mostly in the spring and summer months, ending just after Labor Day. We should have our pick."

We cross a two-lane bridge onto the island and the road becomes four lanes with a divider in the middle, a clear indication of the traffic volume during the high season. Low scrub brush and stumpy trees on the roadside impede our view of the surrounding area. Five minutes later we drive into the sole village on the island; the usual beach town—a hodgepodge of low one- and two-story buildings with the occasional multi-story hotel.

"Want to just try one of these hotels?" I ask.

"Nah," Danny says. "Let's look around a little. Maybe we can find someplace neat. Look! A rental agency. Let's try there." God he's such a big kid!

I find a parking space. "It won't take three of us to find a place," I say. "I'm gonna look around a little. Call me when y'all're ready to leave and I'll meet y'all back here."

The road divides ahead and there's a little triangular park in the center, so I make for that. It's a circular courtyard surrounded by palm trees and a bunch of flagpoles. There's a fountain in the center, a Greek woman with a vase pouring water into a shell held by a child at her feet, and benches around the perimeter. There's a newspaper dispenser with a glass lid and a sign on top that says *Tybee Islander—Free!* I grab a copy, then a a bench, and begin flipping. It's not your typical beach paper just full of ads for local businesses—it's got news stories too. There's an address on the masthead. This may be the place to start our hunt for the Marquis.

I look up back toward the rental agency to see if Danny and M.B. have come out, and do a double take. A VW minibus that looks a lot like the one I saw at lunchtime is turning a corner! He followed us all the way here? I jump up, tucking the *Islander* under my arm and trot that way, crossing again so I can look down the street he turned on. The bus is parked about halfway down and the driver is getting out. OMG, he's one of the biggest guys I've ever seen—when he stands erect, his head is higher than the top of the bus, and he's got a build like an NFL jock. He turns and walks away from me. Way to be paranoid, Nattie! If he was actually following us, he totally picked a terrible vehicle to do it in. The street is filled with shops and restaurants. Tybee Island is a popular vacay spot—it's not too much of a coincidence that two cars on the same Georgia highway could be headed there and I'm sure VW made more than one green minibus. The big guy turns into a restaurant—makes sense, he's hungry after a long ride. Me too. I head back to the rental agency to see how Danny and M.B. are doing.

They're coming out as I walk up. Looks like they're arguing.

"I'm telling you, my *per diem* isn't going to cover even half of this place," M.B. says.

Danny is holding a sheaf of papers. "Don't worry about it," he says. "I'll make up the difference."

Walking up to him, I say, "What'd you do?"

Killers!

"He rented us a palace," M.B. sniffs.

"Hardly," he replies, looking at me. "In the car, you said you wished we were here for a vacation. I just got us a nice place so it will seem like that a little while we're working..."

"For two hundred and seventy-five dollars a day!" M.B. finishes.

"Danny..." I begin.

"Look, I'll pay for it. I'll even pay for all of your part, M.B. This has been kind of a shitty trip so far, and I just want to make it a little better for us."

See why I love this guy?

"Besides, it has a kitchen. We can cook and save money on restaurants."

"Oh, hell no!" I tell him. "I've eaten your cooking."

"But you haven't eaten mine," M.B. says.

We hop in the Jeep and drive five minutes to the cottage. It's a single-story, white clapboard house with a screened porch that wraps around two sides, nestled on a quiet back street near the lighthouse. A plaque next to the front gate reads *Sandcrab Cottage.* The porch has padded rocking chairs and a dinette table. Inside, it's totally done up in white with pastel blue accouterments. I'm instantly in love!

"Yeet! Maybe we can get takeout and eat on the front porch..."

Danny just smiles, while M.B. shakes her head.

Chapter 19

G od, grant us the serenity to accept the things we cannot change, the courage to change the things that we can, and the wisdom to know the difference."

Along with the NA group, Lupe intones the words of the familiar prayer that begins each meeting. It seems more appropriate than usual tonight. She really needs this meeting and the wisdom it may bring. She can't understand why Nattie and Danny aren't treating her as an equal partner. She couldn't go with them to Georgia because she has to work, but surely there's something she could do to help find this monster threatening her family. Nattie thinks that she must protect Lupe from stress, but Lupe knows better. NA has taught her that she's just one fix away from a relapse, but she's also learned that whether or not she takes that fix has nothing to do with how she feels or what's going on in her life. Besides, she'd be under a lot less stress if she were actually doing something to find the Marquis.

Tonight, Lupe is the meeting chairperson. She asks the group, "Is there anyone here at their first NA meeting, or at this meeting for the first time?"

A man stands up in the back of the room, looking at the floor as he speaks. "Me." He's a thirtysomething, with a shock of dark, collar-length hair, a slight build and a boyish face. He's probably the best dressed person in the room, wearing a corduroy sport coat over a yellow Hawaiian shirt and a pressed pair of blue jeans. A white cast peeps out from under the sleeve at his right wrist. He looks too old to be a student, but the State Campus NA group is open to any addict, student or no.

"What is your name?" Lupe asks.

"Theodore."

"Welcome, Theodore! You are the most important person here tonight! Is this your first NA meeting ever?"

"Yes, Ma'am."

"You don't have to call me Ma'am. My name is Lupe, and I'm an addict."

"Oh, I guess I'm an addict too. I forgot to say." He smiles boyishly. "And you can call me Theo."

Killers!

Lupe smiles, hoping to put the newcomer at ease. "You don't have to say you're an addict unless you want to, Theo. No one will think badly of you if you don't."

Lupe directs the members who have volunteered read aloud from the NA literature to begin, and when they are finished, she asks the group for a discussion topic. Theodore raises his hand, and she acknowledges him.

"I totally want to go out and get high right now," he says. "What can I do about that?"

"It was hard for me to admit that when I first came here," responds Lupe, "so thank you for your honesty. Can anyone share some things they have done not to use when they feel that way?"

A girl in front named Sherrie raises her hand. She's a twentysomething State student who does not have much time in NA, a bleached blonde with the bad complexion that habitual meth use generally brings. Lupe is her sponsor. Lupe calls on her, then sets an alarm on her phone to signal when the time for discussion is nearly up. For the next forty-five minutes, various members share; Theodore seemingly hangs on every word. However, Lupe is somewhat troubled. In the months that she's been coming to NA, she's developed a pretty good radar to sniff out people who are experiencing a craving for their drug of choice. While Theodore says that he wants to use, he's not triggering her detector. Lupe knows that not all addicts are the same, but she still wonders if the young man is being truthful about his addiction, or if he just came to the meeting to be the center of attention. It happens, but no matter. The right thing to do is simply take his statement at face value.

Lupe's phone dings. She addresses the young man. "Theo, I hope you got what you were looking for tonight." He smiles at her, nodding his head. She feels a chill go through her at his smile. That's odd—Lupe is a committed lesbian, not generally attracted to men, although Danny is becoming an exception. But she can't deny that Theo is good-looking, and he does have a peculiar magnetism.

She goes through the meeting closing ritual. After the final "Amen", she gathers up her materials and puts them back in the chairman's binder, nodding at the group treasurer who has arrived to take the collection basket. She puts the binder away in a metal cabinet, then goes to the back where a small group has gathered around the newbie. She hears Sherrie say to

100

Theodore, "You look so familiar, dude! I'm sure I've seen you somewhere before."

"Yeah, well maybe neither of us were in any shape to remember it if we've met before," says Theo. He turns, and his face lights up at Lupe's approach. "Hey, Lupe, I want to thank you for making me feel so welcome here." Sherrie frowns, probably because she was so summarily dismissed.

There's that tingle again. "*De nada,* Theo. Did anybody tell you a group is going out for coffee, if you want to come along?"

He smiles expectantly. "Are you going?"

Lupe hadn't planned on it, but WTF—it's not like she has anything special to do at home. Eduardo is still staying with Judy McMasters in the guest house, and will be in bed by the time she gets there. "Sure," she says. Theo smiles even more broadly.

A warning bell goes off in Lupe's head. She'll have to be careful not to let the young man get too attached to her. Addiction is a lonely life, and it's common for newcomers to become infatuated with someone who shows even the slightest interest in them. Relationships formed in early abstinence don't generally work out. Besides, Theo will need a sponsor to help him navigate the early days in the program and guide him through the twelve steps. A relationship could interfere with that.

On the way to the coffee shop, Theo walks beside Lupe, chattering like a squirrel, but she hardly hears him. She's still bummed that Nattie has dissed her—maybe she needs to talk to her own sponsor before she goes to sleep tonight. Sleeping on a resentment can lead to a fix the next day.

Theo sits next to Lupe at the coffee shop. He tries to monopolize her attention, but she doesn't let him, leading others into conversation with him. Sherrie, sitting on Lupe's other side, has her eyes fixed on him. Is she trying to puzzle out where she knows him from, or is she just mad that he's talking to Lupe instead of to her? Clyde is sitting at the head of the table— he's an old-timer, who specializes in the quick indoctrination of newcomers. "You should at least get some phone numbers before you leave here tonight, Theo," he says. "If you're wanting a fix, calling someone in the program is the quickest way not to use."

"Give me your phone and I'll put my name and number in your contacts," says Theo. Clyde obliges. Handing his phone back, Theo turns to Lupe with his hand out. "May I have yours, too, Lupe?" That's one request

Killers!

you almost never say no to in NA. Lupe hands over her phone and Theo punches buttons with his thumbs, handing it back after a minute. Sherrie hands hers to him as well, and after a moment, he takes it. "I promise I won't call any of you unless it's really urgent," he says.

By the time the evening is nearly over, Clyde has consented to be Theo's temporary sponsor, until the young man has met enough people to form a more permanent relationship. As they step out onto the sidewalk, Theo turns to Lupe and takes her hand in his with his uninjured arm. He stares into her brown eyes with his deep blue ones. "I want to thank you for all you've done for me tonight, Lupe," he says. "I totally feel like I'm not ever going to use again after tonight."

"Hey *amigo*, one day at a time, right?"

"Sure." He smiles again, and Lupe feels that smile burning into in her heart.

Theo takes off. Sherrie calls, "Hey Theo, wait up!", trotting quickly after him. A flash of resentment arises in Lupe. What the hell is going on here?

Chapter 20

From the Journal of Rebecca Feiner
July 21, 20____

I's Saturday night. We're at Barrett's. Over the past month or so, we've been exploring various aspects of our new relationship. Barrett has this way of pushing me past my limits: I've been finding out that some things I thought were hard limits, I actually enjoy.

Now he's got me spreadeagled on his brass bed, my wrists and ankles tied to the posts with velvet cords, gagged and blindfolded. I'd never have allowed this a month ago!

We smoked a bong as a prelude to our sexplay—I'm sure he had something else in there besides marijuana. I'm alternating between the utter blackness of the blindfold and an out-of-body experience where I seem to be hovering over the bed, watching Barrett service me. He's playing with my nipples and my sex with his fingers, taking me up slowly, then backing off. He's done this several times already, so I'm getting really uncomfortable.

He abruptly stops. A hard pinch on my left nipple sends a jolt of electricity downward. The pain doesn't subside—he's put on an alligator clip. A second later, another goes on the right one. The metal chain that links the clips is cold against my belly. I squirm some more as warmth glows between my legs.

I ask him in a dreamy voice, "Do me down there some more." My tongue is thick with cotton and there's pressure in my forehead.

Suddenly the probing fingers return, opening me, then they're replaced by a tongue. Yess! The strokes are very light and hesitant— that's not how Barrett usually does me. I want some relief, but I can't get it. I try to push myself against the tongue, but the ropes prevent that. Then the tonging stops.

He reaches around my head to undo the strap, and the ball pops out of my mouth. I close my aching jaws, swallow the saliva that's built up, grateful for the extra freedom.

The tongue returns, flicking, dancing, probing with featherlike touches

"Dammit! Finish me!"

The tonguing stops. "Are you sure that's what you want?"

"Yes, dammit!"

Killers!

The teasing tongue starts, stops, starts, stops again. There's a little jerk on the chain, sending a jolt of pain everywhere. Then more tonging, still light and sporadic.

"Please! Finish me!"

The tongue stops again. "Beg, you slut! And call me Master!"

It's like I have x-ray vision! I can see him looming over me, despite the blindfold, smell the cloying aroma of his sweaty maleness. There's another odor too, sweet and spicy.

"Please Master, please make me come!"

The tongue starts again, harder this time. "Ohhh yesss, yesss..." I'm almost there!

"Are you sure you want to come, little one?"

"Yes, Master! Please!" Wait a sec! His tongue is still swirling inside me. How can he speak so clearly?

"What's going on?" I shout fearfully.

He pulls off the blindfold and a burst of white light sends pain through my head. The light fades to red as my vision comes back into focus. I look downward and see a black-haired head between my legs, nuzzling me. The tongue stops, and she looks into my eyes.

"Wait! No! Red! Red!"

Barrett, standing next to the bed, gives the girl a crack on the butt that had to hurt. She burrows in, hard.

My belly starts to spasm. No! I'm giving in to something I never wanted, again! My eyes close despite myself as I thrust my hips against her mouth, giving myself over to the pleasure. Damn you, Barrett Tybee!

Later—I'm still tied on the bed, Barret on one side of me, the pretty Japanese girl on the other. They're both playing with my tits and my sex. I'm getting hot and bothered again, but I'm still mad that he tricked me into this.

"So Rebecca, have you met Meiko?" Barrett smirks.

"You shouldn't have done this, Barrett."

"I checked our contract. A three-way with another woman wasn't a hard limit for y'all."

"You didn't bring it up when we made the contract."

"Neither did you. What would you have said if I did?"

"I'd probably have said it was a hard limit."

Meiko tweaks my nipple and my hips begin to rotate involuntarily.

"What do you think now?" Barrett asks

Damn you! "I don't know..."

Meiko speaks for the first time. Her voice is like the Chatty Patty doll I had in the 80's. "Didn't you like what I did, Rebecca? You sure seemed to."

"That's not the point..."

"The point is that y'all found out something about yourself. That you like having sex with a woman." Barrett says.

"But..."

"And now, I think you owe Meiko something in return." Barrett motions Meiko toward me. She throws her leg over me, straddling my face. Her funk causes me to stop breathing for a moment, then, "Please! No! Red!"

Barrett kneels between my legs, starts rubbing his hardness against my most sensitive place. My words choke in my throat, and a moan escapes my lips.

Meiko rubs herself harder on my mouth. I open it and my tongue snakes out. There's a sharp pain below as Barrett pushes inside.

Closing my eyes, I give myself over to the moment again.

Killers!

Chapter 21

Ye-ye's and Tyson's hands slide along each other's arms, each one sticking to the other, trying to identify where the opponent's next move will arise and counter it before it begins. They execute a complicated dance away from the pickup to a more open area, without ever losing contact with each other. Each one knows that committing too early can be fatal–if your opponent knows your next move, he can have an attack ready to counter it. These two have trained together for countless hours— each is an extension of the other, one body, one brain.

"I think you have learned things I did not teach you, Larry. That is why we had to part ways," Ye-ye says.

A broad grin lights up Tyson's features "Ah *Sifu*, it has been too long, too long."

"I cannot allow you to continue to harm others." Suiting action to words, Ye-ye stikes, an open palm slap aimed at Tyson's forehead. He senses it before it lands and retreats, robbing it of any force. He tries to grab the old man's wrist and redirect the energy to take him to the ground, but Ye-ye anticipates and his arm, supple as a snake, slithers away from the grasping hand. Tyson is still grinning as the players go back to the rhythmic give and take of pushing hands.

Ye-ye quotes Sun Tzu. "The difficulty of tactical maneuvering consists in turning the devious into the direct, and misfortune into gain."

Tyson responds. "But the *Tao Te Ching* says, men come forth and live; they enter again and die. Of every ten, three are ministers of life to themselves; and three are ministers of death. I am a minister of death. I am true to my nature."

"So you consider yourself part of the natural order?"

"Everything must die, *Sifu*. How a man dies only matters to him."

Now Tyson attempts an attack, a straight hand to the old man's throat. Ye-ye sweeps the attacking hand outwards and down, simultaneously raising his elbow for a *zhou* strike to the chin, but this time Tyson anticipates, redirecting the energy so it becomes harmless.

"We are perfectly matched, you and I," says Tyson. "Our difficulties will not be resolved in this way."

"Then how can we resolve them?" asks Ye-ye.

"What is it that you want from me, *Sifu*?"

"I want you to leave Natalie alone."

"You would demand that the tiger does not hunt? Besides, Natalie will not let me alone. She knows that I killed her mentor and best friend, you know."

At last, an admission of guilt!

"That is true," Ye-ye agrees. "Then what is the answer?"

Tyson smiles and nods, and fear strikes the old man as he realizes that the smile is not directed at him. He has been watching the two men on his periphery, and now they advance on him from either side. He can tell from the way they move that they are not trained fighters. Surely Tyson does not expect them to take him down, even with his assistance.

They rush in simultaneously as Tyson launches another attack. Ye-ye goes limp, dropping to the ground, sweeping his leg behind Tyson's knees, bringing him down as well. Ye-ye rolls away from his former student as his two goons put on the brakes to avoid crashing into each other. The old *sifu* comes effortlessly to his feet, facing the three of them in a relaxed posture. He smiles. Maybe this will not be so difficult after all...

Then Ye-ye senses danger behind him. Suddenly, he realizes where the true threat lies! He whirls around to confront Vivian, too late. The ugly black and yellow stun gun spits, and Ye-ye feels the sharp prongs tear through his shirt, cutting into his chest. Even a Tai Chi master cannot resist the 50,000 volts of electricity that jolt him; a million bee stings inside turn his muscles to jelly. He topples like a felled tree.

Forgive me Natalie. I have failed you...

Chapter 22

On Wednesday morning, I wake to the aroma of coffee, bacon, ... and fish? I turn to see Danny lying on his side, facing away from me, still dead to the world. I hop out of bed and pull on a pair of panties and cutoffs, and a t-shirt. Then I go out to the kitchen.

M.B. is cooking breakfast–bacon, biscuits and fried fish!

"Where'd you get the fish?" I ask her.

She smiles. "Haven't you noticed we're surrounded by water?"

"What, you caught it?"

"Yep. Found some tackle in the porch closet."

"What'd you use for bait?"

"Dead fish I found on the beach that the gulls hadn't got to yet." She uses a spatula to carefully flip the fish in the pan. "Want some eggs with this?"

"Sure." Something about M.B. has been nagging at me for a while. Since we're alone, now would be a good time to ask her.

"A while ago, a police officer told me that the FBI would be investigating this case. Would that be you?"

"Ya got me," M.B. says. "After Chipper passed, I was at loose ends for a while. We had so many plans for retirement—hobbies, travel and the like. All that died along with him."

"I'm sorry," I say.

"Me too. You know that the Bureau considered Barrett Tybee a person of interest in the Marquis investigation. That's why me and Chipper were at LITM; to see if I could get any evidence to indicate he was any more than that. You know I got his DNA and sent it to the Bureau so they could confirm a match to DNA found at one of the Marquis crime scenes."

I nod. M.B. had told me all this while we were in the hospital after LITM burned.

"Turns out that the current political climate is not only sparking a lot of retirements," she goes on, "it's also deterring a lot of young folks from a career in law enforcement. It's hurtin' big city police forces the most, but the Bureau hasn't escaped, either. So, they've started a program to bring recently retired agents back to active duty on a limited basis. They offered me a shot based on the work I did at LITM. If I can get some solid leads on the Marquis, they're willing to give me a task force to hunt him down."

"Yeet! That would be awesome."

"I've got you to thank for helping me get this shot, Nattie."

I feel the heat rising into my cheeks. "No thanks necessary, M.B. I'm just glad I've got you to help get that motherfucker..."

"You know, I've been meaning to talk to you about your language..."

I so don't want to hear it! "What's the plan for today?" I cut her off. Before she can answer, I continue, "I found a local newspaper yesterday. Maybe their office would be a good place to start."

"That it would," M.B. says, displeasure still evident on her face. Maybe I do need to watch my cussin' around her.

I grab the copy of the Islander I picked up yesterday and get the address off the masthead. About that time, the bedroom door opens again and Danny comes out, obviously roused by the breakfast aromas. He's wearing nothing but a bathing suit, and the sight of those pecs, his six-pack and corded legs makes me want to jump his bones right there. M.B. looks like she's considering it too.

Shit. Duty calls.

By the time breakfast is done, I'm sure I won't want anything else until supper. We change into more suitable clothing and head out to find the Tybee Islander office on Venetian Drive with the help of a tourist map.

Venetian Drive is a street tucked on the back side of island, near Tybee Creek. We go around a bend and start taking note of the house numbers: 1202, 1204, 1206... Google said that the newspaper office was 1116—has to be behind us. But how can that be? The road changed from 12th Street to Venetian Drive when we came around the bend. Nevertheless, we turn around, and I spot a row of yellow posts on the side of an unpaved road going off to the right at the curve. I turn, and see that the first house is 1120. We find the newspaper office next door, in a little two-story clapboard house with windows on either side of a white entry door, both cracked to let in the outside air. A dirt driveway runs along one side of the building, terminating at a tin-roofed shed open in front. The hood of an old sedan peeps out on one side, with space for a second vehicle on the other. Tybee

Killers!

Creek sparkles in the sun behind it. I pull the Jeep into the driveway and park so as not to block in the sedan.

We walk back down the driveway to the front of the house. I knock on the front door, but there's no answer. I push on it and it opens; the twin smells of coffee and hot metal wash over me. The room is furnished as an office; an old-fashioned roll top desk flanked by a perpendicular table with a computer monitor sitting on top. Polished hardwood floors gleam in the morning sun shining through the windows, and a large fan dangles from a green pressed copper ceiling. Floor to ceiling bookcases on one wall hold large, leather-bound books, to which a rolling ladder allows access. A half-closed doorway leads to another room in the rear.

"Hello!" I holler. "Is anybody here?"

There no answer, but there's a lot of humming and clattering coming from the doorway—anyone in there prolly would not have heard me.

We go in. The wall where the roll-top is, is decorated with framed copies of newspapers. Moving closer, I can see that they're all copies of the *New York Times.* Some of the headlines read:

Son of Sam Suspect Arrested in Yonkers

Black Man Killed by Mob in Brooklyn

Subway Vigilante Shoots Four Black Muggers

Black Honor Student Shot and Killed by Undercover Policeman in Manhattan

Jury Acquits All Transit Officers in Death of Michael Stewart

All of the stories were written by Samson Weathers.

Since there's no one in the office, we cross the room and push the far door fully open. The hot metal odor becomes much stronger and the noise gets a lot louder.

Inside, an old African-American man sits in front of a keyboard of a machine that resembles something out of an old steampunk movie, spanning floor to ceiling and festooned with pulleys, chains, and wrought iron curlicues. Moving parts inside go up, down and sideways like some funky cartoon contraption. On the opposite side of the room is another machine with a flywheel and rollers. I know what that one is—a printing press! Yeet, does anyone even use those anymore?

"Sir?" I say loudly.

No response.

I raise my voice and holler, "Sir? Can we talk to you for a minute?"

He finally turns and looks at us. He hits a lever, and his machine goes silent.

"Whatchoo say?"

I repeat myself, still in a loud voice.

"I'm old, not deaf," he says. "And you can talk all you want to. It's a free country. Supposedly."

"My name is Natalie. We were hoping you could help us?"

He turns back to his keyboard, like he's going to cut the machine on again. Hoping to stop him, I ask, "What kind of machine is that?"

He hesitates, then, "It's a linotype machine. We do things the old-fashioned way round heah."

"We're conducting an investigation," Danny says.

The word *investigation* stops him. The old guy looks at us with a sour expression—I'm not sure if he's pissed because we've interrupted him or he's just totally not interested in what we have to say.

"Investigation? An investigation of what?"

"We were hoping we might be able to find somebody who might have lived on the island years ago," M.B. says.

"Lotta people used to live heah. Who you lookin'?"

I hesitate. WTF, might as well tell him.

"The Marquis. He's a ..."

"I know what he is." A beat. "I've hunted his kind before."

"We saw your Son of Sam story on the wall outside," M.B. says.

That evokes a half-smile. "Yeah, I worked on that story. I wasn't the one that found him, tho'. Parkin' ticket caught that SOB."

I approach him, hand extended. "I'm Natalie McMasters. That's Maribeth Woodrow and Danny Merkel."

He reaches out. Uncle Amos drilled the virtues of a firm handshake into me when I was growing up, so that's what I give him. He returns it with a strong grip.

Killers!

"Pleased," he says. "Sam Weathers. What makes you think that the Marquis is on the island?" he asks.

"We don't know that he is, but we think he might've come from here. He's used an alias with the last name of Tybee."

"Hmmph. Not many people with that name. One person on the island today, in his eighties."

"The Marquis's real name is Leonard Ashworth," I tell Weathers.

Weather's jaw drops, and he just stares at me as if he doesn't believe what he just heard. "That's a name I do know," he finally says. "The Ashworths were an old island family. But far as I know, Leonard Ashworth is dead."

Chapter 23

Acold front heralds the advent of fall in the capital the next day, bringing blustery winds and grey skies that match Lupe's mood perfectly. She's at work, watching one of the *vieja urraca* she coaches trying not to totally destroy herself on a dancing pole. She woke up with a headache—a quick mental inventory told her she had a resentment because Nattie left her behind. She's also vaguely mad at Sherrie from last night. But why? For running after Theo? Sherrie's behavior worries Lupe, because early sobriety is no place for relationships or sex. That shit will get you high in a heartbeat. But Lupe also recognizes a vague undercurrent. Jealousy? WTF has she got to be jealous about? She's a lesbian, for God's sake.

"Owww!"

Lupe's client, Mrs. Alford, lands her butt on the pad with an audible thump. She's massaging her shoulder like she's pulled something. If only!

Lupe tells her that, given the shape she's in, it would be way better for her to choose something less physically demanding than pole dancing for fitness, but her advice apparently fell on deaf ears. "Mrs. Alford, maybe we had better make that all for today," Lupe says, extending a hand to help the lady to her feet.

Dame Alford gives Lupe a look of pure venom. Hey, it's not my fault you fell off the pole, Señora! Ignoring the helping hand, she struggles to her feet and stalks off toward the locker room.

"You'd better not count on a tip from that lady," says a voice from behind Lupe.

Lupe turns to find Leon Kidd smiling at her. "You made it!" she says.

"You sounded kinda down on the phone this morning," says Kidd, "so I figured I'd better clear the decks and show up. Where would you like to go for lunch?"

"Somewhere close. My next client is due in 45 minutes."

"Better make it Century Lanes, then." Kidd says. "That bowling alley has the best burgers around here. Go figger."

Killers!

"Let me change and I will be right with you." Lupe heads back to the locker room to pull a top and a pair of slacks over her two-piece gym outfit and grab her purse.

They walk next door to Century Lanes. The coffee shop inside is enclosed by glass walls, so the sounds of bowling are muffled. Lupe grabs a table while Kidd goes to the bar to order for both of them.

Lupe is wearing a glum look when Kidd comes back to the table. "What's going on, Lupe?"

She tries hard not to let the tears flow when she answers him. "Why don't Nattie and Danny want my help, Leon?"

"Hey, you're making a big assumption there, kiddo. Why do you think that?"

Is he stupid, or what? "Maybe because they ran off together in Nattie's new car and left me here!"

"Lupe, you know that Nattie loves you more than anything. She's just trying to protect you, is all."

"She should know me well enough to know I do not need protecting. I came to this country from Mexico when I was only a little older than Eduardo is now. She has no idea the things I've seen and done."

"Nonetheless, she has your best interests at heart."

Lupe grits her teeth, then takes the plunge. "I want you to help me find whatever that key that Nattie found in Rebecca's office fits," she tells Kidd.

His eyes widen. "It's likely a safe deposit box, or a mail drop."

"Could we find out if Rebecca had one of those?"

"Maybe. It's not easy—records of things like that are usually not kept where you can get to them." Kidd pauses. "Do you have the key?"

"No. Nattie had it. But I do not think she took it with her. Why would she?"

"Why does Nattie do anything?" Kidd asks rhetorically. "Because she can."

The bartender catches Kidd's eye, indicating that the burgers are up, and he goes to get them. When he comes back and puts a plate in front of Lupe, she asks, "How would we find out if Rebecca had a safe deposit box?"

Kidd thinks a second. "Ask the lawyer. If he he'd talk to us."

"I could check the house some more, too," says Lupe. "Everything stopped the other night after we found the key. Maybe we overlooked something."

Kidd takes a bite of his burger, and his face assumes an expression of pure bliss. Then it reverts to his usual, sour look. "What do you think Rebecca might have kept in this mysterious container?"

"Nattie said she thinks that Rebecca was trying to find Mister Barrett. Maybe it's something to do with that."

"That's possible," Kidd agrees. "But you know, people usually keep things in safe deposit boxes that they need only once in a while. If you're right and it's a record she was continually adding to, it would be a real pain in the ass to keep going back and forth to the bank to get it."

"So it's probably in the house," Lupe says.

"It's a big place. Plenty of room to hide something."

"So maybe I will start looking after I get home from work. My last client today is at three. I will go room by room. If I don't find it, then we can think about safe deposit boxes."

"Sounds like a plan," says Kidd.

Killers!

Chapter 24

From the Journal of Rebecca Feiner
July 23, 20___

Them he Tai Chi farm is about a six-hour drive, mostly on the Interstate. That's a lot of time to think. Too much time.

The law says that I must have my gun locked up when I'm in in the car, inaccessible to me. But what if I need it for protection? It takes about a month to get a CCH—I don't have that kind of time. So, I'm forced to break the law, keeping my gun in the unlocked glove compartment. I should be OK as long as I don't get pulled over and have my car searched.

Traffic is sparse for most of the trip, but as I near Atlanta, it becomes denser. As I'm driving in the right lane, tapping the brake to avoid hitting the jerk in front of me, a car whizzes by on my left, it's horn blaring, scaring the living shit out of me. The initial cold frisson of fear is quickly replaced by anger. Before I even know what I'm doing, I jerk the car into the left lane and lay on the gas, trying to catch the idiot who's now several car lengths ahead. He must realize what's happening, because after a few seconds' time during which I rapidly gain on him, the distance between us ceases to change—he obviously saw me and is speeding up too. I glance down at the dash. Oh my God! The digital speedometer registers 105, 106, 107...! I take my foot off the gas and his car seems to take off like a rocket, rounding a curve and disappearing from sight. I hit my turn signal and ease back into the right lane, suitably chastened. I had no idea how much stress I was feeling until just now. I'm very lucky a cop didn't see me—speeding like that easily could've resulted in a search of my vehicle. If that gun was found, I'd be up on felony charges. Then a more troubling though arises—what would I have done if I'd actually caught up with the guy?

The rest of the ride is a struggle to stay awake as the surge of adrenaline wears off. It's not till I'm just west of Cedar Bluff that I become alert again, searching for a series of increasingly smaller roads to take me to my destination. Finally, on a dirt two-track in the woods, a gate like you'd find in a big city Chinatown looms ahead. I pass through it and drive another hundred yards, coming into a clearing that contains a single-story ranch house with an old barn off to one side and an old pickup parked out front. Pulling up next to it, I feel relieved—at least someone is home. I jerk the parking brake and get out of the car, stretching my muscles aching from the tension of the drive.

I hear a creak and a bang. An old man with a long, wrinkled face, Mandarin-style chin whiskers, and a bald head comes out of the house. He must be eighty or more. He's dressed in a red and black checked flannel shirt and blue jeans. It's got to be hovering around ninety degrees, but he's not sweating.

"Welcome to you, beautiful lady! I am Li-Chin. Who are you who comes to visit an old man, bathing me in your glorious light?"

Oh brother! "My name is Rebecca Feiner. I was here once many years ago with a friend. You called him Xióng jīn?" That's Barrett's Chinese name, which he told me meant golden bear.

His wrinkled face blossoms into a wide smile. "Xióng jīn, shì de! But I have not seen or heard from him for long time." My face must communicate my feelings. I'm ready to get back into my car and leave, but he says. "Please, pretty lady, please come inside. Let me make nice Chinese meal for you." His eyes are so beseeching I just can't say no.

I follow him up the steps to a broad porch furnished with a few broken rockers—I have a vague memory of sitting on that porch with Barrett many years ago, enjoying the music of the night. We enter a large room furnished with Shaker-style chairs, a sofa and low tables, passing through to a doorway on the far side into a commodious kitchen that contains a large, cast iron stove. It must be running, because it's stifling in here. I'm trying to think of a way to tell *Li-Chin* that I have to get out of here before I pass out when he waves me to the back door and out onto another porch overlooking a spacious back yard at the foot of a mountain. The sun is setting over it and a cool breeze wafts down the mountainside.

"You wait here," he says. "I bring tea, then supper soon."

The tea proves to be a smoky black one, served from a blue and white ceramic teapot with a bamboo handle, in thin china cups not much bigger than a duck egg. His dinner is tofu in a peppery sauce with white rice, and boiled wontons stuffed with an unfamiliar green. We eat it out of small

Killers!

bowls with the trays of food between us as we sit on the back steps, watching darkness descend over the mountain.

Li-Chin tells me about his dream to create a place for Tai Chi players to practice and pass on their Art. It took him ten years after he bought this run-down farm to achieve it. His annual festival had been running for about twenty years when Barrett brought me here. "Now I remember you from that visit," he says. "I was so happy that my friend Xióng jīn had found himself a worthy companion. It is sad that the two of you drifted apart. Please, if not too nosy, you can tell me reason why?"

I can see that the old man still has feelings for Barrett, so I don't want to tell him the truth—that the man he remembers so fondly is a serial killer. "It was one of those things. We graduated, and each went our separate ways."

He picks up the pot and pours tea for both of us in the tiny cups. "Ah yes, is tragedy of today's world. One time woman's greatest calling was to serve her man and have many children. In turn, he would protect her." He clicks his tongue in distaste. "You know, Xióng jīn was thinking of making his own place like *Wudangshan*."

My antennae perk up. "Oh really? Did he ever do it?"

"I no think so. He would have invited me." My heart falls. "Mebbe he could not get the land he wanted."

"What land?"

Li-Chin rises, collecting our dishes onto the bamboo tray that he brought them out on. "Wait here. Mebbe I still have..." He takes the tray inside. Thru the screen door, I see him leave the kitchen and go into the back of the house.

I'm quivering as I sit there, and it's not from the chill that comes with the night. Is it possible that I'm finally going to get a line on Barrett?

After about five minutes, Li-Chin calls to me from the kitchen door. I go inside and he hands me a piece of newspaper. "Xióng jīn show me this, say this is place that he wants to buy." It's a newspaper ad for a bankruptcy sale of a place called Tilghman's Landing, on the east coast of Georgia. Apparently the people living there just couldn't afford it anymore. The bank was looking for someone to take over the lease. That would be just like Barrett. Buy the land out from under a bunch of poor, dirt farmers and kick them out of their homes. Suddenly, I start to cry.

"What is wrong, pretty lady?"

"I don't know." That's a lie. I've been working so hard to find Barrett. Now I may have.

The old one places his hands on my shoulders, drawing me to him. He smells strange, of sweat, soy sauce, and unidentifiable herbs. I find myself sobbing into his flannel shirt. I can feel energy radiating from him, going inside of me, driving out the bad. My sobs cease and I look up into his weathered face, smiling kindly at me. I back away, flustered that I showed such intimate emotions to a total stranger.

"Is okay," he says, seemingly reading my thoughts. "I feel much bad *chi* inside you. No good. Must get rid of it." He hesitates, then, "Can show you mebbe how?"

What have I got to lose? "Okay."

"Go outside and wait." He says.

I do as he says. After a while, he comes outside with the bamboo tray he brought dinner on, but this time it contains a long, cylindrical object with a silver bowl placed halfway along its length, a ceramic dish with a hinged top, a small spoon, a pair of tongs and a metal brazier sitting on a footed platform. The sharp smell of burning charcoal is suddenly apparent in the air.

I'm sitting on the steps as before; he places the tray next to me and sits with it between us.

"What is this?" I ask.

"Medicine."

"I don't..."

He places a finger on my lips, shushing me. "Will be good for you. You see. Need powerful medicine to drive out bad *chi*."

He opens the top of the dish, then takes up the pipe and flips up the top of the bowl. With the spoon, he scoops a small heap of brownish powder from the dish and transfers it to the bowl. He puts the spoon back on the tray and closes the lid on the dish, then picks up the tongs. He uses them to remove a coal from the brazier and drops it into the bowl of the pipe, on which he begins to puff. After a minute he exhales a stream of white smoke, then he turns the pipe in his hand to present the open end to me. I take it from him, feeling entirely like someone else as I do so.

"Inhale long draft of smoke deep inside. Hold as long as you can."

Killers!

I have no doubt that I'll be able to do as he asks; my undergrad pot-smoking days have prepared me well. I fit my lips around the broad end of the pipe, not unaware of the phallic connotations, and draw in the hot, acrid smoke, which sears my lungs briefly before the drug it contains quells the pain. Per his instructions, I hold it in, and the world suddenly shifts, then glows with bright colors as I remove the pipe from my mouth and breathe out. Quite involuntarily, I take another hit, then find myself tumbling through a curtain of blackness...

Chapter 25

S amson Weathers leaves his linotype machine and goes into the
next room, the three of us trailing behind. He indicates the shelves
holding the rows of leather-bound books. "The archives of The
Islander," he says. "Go all the way back to 1902." He runs a finger along the
bottoms of the books. "Be in 1992, I think." He extracts a volume and caries
it in both hands to a table by the window. Opening it, he begins paging.
"Yep. Here 'tis."

Looking over his shoulder, I read:

May 20, 1992

SUSPICIOUS FIRE KILLS ISLAND FAMILY

Arson Suspected - Daughter Only Survivor
by
Samson Weathers

Last Saturday, longtime island residents Barrett (42) and
Lorna (39) Ashworth, and their son Leonard (17) were apparently
victims of a fast-moving blaze that reduced their home at 1110
Venetian Drive to ashes in a matter of minutes. The Ashworth's
daughter Lily (8) survived, and was found outside in the yard
by the fire department. The other three residents were burned
beyond recognition, but the remains were consistent with the
descriptions of the Ashworth family.

Fire Chief Chester Goodly averred that the fire had burned
very hot and quickly. "There was really nothing for us to do
but keep it from spreading to other houses," he said. "Anytime
a fire acts like that, we automatically suspect that it might
have been deliberately set."

But neither Goodly nor Island Police Department Chief Asa
Bryan could say with certainty that arson was involved. "We'll
investigate the ruins of the house and the bodies in the coming
days, but the destruction was so complete that I don't hold out
much hope that we'll find anything," said Bryant.

Killers!

When asked about the fate of Lily Ashworth, Bryan said, "I don't think there's any extended family, so she'll likely become a ward of the State."

"Venetian Drive?" I say to Weathers. "That's the street we're on."

"Yes 'tis," replies Weathers. "The Ashworth house was just down where the road ends."

"So, you knew them?" M.B. asks.

"I knew Lennie. His folks and his sister, not so much."

M.B.: "How's that?"

"Lennie started to come over here when he was twelve or thirteen. Bothered the shit outta me. He was fascinated by all the machines—the process of assembling the paper. Finally, I gave him odd jobs to do just to keep him outta my hair."

"So, you were here when the fire happened?" I ask.

Weathers's features harden like he's not pleased with the question. "I was. Fire engines woke me up."

"What did you see?" Danny asks.

"Fire was goin' great guns when I got out theah. I was worried that the trees were gonna catch and the whole damn neighborhood was gonna go. But they got it under control, praise the Lord."

"And you're sure that Leonard Ashworth was killed in that fire?" I ask.

"Ain't sure of a damn thing," he says in an angry tone. "But they found three bodies in the ruins of the house, like my story says. One was a boy about Lennie's age." He pauses. "I guess you're telling me that that body wasn't Leonard Ashworth's. How do you know?"

"The Marquis sent me a threatening letter a while ago. He signed it Leonard Ashworth."

"But why would he do that if he tried to make it look like he died in the fire?" Danny asks.

"A psychopath doesn't need much more of a reason to do something than that he feels like it," M.B. says. "That fire was almost thirty years ago. Maybe he just doesn't care anymore if we know who he really is. Or was."

"Maybe the Marquis just heard about the fire and took dead Leonard Ashworth's name?" I offer.

"I don't think so," says Danny. "I distinctly heard that crazy old woman who died on Rattlesnake Mountain call Barrett "Brother Leonard". And she

122

called herself "Sister Lily." He points at newspaper article. "Lily is the Ashworth girl's name."

"Assuming it was him that set the fire," I say, "Leonard must've substituted the body of another boy about his age." I turn to Weathers. "Did any other boys that age go missing on the island about that time?"

"Nope. This heah's a tight-knit community. I would remember."

A thought occurs to me. I ask Weathers, "Leonard didn't say anything to you about something being wrong at home around the time of the fire, did he?"

"No, he didn't!" Weathers snaps. "The two of us weren't like that. He just cleaned up, delivered papers, that kinda thing. We weren't pals."

Weathers angry tone surprises me. Maybe my question hit a nerve?

"So, I guess we should check surrounding communities, especially Savannah, for disappearances of young men in that age group," says M.B.

"To what end?" asks Danny. "What does it matter now who the vic was?"

"When you're investigating, you document everything. You never know what might become important." M.B. says.

"You told me that before," Danny says.

"Well, you obviously didn't pay attention the first time," M.B. snips.

Trying to nip this in the bud, I say, "Maybe Leonard didn't kill anybody. He could've gotten a body any number of ways. Stolen from a funeral home. Dug up from a graveyard. A fire like that would make it hard to tell."

"That's not an investigation for us," M.B. says. "Too many variables." She pulls out her cell phone and heads outside, saying, "All it will take is a call to Quantico to get the ball rolling on that."

After she's left, Weathers asks. "Quantico? She's FBI? She's a little old, ya think?"

That just hits me wrong. "Ain't you a little old to be running a newspaper?"

He replies with a scowl, "Old reporters never die, they just end up on the nursing home beat." Yeet! It seems like Weather's has totally developed a case in the ass for us.

"Is that what the Islander is—a nursing home newsletter?" asks Danny.

Killers!

"Mostly," says Weathers. "Of course, that's what I wanted when I bought it. I had all I could stand of so-called real journalism when I was in New York."

"How so?"

"Another version of that old joke says that old reporters never die, they just get depressed. Well, that's what happened to me. New York City in the late seventies/early eighties was surely a depressing place, especially for a black man." Weathers walks over to the wall where the *Times* stories are displayed and points to one. "In June of '82, Willie Turks, a 34-year-old African-American MTA worker, was killed by a white mob in the Gravesend section of Brooklyn. Two of his black co-workers were also beaten up. My editor put me on the story. They arrested a white kid for the killing. A mostly white jury convicted him of assault, not murder."

"So you quit because of that?" I ask.

Weathers glares at me. "Hardly." He indicates another of the framed newspapers. "In September of '83, Michael Stewart, another black man, was beaten into a coma by New York Transit Police officers. He died from his injuries at Bellevue 13 days later. By this time, my editor had assigned me to the nigger-beating beat as the token black reporter. The six white officers that killed Stewart were acquitted on all charges." He points to yet another frame. "Then in '84, a mentally ill black woman named Eleanor Bumpurs was shot and killed by police as they tried to evict her from her Bronx apartment. The cop that done it was acquitted on charges of manslaughter and criminally negligent homicide."

"Hey, I used to be a cop," says Danny. "It's pretty damn easy to second guess the cops in these kinds of incidents when you're not on the scene."

"It wasn't only the cops," spits Weathers, indicating another posted headline. "A few months after the Stewart killing, a crazy white sumbitch called Bernhard Goetz shot and wounded four unarmed black men on the number 2 train, who he claimed tried to rob him. He was acquitted of the shootings—they got him for criminal possession of a firearm and gave him six months in jail, a year's psychiatric treatment, five years' probation, 200 hours community service, and a $5,000 fine. Whoop, whoop. Some of the vics managed to get a civil judgment a'gin Goetz for millions, but last I heard, he never paid a penny of it. But the case that finally got to me was Edmund Perry's."

"Who is Edmund Perry?" I ask.

"Was, not is", says Weathers. "Edmund Perry was a 17-year old black graduate of Phillips Exeter Academy in Exeter, New Hampshire, one of the most prestigious private schools in the country. Honor student. You couldn't find a better black teenager if you tried. Edmund got shot to death in Harlem by a plainclothes cop who said Edmund and his brother Jonah tried to mug him in Morningside Park. Jonah managed to get away. The cop was acquitted of the shooting the following month. They tried Jonah Perry for assault, but they couldn't convict him either. Says a lot when you can't convict a black kid for assault on a white cop, don't it? After that, I had all I could stomach of the big city. I came back down heah to Georgia. It ain't perfect, but it's a damn sight better than New York City."

"Sounds to me like you just cut and run instead of trying to do anything positive," says Danny.

STFU, Danny! I think. We need this guy to help us find the Marquis, and you're pissing him off.

"Who the hell are y'all to judge me, white boy?" snarls Weathers.

"Somebody who nearly got his ass shot off both as a cop and a Marine so you could be a journalist in a free country," says Danny. "I don't deny the system sucks—I've seen my share of police corruption and racism. But nobody ever solved a problem by running away from it."

"Maybe I don't want to solve it," says Weathers. "Maybe I just want to make sure I'm not the po' nigger what gets killed by the cops."

I'm frantically trying to think what I can do to save the situation and get Weathers back on our side when he says, "Look, y'all got what you came foah. Whyn't you just get outta here and leave an old nigger in peace."

I can't help it. "I wish you wouldn't use that word," I say.

"What, nigger? Why not? Y'all's the ones taught it to me."

"C'mon Nattie," says Danny. "This gentleman obviously doesn't care about the two dozen people that the Marquis killed, or any others he might kill in the future. Help from the likes of him we don't need."

Weathers, tears in his eyes, gives Danny a look of pure venom, but he doesn't say anything else.

We meet M.B. coming back in as we're leaving. "What..." she begins, but I just take her elbow and steer her out.

Killers!

When we're in the Jeep on the way to Sandcrab Cottage, M.B. asks again, "So what just happened back there?"

Danny starts in, "That guy's just an old racist..."

I cut him off. "I don't think so. He was fine until we started talking about the fire. I think he knows something."

"Like what?" Danny asks.

"Like what really happened to Leonard Ashworth."

Chapter 26

At Hyacinth House, Lupe is searching the master bedroom for the key that Nattie and M.B. found. She could just simply call Nattie and ask her where it is, but she's afraid that Nattie will tell her it's none of her business. Not asking her to go along on the trip with Danny and M.B. speaks volumes about Nattie's attitude towards her.

The bedroom still contains a lot of Rebecca's clothes and other things, so Lupe feels vaguely guilty going through it all. It's actually a relief when her phone titters. She looks at the screen—Unknown Caller.

"Hola. This is Lupe."

"Hi, Lupe. It's Theo. From the meeting last night?"

"Oh, hi Theo. How are you?"

Silence. Then, "Not so good. I been wanting to use all day."

"Did you?"

"No, not yet."

"Do you have any?"

"Yeah, I gotta bag."

"Then flush it. Right now! I'll wait."

"But..."

"Right now! Or hang up. It won't do any good to talk if you are high."

More silence. "Okay. Just a minute." A soft clunk as he puts the phone down, followed by rustling sounds. Lupe hopes they mean he is disposing of the drugs, not consuming them. A minute later, he comes back on the line. "Okay, I did it."

"Good. Now get yourself to a meeting."

"What meeting should I go to? Are you going?"

Lupe surveys the mess she's made of the master bedroom. "No, I was not going to go out tonight."

"Oh." It's amazing, the amount of pitifulness he can cram into one syllable.

Dammit! "Okay. You know that the State Campus Group meets every night, right?"

"I didn't know that."

Killers!

"I'll see you there tonight. You can go early and help them set up and make the coffee if you're uncomfortable where you are."

"I'll do that. Thanks, Lupe."

"*De nada.*"

She disconnects. Lupe now knows that she has a problem. Sometimes a newcomer fixates on one person at their first meeting, even though that person may not be the best one to help them on their journey to sobriety. Lupe realizes that she does have a duty to Theo—nobody turned her away when she first came into the program—but that does not mean that she must become his primary contact or his sponsor. She needs to go to that meeting tonight and help him get involved with somebody else.

Theo is at the meeting when Lupe arrives. Tonight it's a speaker meeting, where a couple of people who have been in the program a while tell their stories. One of them is Clyde, who took an interest in Theo last night. Clyde is a heroin addict from Manhattan who has been clean for a decade after living on the streets for two—he would be a perfect sponsor for Theo, Lupe thinks. As things are getting ready to begin, Theo plops down beside Lupe with a boyish grin, and again that tingle dances along her nerves. She resolves to ignore it.

The speakers are great, Clyde in particular. He can have you laughing your ass off one minute and crying the next. Lupe glances at Theo, who seems enraptured with the older man's story. Good. She also notices Sherrie, sitting a few tables away, staring intently at Theo. He doesn't seem to notice.

After the final prayer has been said, Theo turns to Lupe and says, "You know, you totally saved me from using tonight. I was this close."

"I am happy that you did not," Lupe answers. And she is. But why does she still feel like Theo is being insincere?

"Are you going for coffee?" Theo asks.

"No, I have to do some work at home to do before I can go to bed. But you should go. Talk to Clyde; he would make a great sponsor for you."

"How bout you? Could you be my sponsor?"

Ai carajo! "A woman is not the best choice as a sponsor for a man," she tells him.

"Why not?"

"Other things can get in the way. Like sex, for instance."

"But you like girls, not guys."

Anxiety grows in Lupe's belly. "How do you know that?"

"I asked around about you when I thought about getting you to be my sponsor. I hope you don't mind?"

A normal and natural thing to do. But Lupe does mind. "Let me think about it. In the meantime, why do you not go for coffee and talk to Clyde?"

Theo looks like a puppy that's been kicked. "Okay, if you say so. But when will I see you again?"

Against her better judgment, Lupe says, "I can come back here tomorrow."

Lupe and Theo go outside, where the coffee group is gathering on the New Commons. Lupe squints at the glare of the high-powered street lights that ring the courtyard, installed a couple of years ago after repeated requests from campus women's groups. She points out Clyde to Theo and gives him a little push, then watches as he walks towards the older man. Out of the corner of her eye, she sees Sherrie holding her cell phone in front of her face. *Is she taking Theo's picture?* That's highly irregular—NA is supposed to be anonymous. But Lupe can't deny that even she feels attracted to Theo. Is Sherrie developing a crush on him? As Sherrie's sponsor, Lupe will have to address this with her very soon.

The coffee group heads off for Lee Street, and Lupe goes the other way. It's a five-minute walk across the New Commons to the parking lot, giving her time to think. Normally, she likes working with newcomers of any gender, but Theo somehow gives her the creeps. She's chagrined to realize that with all of the emphasis she's placed on searching the house and NA, she hasn't even seen Eduardo today. She checks her phone. 9:15 p.m.—still early. She decides to drop by the guest house before she turns in for the night.

Back at Hyacinth House, Lupe activates the door opener on her dash and pulls into the sizable four-car garage. Danny's pickup and Judy McMasters's minivan are both here. She still can't believe that she's living in a place like this; a far cry from the adobe hovel in Sinaloa where she began life. She smiles—the American Dream is real! She parks beside Danny, closes the garage door with the remote, then gets out of her car and goes outside through the rear door. Hyacinth House occupies a wooded five-acre lot in the northern suburbs; the guest house is a smaller A-frame about 50 yards

Killers!

from the main house in a grove of trees, which can't be seen until you're almost on top of it. As she approaches, she notes the lights are on—good, Judy is still up. Even though it's nearing 10 p.m., Eduardo probably is still awake too; like grandmothers everywhere, Mrs. McMasters spoils her grandson shamelessly.

She presses the lighted doorbell; Judy has told Lupe that she's free to just walk in, but that would offend Lupe's considerable sense of propriety. She waits until Judy opens the door and she hears Eduardo screech, "Mama Lupe!" at the top of his lungs. She holds her arms open as her son dashes across the room and leaps into them, then she hugs him tightly, kissing his face and hair.

"How has he been today, Mom?" Lupe asks, carrying her son into the living room.

"A handful, as usual," Judy replies. "He's into everything, especially since he found that safe in the main house the other day. He's convinced that there's buried treasure in this house too, and he isn't going to rest until he finds it." She addresses Eduardo. "Okay, bucko, kiss your Mama goodnight and get off to bed. You've got school tomorrow."

"Yes, *abuelita*." He gives Lupe another kiss, then jumps down and runs to his bedroom in the back of the house.

Lupe surveys Judy, an attractive, dark-haired fortysomething who doesn't look a bit like Nattie. "I just want to say again how grateful I am that you are taking care of Eduardo for us."

"What else would I do?" says Judy. "I can't let a bunch of bureaucrats consign my grandson to a group home. Your family may not be traditional, Hon, but it is most definitely a family. It will just take a few years for everybody else to catch up with you." She steps forward to give Lupe a hug. She continues, "I know you don't drink alcohol anymore because of the drugs, but I'm going to have a glass of wine. Could I interest you in a cup of herbal tea and some company?"

Lupe readily agrees. She's found that she can discuss things with Judy that she can't with the more volatile Nattie. Besides, Nattie's mom reminds her own mother in Mexico, whom she hardly knew. The two women spend a pleasant hour talking and relaxing, before Lupe reluctantly calls a halt.

"Mom, I have really enjoyed this, but I have a client coming in at ten tomorrow."

On her way back to the main house, Lupe reflects again on how lucky she has been—meeting Nattie, Danny and Judy, and gaining the love and respect of such fine people. Surely Jesus cannot hold her unusual marriage against her, or he wouldn't have given them to her.

Killers!

Chapter 27

I**t's Thursday evening at Sandcrab cottage. We're eating a totally** ripped fish dinner with all the trimmings, cooked by M.B. from her day's catch. After our disappointment at the Islander office yesterday, we're fresh out of leads, so we decided to take the day to chill and talk over what comes next. The weather was beautiful today, only 80 degrees and balmy sea breezes. Me and Danny hung out on the beach while M.B. went fishing. I'm definitely coming back here after this is all over.

I'm getting some slaw on my fork with my fish when the house phone rings. I "That's weird," I say. "Who knows we're here?

"Nobody, other than the rental agent," M.B. says.

I go to the living room and pick up. "Hello?"

"Sam Weathers. Did some thinkin' last night after you left. We need to talk some more about Lennie Ashworth."

Hmmph. Maybe he has a conscience after all. "What about him?" I ask him.

"Not on the telephone. How 'bout you come over here later this evenin'?"

His voice has a peculiar tone–like he's stressed out. "Is anything wrong, Mr. Weathers?"

"Naw. You jes' get ovah here in a little while." He hangs up.

I tell the Squad. "He almost sounded like he was gonna cry," I finish.

"Weird old bird," says Danny. "Maybe he got an attack of conscience."

"What do you mean?" M.B. asks.

"I've been thinking," Danny says. "I agree with what you said last night, Nattie. I'll bet Weathers knows that it wasn't Leonard Ashworth who died in that fire, and that he knows what really happened to him."

"How do you figure?" I ask.

"Couple things. He played the race card to get us out of there so he didn't have to pursue the subject. And did you notice that he called Ashworth Lennie? That could mean that the two of them had a deeper relationship than Weathers let on."

"What kind of relationship, do you think?" M.B. asks.

"They were neighbors," Danny answers. "Could have been that the kid just liked to hang around the paper. Could have been sexual. But suppose Leonard did set that fire. He must've had a reason."

M.B. breaks in. "A psychopath doesn't need..."

"...a reason," Danny finishes. "You said. But if Leonard and Weathers were close, maybe the kid gave him a reason. Like he was being abused, maybe."

"Psychopaths are great manipulators." M.B. agrees.

"So he goes to Weathers that Saturday night, tells him what he's done, and asks for help. I could see Weathers agreeing if he thought the kid got a raw deal."

"So what does Weathers do?" I ask.

"Hides the kid, maybe gets him off the island," says Danny.

"Then Weathers had to know about the third body in the house," M.B. says. "Hell, maybe the two of them even planned it together. Weather's might have even helped Leonard get the body."

"You do realize you're accusing Weathers of condoning arson and murder, don't you?" M.B. says.

"Ain't accusin' nobody of nothing," Danny retorts. "I'm just playing what if."

"Then why don't we quit speculating and just go see what Weathers has to say?" I ask.

M.B. barks, "Not so fast, Nattie. I busted my butt cooking this dinner. Let's finish it first. Weathers ain't goin' anywhere in the next hour or so."

Night has fully fallen by the time we leave the Sandcrab Cottage, but a three-quarter moon illuminates the neighborhood nearly as brightly as daylight. There's hardly any traffic on the road, and the Islander office is only a ten-minute drive. I pull the Jeep into the driveway and punch the button to shut it down. The headlights stay on and looking down the driveway, I notice that there are two vehicles in the shed at the end.

We all get out, and Danny and M.B. head for the front door.

"Weathers has company," I say. "Maybe that's why he doesn't want to see us."

"Whatever," says Danny.

Killers!

There's something familiar about the front end of the second vehicle, but the Jeep's headlights go out, so I can't tell what it is. "Hang on a minute; I'll be right back." I go down the driveway to take a closer look.

Coming into the back yard, I can make out a logo on the front of the vehicle. A large circle, letters inside. V... W... I get close enough to touch and use the flashlight on my phone. Holy shit! It's green! It's the microbus that followed us here from the mountains?

I turn around to tell Danny and M.B., but I see her standing next to the Jeep looking straight at me, her posture unusually rigid. She beckons with her right arm, calling me to come forward.

Something ain't right...

Chapter 28

From the Journal of Rebecca Feiner
July 23, 20____

*R*d *light blazes, suffusing everything. The scents of mold, dirt,* and old metal hang in the air.

***

Fade in.

I'm wearing a black mesh body suit, thigh-high patent leather boots.

A white hand freckled with golden hair holds a syringe. It presses the plunger and the yellow liquid inside flows into to an i.v. in my wrist vein. The world spins.

Fade out.

Fade in.

A large room, brick walls. Chains dangle from the rafters, clanging like church bells. A St. Andrew's cross against one wall, leather straps hanging from the ends of the X. A pegboard holding whips, knives, restraints on another wall.

A naked woman strapped to a metal table, wearing a black leather hood and a ball gag. Barrett, nude and rampant, looms over her, a silver knife gleaming in his hand.

He reaches down, jerks off the hood—oh my God, it's Meiko!

He bends over her face, does something with the knife. Her screams rend the air. Blood spurts. So much blood!

He turns, smiling, shows me something held between his thumb and forefinger. Her eye! My God, it's her eye!

I'm drawn closer. I don't want to see, but I have to. Poor eyeless Meiko, her belly laid open like a frog on a dissection board, white intestines spiraled with red veins. Barrett beside her, his head thrown back, masturbating furiously. The tendons on his neck stand out like cables. He shouts in ecstasy as he ejaculates on her insides.

Will her screaming never stop!

135

Killers!

Later, in a van, driving through the night, Barrett next to me, riding shotgun It's raining. The streetlights are rimmed with yellow halos and the twin odors of car exhaust and smoke permeate all.

Barrett says, "Stop here."

I stop, and we get out.

He opens the van's rear doors. Inside is poor Meiko, wrapped in a transparent plastic sheet. Her face seems fractal, like a bizarre piece of modern art.

"Take her feet," Barrett says. He takes her shoulders. We pull her out of the van. Blood sloshes beneath the plastic.

We carry her a ways, sidestepping broken pieces of furniture and piles of trash. Swing her back and forth—one, two, three, let go! She flies through the air, crashes into a mound of garbage and tumbles down the other side.

"Remember, you were part of this!", Barrett says.

Fade out.

***

Fade in.

Creak, creak, creak, creak...

It's cold. Where am I?

I see chains, smell dirt, pine trees. I know! I'm in the hanging swing on Li-Chin's porch.

OMG! What did I do?

Chapter 29

I t's pushing 1:00 am as Lupe is getting ready for bed. **Hyacinth House** is eerily silent and cavernous, and the loneliness is palpable. Lupe misses her wife, her husband and her little boy terribly, even though she's just seen Eduardo and he is only a few hundred yards away. The sound of her phone chittering literally makes her jump and her breathing stop. She looks at the screen–it's Sherrie. *Shit. Don't tell me she's getting ready to use again.* As much as she wants to let it go to voicemail, Lupe knows she can't ignore a call from a fellow addict, especially at this hour. She presses the button. "Hola, Sherrie."

"He's here! It's Tommy...", Sherrie croaks. There's a clattering on the line. The screen goes dark.

Lupe sits with her jaw dropped, staring at the dead phone in her hand like it's a live grenade ready to blow. Who the hell is Tommy? What now?

Call Nattie? Call 911 and send them to Sherrie's place? Or just go over there herself?

Lupe has gotten calls from addicts when they're high before. They're apt to say or do anything. She grabs her phone, pulls up her recents and taps Sherrie's number. Straight to voicemail. *Shit.*

Lupe knows that Sherrie lives in a dorm on the fringe of campus—she walked Sherrie home from the NA meeting a couple of times. She could be there in fifteen minutes.

Her mind made up, she digs out her keys.

Traffic is non-existent on the midnight drive. Lupe turns off Lee Street onto campus at Pickens' Tower, a crenelated battlement constructed during the War Between the States that's the most recognizable symbol of State University. She pulls up in front of Williams Hall, a three-story WPA red brick building on the fringe of campus. Only a few windows show light; most of the students are likely in bed this early on a Wednesday morning. She parks in a space painted with white diagonal lines in front of the main entrance and hops out of the car, praying silently that the notorious campus tow trucks will be idle at this hour. She hurries up the stairs and through the wooden double doors into the lobby.

Killers!

The lobby, a two-story room painted in institutional beige with a tan and beige tiled floor, is brightly lit by fluorescent bulbs in ceiling fixtures. Curved staircases on either side of the entryway lead up to a balcony spanning three sides of the room that gives access to the second floor. Straight across from Lupe sits a massive mahogany clawfoot desk, occupied by a woman with her head face down on the desktop, encircled by her arms. Stepping forward, Lupe sees a dark pool beneath the woman's head. Is that blood? OMG!

Lupe snatches her phone from her pocket and punches in 911.

"911. What's your emergency?"

"I am in the lobby of Williams Hall on campus. Something terrible has happened! I think the receptionist has been injured! Send someone quickly!"

"Ma'am, could you please tell me your name and a little more about the situation..."

Lupe disconnects and jams her phone back into her pocket. She rushes to a doorway on the right; she knows it opens into a corridor where the residents' rooms are. Sherrie's is halfway down. Reaching it, a bolt of fear stabs her belly. The door is ajar!

Lupe pushes the door open and literally stops breathing. The room is cramped, with a raised bed on either side of the doorway and a single window on the wall opposite the door. The occupants tried to give the space some ambiance by covering the overhead fluorescent fixture with blue cellophane, so the blood pooled on the floor beneath the women's bodies looks black as tar. Both corpses are clad only in t-shirts and panties—since both are headless, Lupe cannot be sure which, if either, might be Sherrie. A fecal odor hangs in the air–one woman emptied her bowels during the slaughter. Lupe's gorge rises and she abruptly spews herbal tea all over the floor before falling to her knees like a mourner at a graveside.

A few minutes later, the two female campus police officers responding to her 911 call find her kneeling in front of the corpses, her hands clasped as if in prayer.

"Get this one out to the lobby, Jackson," one cop orders in a shaky voice. "I'll call this in."

Officer Jackson, a petite brown woman with broad features, reaches down and cups a hand beneath Lupe's elbow to help her up. "C'mon, Hon, you just come with me now. You'll be all right..." She squires Lupe out to the lobby, glances at the grisly scene at the reception desk, then keeps on going through the front doors. She takes Lupe down the stairs to the patrol car parked in front, removes her handcuffs from her belt and eases Lupe's right hand behind her back. Lupe doesn't have a clue what's happening until she hears the metallic rasp of the cuff closing and feels the cold steel against her wrist.

"What are you doing?", she shouts, but Jackson already has her other hand behind her and cuffs it fast. She opens the patrol car door.

"This is for your safety and ours," Jackson repeats the phrase she learned by rote. "You just wait here and take it easy until the detective has a chance to talk to you." She goes back inside.

Lupe is scared to death. Being handcuffed in the back of a police car in Mexico can have an entirely different outcome than in the U.S. She struggles, pain arching through her shoulders and begins hyperventilating. Everything turns grey, then black.

The next thing she knows, someone's shaking her. She opens her eyes. A youngish thin brunette woman hovers over her, looking into her eyes. "Miss! Are you okay?" she asks.

Lupe begins to struggle again. The woman says, "Stop, please. No one's going to hurt you. Let me get you out of there and get those cuffs off of you."

The woman's voice is calming, so Lupe allows her to help her out of the car. She steps behind Lupe, and in a moment, the cuffs fall away. She helps Lupe turn to face her, then extracts a leather folder from an inside pocket, flipping it open and dangling the credential inside in front of her.

"I'm Detective Julia Sykes, Campus police. And you are?"

"Lupe Ibáñez."

Sykes does a double take on hearing Lupe's name. "You're Natalie McMasters's wife," she says.

"That is right," says Lupe. "How do you know this?"

"Never mind," Sykes replies. "I'm sorry my officers locked you up, but it's policy, for your safety and theirs." Again the canned phrase. "Will you promise to remain here while I go and see what's happened inside? I'll want to talk to you when I come out."

Killers!

As a former undocumented person, Lupe has never been comfortable talking to the police. "I do not know anything," she says, a hint of fear in her voice.

"Will you stay here?" Sykes asks again.

Fearing that she'll be cuffed again if she refuses, Lupe says, "Yes. But I really do not know anything about what has happened in there."

"We'll see," replies Sykes, heading inside.

Every fiber of Lupe's being is screaming at her to run, get Eduardo and get a far away from this city as she can. But that's how she's always handled things like this until now, and she's always gotten in more trouble. She steels herself and decides to wait for the detective.

After a while, Sykes returns. Lupe is sure she is a couple of shades paler than she was before going inside. She leads Lupe up the stairs, helps her to a seat on the low wall that surrounds the porch, and takes a seat beside her. This close, Lupe is surprised to see tears on the detective's cheeks. Sykes takes out her phone and says, "Ms. Ibáñez, I'm going to record this interview, if you don't mind."

Do I have a choice? "That is fine," Lupe says.

"What do you know about what's happened in there?" Sykes asks.

Lupe tells Sykes about the phone call from Sherrie.

"Wait a minute. You're sure she said that Tommy was here?"

"Yes."

Sykes does something with her phone, then holds it so Lupe can see the screen. It's a picture of a young man with dark hair, a roguish smile on his youthful face. "Do you know this man?"

"Yes. His name is Theo. I just met him the other day." Lupe doesn't say where. NA is supposed to be anonymous.

Sykes bores into Lupe's brown eyes with her own. "His name is not Theo. It's Tommy. Tommy Burke."

Lupe looks at her uncomprehendingly. "Who is Tommy Burke?"

"Tommy Burke is a serial killer, Ms. Ibáñez. We think he's responsible for the murders of over two dozen women."

Chapter 30

I'm unsure—M.B.'s demeanor indicates trouble. Should I go to her, or run away and get help?

"What's wrong?" I holler.

"Just come here," M.B. says. Her voice is high pitched and shaky.

Shit. I walk toward her, while she faces the front of the building. I pass the structure and turn so I can see the front door.

WTF! Danny's on the steps, and the huge man who I saw downtown the other day is standing in the doorway. Oh, shit! He's got a gun! He's pointing it at Danny!

Danny is a big guy, six two, nearly two hundred pounds, but the dude with the gun is a true Frankenstein monster. He must be nearly seven feet tall! Danny looks like a kid standing in front of him.

"Just keep on coming, ladies," says Frankenstein. "Keep your hands in view, or I'll shoot your friend."

"Listen to him, Nattie," says M.B. "Trust me, he'll do what he says." She acts like she knows this guy?

Frankenstein looks away from Danny to speak to us, and Danny takes advantage of that momentary lapse of attention. He grabs the guy's gun in his left hand and pushes upward, trying to get the weapon above his head, while driving his right fist into the giant's solar plexus. His gun arm travels upward a few inches, then the big man catches on and tenses his muscles. His pistol is pointed right at Danny's face! The blow to the big guy's torso had as much effect as if Danny punched an oak tree. Danny's still got hold of the gun, but the giant twitches his arm and Danny goes flying off the steps, landing on his back on the ground.

The big guy brings the gun down and it cracks once, flame from the muzzle lighting up the porch. Danny's hands fly to his lower abdomen.

"No!" screams M.B.

OMG! He shot Danny! The motherfucker just shot Danny!

"Do as I say ladies, or he gets the next one in his face."

Ignoring him, I run over to my husband. Danny's face is a mask of pain, and rich red blood wells up between his fingers.

Killers!

"Leave him be or I'll kill him!" The big man snarls as M.B. runs up next to me. "On second thought," Godzilla says, "bring his ass in here."

I stare defiantly into the monster's face. "Look at me, asshole! There's no way I can pick him up!"

"Each of you grab a leg, and drag him in here. Do it or he's fucking dead!"

We have no choice. I get Danny's left ankle in both hands and M.B. takes his right. Thank Christ there are only three stairs to the front door; anymore and we'd never get him up. Danny moans in agony as he bounces on the stairs, leaving a trail of blood behind. Keeping his pistol trained on us, the big man backs into the newspaper office to give us room to pull Danny inside. Finally, we wrestle him in far enough so his head clears the doorsill.

"Close the door, Natalie," the big guy says. WTF, he knows my name?

As I turn away to do as he says, I decide to take a gamble. I drop my left hand, unclip the Microtech from my pocket and palm it.

"Hands where I can see them!" the big guy snarls.

I bring my hands up so he can see them, my palms facing me, the long skinny stiletto hidden behind my fingers. "Please let me get help for my husband before he bleeds out," I plead.

"Don't waste your breath, Nattie," M.B. says. "This is Eugene Knott. He's killed ten people that we know about, nine women and one man."

Knott looks at M.B. "How do you know me?" he asks.

"I hang out in post office lobbies a fair bit," says M.B.

"Funny," says Knott. "And it's eleven people now, and two men." He steps aside and motions us into the press room. "Get in there."

I lower my arms to my sides and he doesn't say anything. Still hiding the Microtech, I walk past him and into the press room. I'm aching to spin around and stick him, but it would be suicide with that gun on me. I've got to wait until he's distracted and hope he doesn't spot the knife in the meantime.

As we enter the back room, I stop and stare in horror. The nude body of a black man hangs by his arms from the linotype machine. Sam Weathers! His belly has been cut open, and a red rope of intestines dangles into a pool of blood beneath him.

"See, I told you," Knott says. "Two men." He waves his gun at M.B. "Come over here, old woman. Keep your hands up over your head."

M.B. does as she's told, and Knott searches her with one hand while holding the gun on her with the other. He removes her pistol and handcuffs and tosses them on the floor in a corner.

All the while I'm thinking, how can I get to him? I've got to do something, or Danny's fucking gonna die!

"Go stand over there," he says to M.B., motioning toward the printing press. Then he faces me. "Your turn, Natalie."

I walk toward him with my arms at my sides, thinking it will help me keep the Microtech concealed. "Put your hands up," he says again and I do it like before. He runs his rough hands over me, not even trying to cop a feel. He finds the Sig and tosses it in the corner with M.B.'s gun.

Every muscle in my body is quivering with fear and anticipation. My hands are high above my head, just about at Knott's eye level. Surely, he must notice the Microtech! If he sees it, what will he do? He's demonstrated that he'll maim and kill with little or no provocation. I feel a warm trickle between my legs as my nerves cause my bladder to let go.

There's a scraping sound from the other room. I look that way and see Danny in the doorway, one hand holding his belly wound and his 1911 in the other. His pistol belches flame and my ears immediately fill with a loud ringing. I see the muzzle flash but don't even hear it as Knott shoots back, and Danny goes down again. No! I whirl around, working the switch on the stiletto with my thumb. Three and a half inches of razor-sharp steel shoots out the front of the handle. Powered by all of the adrenaline in my body generated by fear, desperation and hatred, I stab at Knott's belly just above his navel, sinking the blade in to the hilt. I savagely jerk the knife sideways and the serrated edge cuts through fat and muscle like butter, gutting him like a fish. He grunts, and a yeasty odor chokes me as warm, rich, red liquid cascades over my hand and forearm. I stab him again, just above his groin, pulling upward this time, and his tripes spill out like Sam Weathers'. Bellowing like a wounded gorilla, he backhands me across the face with his pistol. I frantically dodge, but not in time. A glancing blow hits me in the mouth, lights explode before my eyes, and I tumble to the floor. Spitting out pieces of teeth, I roll over in time to see muzzle flashes from the corner as M.B. wildly empties her pistol at Knott, who's shooting back just as fiercely. Even though she's still working the trigger, the flames from M.B.'s Glock cease, and Knott fires once more, bringing her down. He swings the muzzle

Killers!

of his gun towards me, a rictus of agony and laughter on his face as a gout
blood   erupts   from   his   mouth.

Chapter 31

From the Journal of Rebecca Feiner
July 24, 20___

Since I've been back home from Alabama, I've hardly slept. I'm tired all the time, I have trouble concentrating, remembering details, and making decisions.

I searched the online Baltimore newspaper archives for the period Barrett and I were at Hopkins. Sure enough, I found an article about the unexplained disappearance of a grad student named Meiko Hattori.

Did I really watch as Barrett butchered that poor girl and help him dispose of her body in a landfill? I don't want to believe that I could do that, but I must have. There really is no other explanation.

If that's true, I'm as guilty as Barrett, at least in the eyes of the law. I could go to the police or the FBI, but what purpose would it serve? They already know that Barrett is the Marquis and they're actively searching for him. Since I have no inkling of his present whereabouts, I don't see how my coming forward will help. All it would do is make a great deal of trouble for me. And I surely have enough trouble right now.

The silver revolver I bought in a moment of weakness lies on the desk in front of me. What a feckless idiot I was to think it would save me if Barrett came after me. For a young, naive person like Nattie, a gun is a perfect solution. Just blow away the bad guy, no more problems. Isn't it wonderful when your life is so simple?

Even if I did kill Barrett, it wouldn't expunge the guilt that festers within me. I helped him dispose of that poor girl's corpse and my traitorous mind blanked it out, because I knew innately that I didn't have the moral fortitude to deal with it. Whatever possessed me to get involved with that man in the first place and become his sex slave? If that doesn't speak to a lack of character on my part, nothing does.

Picking up the silver revolver, I turn it in my hands, stare down the dead black barrel, see the coppery heads of those little messengers of death in the cylinders. My finger brushes the trigger. How easy would it be to end my guilt and my misery. I wouldn't even hear the explosion. It would be a

Killers!

fitting end for one as worthless as I. I cock the hammer and the cylinder turns. Open my mouth, put the barrel inside, close my lips around it. The steel is cold and the gun oil tastes sweet. I touch the hammer with my thumb...

Suddenly my bladder releases, smelly warmth cascading over my legs, onto my chair then on the floor, followed by a rapid chill. What am I doing? I rip the gun from my mouth, tearing my lip; my finger jerks the trigger; there's a blinding flash and my ears go dead from the loudness of the blast. The resultant tinnitus tells me I'm still alive. Disgusted, I hurl the gun away from me and it hits the wall, knocking out a chunk of plaster before falling to the floor. My head drops onto my folded arms on the desk and I'm weeping madly, for Meiko, for all of Barrett's other victims, and mostly, for me.

Eventually, I stop crying. I know I have a decision to make. Do I want to live or die? I look at the revolver on the floor. There lies the means to accomplish the latter. But if I truly want to live, I have much work to do.

I go over to the gun and pick it up by the grip, pointing it at the floor, ashamed of myself that I ever purchased it. I'll lock it away, along with this journal. Tomorrow I will get myself a new book to write in. It will be the symbol of a new life. A life without Barrett.

I think again about Natalie. Fighting so hard to save the world, striving to become all that she can be. Helping her and others like her is my life's work, and it is a noble one. I owe it to her to heal myself so I can return to it.

Suddenly, a sobering thought. Barrett is still out there and may come for me like he promised. If he does, there is a way I can take care of Nattie even if he succeeds in taking my life. I go to my desk, look up a phone number on my PC, then pick up the receiver and dial.

"Willy, Talbott and Hightower. How may I direct your call?"

Chapter 32

At two-thirty in the morning, Lupe sits alone in a plastic cafeteria chair in front of a huge, gray metal desk in Sykes' cramped, windowless office, staring at the orange and blue State banner hanging on the back wall. One corner has become undone and flops over limply; it's a perfect reflection of Lupe's feelings.

The smell of commercial deodorizer mixed with sweat is vaguely nauseating and brings back unpleasant memories of Mexico. The first time she was sexually assaulted in her village by a *sicario*, Lupe, a child at the time, had been foolish enough to report it to the police. She had been brought to the local *comisaría* and placed in a similar room to wait for the *capitán* to interview her about the incident. When he finally arrived, he asked her many questions, stopping her when she responded to ask for more and more details. Finally he had said, "Perhaps, *chica*, it will help if you can show me on your body exactly where he touched you." That's when Lupe figured out exactly what was going on, but it was too late, for the *capitán* also had his way with her before turning her out into the street. Needless to say, the next time a *sicario* assaulted her, she did not report it.

Lupe feels a cold draft on her neck as Sykes enters, carrying a manila folder. The detective sits in her chair, placing the folder on the desk in front of her and opening it.

"Why did you bring me here?" asks Lupe. "I have already told you everything that I know about Theo." It was not much.

"Did you now?" asks Sykes. "Let me tell you a little bit about me. I grew up in a little town in North Carolina called Liberty. The highest aspirations of most of the girls from there were to marry a rich farmer and have lots of babies. But I wanted more. I studied hard in school, got admitted to State in pre-law. Unfortunately, my grades weren't good enough to get into law school, nor were they good enough to get into a federal agency. So I started applying to police academies and what do you know, CCPD said yes. I did really well at the academy and made Rookie of the Year. But I was told it would take at least five years for me to become a detective. Then I heard that my alma mater was hiring, so I got an interview. Turned out they liked me so much that they said if I jumped ship and came on with them, I could be a detective in a year if I did well. So here I am."

And why are you telling me all of this? thinks Lupe.

Sykes picks up a sheet of paper from the folder. "No one knows when or where Tommy Burke killed for the first time. It could have been when he was a teenager or in his early 20s in the mid-1990s. It might have been in Florida, where he was born and lived as a young boy, or anywhere else in the Southeast. But by 1999, his reign of terror and murder was underway. All over the Southern States, attractive female college students went missing. In several cases, a young man on crutches or with an arm in a sling was identified in the company of the victims shortly before their disappearance. Later, it was discovered that Tommy Burke often faked an injury to evoke sympathy from his victim. He was arrested for the first time in 2000, in Atlanta, after his minivan was pulled over, suspicious items including handcuffs, rope, and a ski mask were found. Of course, it's not illegal to possess any of those things, so there wasn't enough evidence to hold him."

Lupe turns her head so Sykes won't see her roll her eyes. She doesn't see the point of the history lesson.

Sykes goes on, "In 2001, Burke was charged with killing a spring-breaker in Palm Beach, but he escaped from a third story room in the courthouse and disappeared. A federal arrest warrant for unlawful flight to avoid confinement was issued, and a $250,000 reward was offered for his capture.

He was arrested again in 2002 in North Carolina on suspicion of murder, but he escaped again, this time from a county jail. A nationwide manhunt followed, with the FBI playing a central role, but Tommy Burke had appeared to have dropped off the map.

After 2003, murders featuring Burke's MO occurred sporadically. A man with an arm in a sling was reported to have been spotted near the home of one victim, but no trace of Burke was ever found. Police speculated that he had found himself a secure bolthole somewhere, where he would retreat between crimes."

Now Lupe can't hold her tongue any longer. "Why do you tell me all of this?"

"To show you that I am ambitious. I would love to catch a serial killer that the FBI couldn't—maybe then everyone would stop looking at my grades. And I want to convince you that you must abandon the anonymity that you NA folks treasure so much and tell me all you know about the man you knew as Theo."

Lupe replies, "I have already done so."

Sykes' expression plainly indicates that she doesn't believe it.

"OK. But If he calls you again, let me know immediately. If he wants to meet you, say yes, but don't invite him to your home. Set up a meeting in a public place and call me right away."

Now Lupe is looking at the floor, eager to be away.

"This man is incredibly dangerous!" Sykes says. "Don't mess with him!"

"Can I go now?"

Sykes picks up a stack of papers in both hands and taps the bottom on the desk to arrange them before slipping them into the folder. "Yes. But remember, I'll be watching you."

"Good. Then you will catch that bad man if he tries to hurt me."

It's after three a.m. as Lupe trudges across campus to her car, acutely aware that she has the disagreeable Mrs. Alford coming in at ten for a session on the pole. If she can be in bed in half an hour, she thinks, she can sleep until nine-thirty and still be on time.

The dash clock tells her that it's just past three-thirty as she pulls up in front of the garage at Hyacinth House. She activates the door opener and watches the door rise through bleary eyes. She pulls inside, takes the car out of drive, jerks up the emergency brake lever and kills the engine prior to getting out. As her foot touches the concrete, a voice says,

"Just keep on coming, Lupe. Don't turn around."

She doesn't have to. She knows that voice. It's Theo—Tommy Burke!

Killers!

Chapter 33

Someone's shaking me. Go away! I don't want to get up. He shakes me again. "Miss. Miss!" It's like he's speaking through cotton.

My eyes pop open. It's Danny! But what's he doing in a police uniform? Wait, that's not Danny...

"Miss. Are you hurt?"

Fuck yes! I feel like somebody beat the shit out of me. I sit up. I'm on the floor. I have a splitting headache. I rub my forehead with my hands, run my tongue over my front teeth and feel sharp edges. I taste blood. Everything comes rushing back.

"Danny!" I try to get up, but the cop puts a hand on my shoulder and holds me down. "My husband! Danny... he got shot..."

"He's alive," says the cop. "The EMTs are with him. We've called a chopper."

"I want to see him!" I struggle to rise again. This time, the cop helps me to my feet.

Danny's by the doorway where he fell, laying in way too much blood. A couple of dudes are with him, one holding a plastic bag of clear fluid over his head, a tube running down into Danny's arm, the other holding a plastic mask over his nose and mouth, slowly pumping an attached bag with his hand. A white guy in a dark blue uniform with two silver bars on the shoulder stands nearby. I try to run over there, but the cop takes my arm and holds me back.

"Let the EMTs do their job, Miss."

I suddenly remember M.B., and I look to the corner. She's there, propped up against the wall. Her blouse is gone and her bra is unhitched on one side so the woman can wrap a bandage around her shoulder.

"M.B., are you OK?"

"Yes," she says. "You?"

I take inventory. I hurt like fuck, especially my head and face, but I don't seem to be bleeding anywhere but my mouth. Abruptly, I remember cutting Knott. There he is! On the floor, in front of poor Sam Weathers, who's still

150

by the linotype machine. A lake of blood surrounds the two of them. Weathers's bonds have been cut and he's prone too.

"Are they both... dead?" I ask no one in particular.

"No, Miss," says the cop. "The big guy is. His abdominal aorta was cut, and he bled out. The old guy is hanging on, but I don't know how." A beat. "We'll want to talk to you about what happened here, when you're able."

I start to respond, but M.B. says "I don't think so." Still lying on the floor, she reaches into a pocket, pulls out a small leather folder and flips it open. "I'm SSA Maribeth Woodrow, FBI. That's Eugene Knott over there. We've been looking for him for a while, so I'm taking charge here."

The guy with the bars on his uniform speaks. "Respectfully, ma'am, you're in no shape to take charge of anything. We're flying y'all to Savannah. You can contact your office on the way and get somebody down here, if you want."

A thrumming begins to permeate the room, getting louder. It reaches a peak, then abruptly lessens. In a moment, two guys push a gurney into the doorway and load up Danny. The EMT puts his hands on my shoulder. "Can you walk?" he asks.

"I think so." I get up and start to follow them outside, then I turn to the EMT. "Let me say something to Mr. Weathers," I say. "I don't know if I'll ever see him again."

The EMT nods, and I go over to Weathers. They've wrapped a sheet around his middle, but his eyes are open. I lean down and say, "You know what happened to Leonard Ashworth, don't you?"

He nods, and his lips begin to move. I get closer so I can hear over the din of the chopper outside.

"Sent him to my brother Stoney," Weathers croaks. "Tilghman's Landing..." His eyes close.

Stoney was Samson Weathers's brother! Does he even know that he's dead?

"We've got to evac this man now," the EMT says, thrusting me aside. They pick up the stretcher and rush it out front. I follow, and see a large olive drab helicopter awaiting, a red cross in a white rectangle on its side, its rotors slowly turning. They lay Weathers and Danny inside on the deck. One of the EMTs comes over and takes my elbow to lead me to the chopper and help me board. M.B. goes too.

Killers!

The flight to Savannah is short, about five minutes. We land, and exit the copter in the glare of floodlights that illuminate the helipad in front of the hospital. They separate us, me and M.B. going to the emergency room, while Weathers and Danny disappear into the bowels of the building. I tell the EMT I want to go with my husband, but he won't let me. "We'll bring you to him after he's out of surgery," a nurse tells me.

She sticks me in a curtained enclosure, tells me to take my clothes off and get into a hospital gown on the gurney. I do so. In a minute, a pretty brown intern about my size pulls the curtain aside. "Hi, I'm Patty," she says. She begins cleaning up my bloody face with soap and water and alcohol, which stings like fuck. "You've got two broken incisors and you'll need a couple of stitches in that cut on your forehead," she says. Great, another scar, and broken teeth? Pretty soon I'll look like an MMA fighter. "What happened?" Patty asks.

"I fell." I totally don't want to get into it.

"Well, you'll have to see an oral surgeon after you're released." she tells me. "We don't do teeth here." She shoots a local into the cut, which stings for a sec before it goes numb, then she begins stitching it up.

"When can I get out of here?"

"I'll have to talk to my boss. Since you have a head injury, he may want to keep you overnight."

Her boss does indeed want to keep me, which is Gucci with me. My car is twenty miles away. Patty tells me they're keeping M.B. too, since she's been shot in the shoulder and the leg. She promises to get me info on Danny's and Weathers as soon as they're out of surgery. "We can put you and your friend Agent Woodrow in a semi-private room together, if that's OK with you," Patty says.

"Great."

They roll me out on the gurney, leaving my clothes on the chair in the cubicle. "My stuff..." I say.

"Your clothes are a mess," Patty says. "Someone will bring your wallet and phone to your room."

She rolls me through busy corridors and into an elevator. We get off on an upper floor and she brings me into a room. M.B. is already in the other bed, a nurse hanging an i.v. on a hook at the head.

A few hours later, a little black doctor in a white lab coat comes in. He looks about sixteen. "Ms. McMasters? I'm Doctor Ramnarine, Mr. Merkel's surgeon. I'm happy to tell you he's in recovery and appears to be doing well. However, we had to do a bowel resection, so we've got him on heavy antibiotics in an induced coma. He'll likely be here for at least a week until we're sure the danger of peritonitis has passed and that his wounds are healing satisfactorily. I'm recommending limited activity for at least eight weeks."

Yeet! Danny's out for the duration, then. "Do you have any news about Mr. Weathers?"

His face falls, and I know.

After the doctor has left, I ask M.B., "How are you?"

"Fair. I got a through-and-through in the shoulder and they had to dig a slug out of my thigh. I can walk if I have to, but I won't be doing any dancing for a while. They did say they'll probably be letting me out of here in a couple of days."

"So I guess the hunt for the Marquis is over, for now at least. Godammit!"

"Looks that way," she agrees. "But I'm not giving up. As soon as I can motorvate again, we can get back on it."

"And when will that be?"

"A few weeks, I guess."

Shit.

M.B. continues, "What I really want to know is what the hell Eugene Knott was doing on Tybee Island."

"He probably followed us all the way from Greypeak, you know," I tell her.

"No, I didn't know," she says. "When did you find that out?"

"When I saw his microbus parked in the shed behind the Islander office. I'd noticed it at a gas station on the way to Tybee Island, then I saw it again when y'all were in the rental agency. I saw Knott too, from a distance, but I didn't know who he was, of course."

"Why didn't you tell me about it?"

"I didn't think it was important—I thought he was just another tourist. And I didn't have a chance to tell you when I found the microbus in the shed at the Islander office, because the shit had already hit the fan."

Killers!

"Dammit Nattie, didn't I tell you everything's important in an investigation?"

"You did. Several times." I pause, then, "Don't you think it's odd that we should run into a different serial killer than the one we're hunting?"

"Odd, yes." M.B.'s voice assumes a lecturing tone. "But partnerships between serial killers are not unheard of. Henry Lee Lucas and Ottis Toole went on a killing rampage across the US in the 70s, claiming dozens of victims. The Hillside Strangler murders in LA, also in the 70s, were finally recognized as the work of a pair of killers, Kenneth Bianchi and his cousin, Angelo Buono. More recently in 2013 and 2014, Steven Dean Gordon and Franco Cano abducted and murdered five women in Santa Ana and Anaheim, CA. So it's feasible that the Marquis and Eugene Knott crossed paths somewhere and got together."

"So if the Marquis sent Knott, it's a safe assumption that he knows we went to Tybee Island to get the dirt on him. That's probably why he had Knott kill Sam Weathers."

Her eyebrows go up. "Weathers is gone?" I nod. She continues, "That's a shame. But realize that Eugene Knott didn't really need a reason to kill anyone. It's what he does..." Her voice trails off, and her eyes close.

That i.v. bag must contain a sedative. I hurt too, but I'm not sleepy; apparently they don't think it necessary to knock me out. I buzz the nurse and ask her about my stuff, and she says she'll look into it. "You won't need anything until tomorrow anyway, Shug."

"But my wallet and phone are in the pockets..."

"Nobody will mess with them. I'll see that they get up here. If you want to make a call, buzz for a nurse and she'll bring you a phone."

I debate calling Lupe to tell her what's happening, but I decide to wait until I have more positive news about Danny before I do.

My dreams that night are full of demons. I see Danny being shot down over and over, there's blood everywhere and I just know he's not going to make it. When I finally wake up, I can't tell if it's day or night because the window shade is down and I can't see outside. I still don't see my clothes, but there's a closet in the room. But I can't get out of bed because the bars on the side are up.

I buzz the nurse. It's a different one from last night, a middle-eastern-looking guy. His name tag reads Ali.

"Is there any news about Danny Merkel?"

"I haven't heard. I will ask, though."

"What time is it?"

"Six-thirty in the morning. You're awake early."

Great. I'll be short on sleep. "When can I expect to get out of here?"

"Doctor will be by in an hour or so. Once she authorizes your release, it can be anytime afterwards."

"Did my clothes ever get up here?"

"Your wallet and cell phone are on the table by the bed." He's right. He looks in the closet. "Yep, your clothes are in here. You really don't want to wear them, though."

I can imagine. "Thanks," I say bitterly. "Can you put the rail down so I can go to the bathroom?" He does so, then leaves me to my business. After I've finished, I check out my clothes. They're way filthy and full of blood. No way I can wear them, and all of my others are still on Tybee Island.

Ali returns in about fifteen minutes. I tell ask him about clothes.

"Let me see if I can get you a set of scrubs to wear for discharge," Ali says.

He returns about twenty minutes later with the scrubs. "I asked about Mr. Merkel," he says. "They say he's resting comfortably. But Doctor doesn't want him to have visitors for a few days."

It's almost eleven before Ali wheels me out the front door of the hospital. He's told me that the nearest hotels are a couple of miles away, and of course, the Jeep is still on Tybee Island, some twenty-five miles from here. "How can I get to Tybee Island from here? My car is there." I ask.

"Uber or taxi. There is no bus. Would you like me to call one for you?"

"Sure."

"You won't need it," says a familiar voice from behind me. I turn and my jaw drops.

It's Sheriff Frank!

Chapter 34

Tommy Burke has an ugly black pistol leveled at Lupe's belly. He no longer has the cast on his arm. "Go," he says, "To the guest house."

OMG, Eduardo and Judy are there!

Burke marches her through the garage and out the back door, where a broad expanse of lawn separates the main house from the copse that conceals the guest house. Floodlights come on as the pair steps onto the grass; more light their way as they near the trees. A twisting path of stepping stones is illuminated by small lanterns at ground level, which also light up one by one as they go. Rounding a bend, Lupe sees the windows glowing in the small A-frame guest house ahead.

"It's unlocked," says Burke.

Lupe turns the knob and goes inside. The first floor of the cottage is mostly one large room, still smelling of tomato sauce, garlic and hamburger from the kitchen that opens in the rear. A door to the downstairs bedroom where Eduardo sleeps, is next to it. A spiral staircase in the center of the main room gives access to the upper master bedroom, which is Judy's.

A nude Judy McMasters is duct-taped to the staircase. Her arms are extended, pulled back and secured at the wrists to the metal struts, causing her pendulous breasts to jut forward. Her ankles are held in a similar manner. A band of tape around her neck forces her head upward. Lupe notices several red wheals across her belly, as if she'd been whipped with a belt.

A boy's voice cries, "Mama Lupe!" Eduardo, sitting on a couch across from his grandmother, starts to slide off onto the floor. Burke's voice stops him:

"What did I tell you would happen if you got off that couch, little man?" The barrel of his gun travels to cover the boy, and Lupe nearly pees herself.

Eduardo looks at Burke with fear in his eyes, and pushes himself back onto the sofa.

"There's a good boy! Do as you're told and I won't hurt Mommy and Grandma."

Judy cries, "Oh no, Lupe!"

Lupe's fear changes to anger and she glares at Burke, feeling the hatred burning in her eyes. "What have you done, *hijoputa*? They have not hurt you. Let them go!"

Burke tucks the pistol into his waistband. "Such language! Perhaps if you do as you're told, I might indeed let them go."

"What do you want from me?" Lupe says, afraid of the answer.

"You can start by taking off your clothes."

Lupe is a former stripper and totally comfortable naked in a room full of people, but that certainly does not include Eduardo and Judy. "Not in front of my son, please!"

"I think his little pecker was getting hard when he was watching Grandma strip down," Burke chortles. "Isn't that right, kiddo?" Eduardo doesn't answer. "Do it!" Burke snarls at Lupe.

"Please let him leave the room," Lupe pleads.

Burke looks at the ceiling, pantomiming deep thinking, then, "OK, you can run and play, little man, but don't go outside. He extracts a knife from his pocket, thumbs open the blade, which glints evilly in the yellowish light from the ceiling. "You know what happens to mom and grandma if you do."

Eduardo nods, slides of the couch and vanishes into his bedroom.

"Now, strip!" barks Burke.

Lupe does not think that the killer has any intention of letting them go, but she has no choice. She unbuttons her blouse, revealing ample breasts encased in a lacy bra. Burke stares at them, eyes glistening, and his tongue snakes out of his mouth to wet his lips. Lupe reaches behind her to undo the bra, letting her tits fall free. As a former striper, Lupe knows how to promise a man everything with her eyes, her lips and her body. She tries to smile at Burke—if she can just get him to come over and grope her, maybe she can get his gun. She undoes her jeans and sidles out of them to reveal panties that match her bra. She slides them off her hips and lets them fall to her ankles, kicking them in his direction. She plucks at her pussy hair with her fingernails, looking at him coyly (she hopes!). Smiling, Burke picks up her panties in a bunch and holds them to his nose.

"Sit on the floor," is his next command.

Oh no! Burke's smart—he knows that she won't be able to get any purchase to attack him from that position.

Killers!

"Spread your legs. Play with yourself."

Lupe looks at Judy, whose eyes are full of tears. She says, "It's okay, Hon. Do as he says."

Lupe begins to rub herself with two fingers.

"Spread your lips," he says. "Show us what you got."

She obeys. Her genitals are is so dry that her touch is painful.

Burke says, "If you want this to be over, tell me what Natalie McMasters has found out about the Marquis."

Surprised, Lupe stops rubbing herself. Burke glares and makes a gesture of impatience with the gun, so she starts again. "I don't know what she knows," Lupe says. "I have not talked to her."

"Bullshit. She's your wife. I bet you talk every day."

"It is not bullshit. She does not want me involved with this. She left me here to keep me safe."

"Funny how that worked out, ain't it," he grins.

CLUNK! Something hit the floor in the kitchen?

Burke turns in that direction, jerking his pistol from his pants.

Sykes stands in the kitchen door, a silver semiauto pistol leveled at Burke. Seeing the gun in his hand, she shoots. And misses!

Burke returns fire and a crimson rose blooms on Sykes' chest. She collapses to the floor, falling behind the kitchen counter.

The killer grins. "Gotta love these isolated houses!" he says, "Nobody hears shit!"

He goes over to Sykes, and kicks her gun into the living room. Going further into the kitchen, he puts his gun away again. He comes out wielding a foot-long chef's knife. Approaching Judy, he grabs her breast, pulls it upwards and lays the edge of knife beneath it, where it meets her torso. He draws it back just a little, and she hisses sharply as rivulets of rich red blood seep beneath the knife's edge and run down her white skin.

He says to Lupe, "One more time, bitch! Tell me what McMasters knows, or I'll cut off grandma's tittie and feed it to her and that brat of yours!"

Lupe closes her eyes, remembering the carnage this man wrought in Sherrie's dorm room. She knows he will do what he says, and there's absolutely nothing she can do about it.

A gunshot splits the air. Sykes again? But Burke kicked her gun away. Lupe's eyes snap open to see Burke standing with his hands clapped to his shoulder, an incredulous look on his face.

Eduardo is in the doorway of his bedroom, looking stupidly at a smoking silver revolver on the floor where he dropped it. As Burke's hand flails for the pistol in his waistband, Eduardo pounces on the revolver, pulls back the hammer and shoots Burke again, in the chest this time.

Blood spurts out of the killer's mouth as he crumples to the floor.

Killers!

Chapter 35

Sheriff Frank is the last person I expected to see here. She's not wearing her uniform; she's dressed like a tourist, in a hideous, multicolored sleeveless top and knee-length cargo shorts. The pockets are big enough to hold a gun.

"What do you want?" I ask her.

"Barrett wants you." Her right hand drops into her pocket.

I don't have my gun or my knife; the Tybee Island cops took them. "My wheels are still on Tybee Island," I tell her.

"I'll take you," she says. My eyes stay riveted to her right hand. Is she going to pull a gun and kidnap me right here?

I ask another question to stall for time. "How did you even know I was here?"

Her eyes go up and her chin goes down. "We heard a news report about a medical evacuation from Tybee Island and your name was mentioned. Where else would they take you?"

I try to throw her off base. "Where is Barrett? Tilghman's Landing?"

Now her eyes get bigger, telling me I hit the mark. She takes her hand out of her pocket and it's still empty. "How do you know about the Landing?" I don't answer. "C'mon, I'll take you to him. I've got a car here."

"You've gotta think I'm way stupid," I tell her. I turn to walk away.

She stops me in my tracks. "Your friend Ye-ye is there," she says.

What did she say? I face her again. "Ye-ye? What has Barrett done to him?"

"Nothing. He's had an accident. Barrett's taking care of him."

"What's happened?"

"Barrett will tell you. Let's go."

That little voice in my head that I never listen to is telling me I'm an idiot for even considering this. I know she's got a gun in that pocket—I should holler for a cop. But she's a sheriff; a cop prolly wouldn't even do anything. What would Ye-ye do if it was you in his place? I think. I make my decision.

"OK, I'll go. When do we leave?"

"How 'bout right now?" She leads me through a row of palm trees into the parking lot and a nondescript gray Nissan Versa a couple of years old. Opening the driver's door, she says, "It's not locked," so I get in the shotgun side. She fires it up and pulls out into the city streets.

This is bad—not a soul knows where I'm going. I glance at Frank, her eyes on the road as she navigates city traffic. It's worth a try. I slide my cell out of the back pocket of my scrubs, keeping it hidden from Frank between my body and the car door. I hit the home button and the screen brightens, then I thumb the phone icon at the bottom of the screen to get into my contacts. I pull up M.B. and tap her number. I can barely hear the ringing after the phone connects—I look at Frank again, scared she'll hear it, but she's still focused on her driving. The muted ringing stops and M.B.'s voice begins reciting her voicemail message. A muted beep indicates it's now recording.

I sidle over a little and place the phone on the seat beside me. "How far is Tilghman's Landing?" I ask, I hope not too loudly.

Frank looks at me sharply. "I'm not deaf," she says. "I haven't said that's where we're going."

"Whatever. I hope you're planning on bringing me back here, Sheriff," I say.

"Don't worry about it." Easy for you to say.

"So can you tell me what's happened to Ye-ye?"

"I think Barrett'd rather do that himself," Frank says. She reaches down and flips on the radio and a sappy country song fills the car. I'm not even sure that our convo was picked up by the phone's mike, and now there's no hope that any more will be, so I tap the little red phone icon to kill the call. Another few seconds, and my cell is safely back in my pocket.

It's not long before we're out of the city on I-95, heading south. The further we get from Savannah, the more I'm tempted to grab the keys out of the ignition and run when the car stops—no one in the world knows where I am, and I've got a totally bad feeling about this. After about an hour and a half, we get off the interstate and turn east onto a two-lane rural road. We pass through a couple of small towns that have more churches than houses and seem like they're stuck in the 1950s. Civilization becomes even more sparse after that; just some scattered double-wides and salt marshes.

Killers!

We turn onto a one-lane paved road that runs next to a muddy brown river. Warm, moist air carrying the scent of ancient fish blows into the car; Frank wrinkles her nose and pushes a button to roll up the windows, then cuts on the AC. After a mile or so, the road changes to gravel, and a few minutes later we roll into a settlement of decaying, unpainted wooden buildings and rusty double-wides. A sign on the right tells me I'm at the Tilghman's Landing General Store & Vacation Cabins.

Frank stops the car. "This is it." She turns off the AC, kills the engine, then opens the door to get out. The sulfurous smell of swamp gas rolls into the car, making me gag. I undo my seat belt and get out. I look around and see absolutely nobody, then I catch motion out of the corner of my eye. Looking that way, I spy a couple of black kids darting behind a building. Where there's kids, there are generally adults, so somebody does live here after all.

I follow Frank across a packed dirt lot with a couple of green-and-white antique gas pumps in the center onto the porch of the general store. This place makes the Rexall in Greypeak look positively upscale—it's a bare wood two-story building that has two large, filthy windows you can't even see through, entirely covered with a black metal grille. Reminds me of an inner-city slum, or a prison.

Frank pulls the screen door open and the squeal sends shivers up my spine like nails on a chalkboard. Inside is one large room with plank floors, reeking of food, beer and b.o., all intermingled with swamp gas seeping in from outside. A bar with stools in front runs the length of the wall on my right, with a scattering of tables and chairs nearby. The left half of the room is crammed with free-standing shelves holding groceries, household items and even cans of oil, antifreeze and fan belts, all so fucking old I wonder if any of it is even worth a shit. A row of coolers along the back wall holds beer, wine and soft drinks. A neon Budweiser sign on the wall above flickers red.

A big black man wearing a filthy apron that used to be white over a t-shirt and denim shorts is behind the bar. He's bald as an egg and looks about sixty. A white guy of similar age in a camo shirt and black jeans sits across from him on a barstool. Both turn to stare at us as we enter. I see a smirk appear on Whitey's face-a lech if I ever saw one. Now I know what a mouse in front of a cat feels like.

Frank knows them. "Trevon, Lucas. Have you seen Barrett?"

Before Lucas or Trevon can answer her, the screen door squeals again. A familiar voice says, "Heah I am."

OMG! I spin and there he is! Standing by the door. He's lost some weight and he's bald as an egg, wearing a pair of filthy camo coveralls that are a far cry from the totally lit rags he used to sport a few months ago. He looks way different from the debonair host I knew, but I'd know those eyes anywhere. It's Barrett Tybee, aka the Marquis!

Killers!

Chapter 36

I **know Barrett's not his real name, but it's how I think of him. I ask** him, "What have you done with Ye-ye?"

"I'll take y'all to him. Francine, you can come too."

"Yes, Barrett," the sheriff says deferentially.

God, she's looking at him like a puppy at its master. I'm getting a totally bad vibe. "Why can't Ye-ye come here?"

"He's not well," says Barrett.

"What's wrong with him?"

"He's an old man. He's sick."

"I call bullshit. Since I've known him, Ye-ye's never been sick a day."

"Do you want to see him or not?" Yeah, like you're just gonna let me walk outta here if I say no. I nod in agreement. "Then let's go," Barrett says.

As I turn to head for the door, I notice Trevon and Lucas grinning broadly, like they know something I don't. We go outside where the humidity about takes my breath away, and walk across the road toward a rusty, corrugated metal building on a concrete pad that looks as if it's about to fall into the canal. There's a dock built of logs next to it and a flat-bottomed boat covered with peeling light green paint tied to the decaying pier. It has half-a-dozen seats and canopy over the top—it looks like a former tour boat. Barrett waves us to seats and goes to the rear. He flips a switch on a large outboard motor and yanks a lanyard a couple of times. It runs raggedly at first, almost stalling, but Barrett fiddles with something on top and the motor settles into a mostly steady drone, popping just now and again. He casts off the rope, and taking a seat next to the engine, he engages the prop and steers the boat into the center of the channel.

We chug along, turning at so many junctions I quickly lose track of our route. The river banks are forested with pines and deciduous trees hung with dirty gray Spanish moss; thick trunks of live oak trees rear up out of the dark water like misshapen monsters. The motor is too loud for convo and that's a good thing. WTF am I doing? Going off into a swamp with serial killer and a corrupt sheriff; how can this end well? Stoney's battered corpse under Rattlesnake Mountain flashes in my head and I tremble inwardly–what's to say that this monster hasn't done the same to Ye-ye?

After about fifteen minutes, we enter a large pool full of bright green floating plants. A ripple in the black water catches my eye. Holy shit! A scaly head nearly the same color as the water disappears under the surface. An alligator? There's another one, not ten feet away! It's swimming alongside us and is nearly as long as our boat! I shudder to think what might happen if we capsized and ended up in the water with that thing. It turns lazily toward us and bumps the prow with its nose; I can feel the boat skew a little as it hits. Barrett simply compensates by turning the motor slightly to keep us out of the floating plants.

We come around another bend and forge into open water; the gator stays behind in the shelter of the floating vegetation. A spit of land surrounded by water on three sides looms ahead, so thickly forested I can't see much past the bank. Barrett pilots the boat to the right, passing the shore; now it's evident that the land is a good-sized island. We come around the back end and a structure emerges on the bank—a house with a large porch on posts hanging over the water, the rear extending into the trees, onto the island itself. Once white, the clapboards now have a coat of brown-red mud and green algae. There's a wooden dock under the porch, with a flight of stairs leading upward to a trap door. As Barrett expertly steers the boat into a bay next to the dock, an alligator at least ten feet long swims up, bumping our boat with its snout so hard that it actually moves us.

"What the fuck!" I shout.

"Don't worry," says Barrett. "They're just playing. They know this boat—I use it when I feed them."

He feeds them? Of course, he does. And I don't want to think about what he feeds them...

Frank grabs a line and jumps to the pier to make us fast. Barrett kills the engine and says, "Home sweet home." The gator has been joined by two of his friends, and they're all bumping the boat, making it difficult to get out. Barrett comes forward and reaches for my arm, but I dodge and step up on the dock unaided. A glimmer of darkness passes over his features, quickly vanishing.

"Is Ye-ye here?" I ask.

"Upstairs," Barrett says.

Killers!

I check out the stairs; there's a railing on either side, but they seem none too sturdy. Frank goes first and I follow. At the top, Frank pushes on the door with both hands when she's close enough, swinging it upward to fall with a crash inside. I follow her in.

We emerge inside the screened porch. It's dank and smells moldy. It's furnished with cheap metal chaises, a sofa with hideously flowered vinyl cushions and a faux glass table surrounded by plastic chairs. There's an oil lamp on the table and lanterns hang on the walls—no electricity here, people. A door in the center of the far wall gives access to the rest of the house.

Barrett's bald head appears in the opening, followed by the rest of him. "Where's Ye-ye?" I ask him again.

"You'll see him soon," Barrett says. "But first, you'll have to do something for me."

I know what; I don't need to ask. WTF. It's just sex.

"Sit down, Natalie," he says. He lifts up the trap door and lets it fall closed with a crash. I sit on the edge of one of the chaises, wondering if he's gonna rape me right here and now. Instead he asks, "How much did your friend tell the FBI? Do they know about the Landing?" He actually sounds nervous.

"She mentioned the Landing to me before I told her anything about it, Barrett," Frank says.

Barrett looks at me with dark eyes, and I shudder. "How did you find out about the Landing?" he asks

I could lie, but what would that gain me?

"Sam Weathers said he brought you here after the fire on Tybee Island to live with Stoney." I steel myself and glare right back at him. "How could you do that to somebody who took you in?"

"I told you they got into the mine," says Frank, a tremble in her voice.

'Don't worry about it," says Barrett to Frank. To me: "Who else knows I'm here?"

"Nobody." He visibly relaxes. "Yet," I add, and he tenses again.

"What do you mean?"

"I left a note for M.B. at the hospital," I lie. I'm trying to buy time here, people.

He looks into my eyes again. "You're lying," he says finally. I try to maintain my gaze, but I look away.

"Good," he says. "I've got quite a bit invested in this place, and I'd hate to lose it."

"What do you mean?" I ask him.

"After I killed my worthless parents, I lived heah with Stoney and his family for about five years. The village of Tilghman's Landing was on its last legs—just a few Gullah families that didn't have the resources to leave their ancestral home. I got out when I was old enough and enrolled in college."

"How did you manage that?

"In addition to being a child molester, my daddy was an unreconstructed confederate who didn't trust banks. I took his stash of gold with me when I left the house the night of the fire." He smiles. "Gold will open many doors."

He's looking at me like a cat looks at a mouse. I'm pretty sure what he has in mind. Keep him talking, Nattie! "When can I see Ye-ye?"

"In a little while." His picks up his story again. "After I left for college, I came back to the Landing from time to time. A few years ago, when times got hard and the residents couldn't afford to pay their leases anymore, I decided to spend some of my money, buy it, and revitalize it. The residents were only too happy to have me as their landlord."

"It sure doesn't look revitalized to me. Who would come here and stay in those stupid tourist cabins?"

He smiles. "Men who need a safe place, away from the people who are persecuting them. Y'all met two of them at the general store in the Landing—Terry and Lester."

"I thought they were Trevon and Lucas," I interrupt.

"Those are their assumed names. Trevon is Terry Atwater—he got himself in a little trouble in Florida about ten years ago because of his predilection for little boys. Lucas is Lester Wollenz, aka the Riverside Killer. Lucas is partial to whores, but unfortunately, few have survived their encounters with him. And you met my very first client on Tybee Island. Eugene Knott. You didn't treat Eugene very nicely, I heah."

I can't help myself. "I knifed the son of a bitch. He shot Danny and M.B. What do you think you are doing, giving serial killers a place to hide?"

Killers!

Barrett smiles. "Everyone needs a friend sometime in their life. Including me. I met Eugene by happenstance when we were both in Baltimore—because of his size, he's a fairly recognizable character. Once I convinced him that I wasn't going to be easy to kill, I persuaded him that our association could be mutually beneficial. Eugene is a very smart fella; he told me that his IQ tested at 165, and I'm no slouch myself. The two of us actively started hunting for others with a similar predilection, and we were able to track down Tommy Burke after his bold escape from jail made the national news. Tommy should be introducing himself to Miss Lupe right about now."

What did he just say? Everybody knows who Tommy Burke is. He was arrested for butchering a houseful of college women, but after he got away, the cops couldn't find him again. Now I know why.

"No! Please don't let him hurt Lupe!"

"Well, Miss Natalie, I think that will depend upon you," he says, smiling broadly.

I know just what he wants.

Chapter 37

Barrett ushers Frank and me into the house. We pass through a living room/kitchen area cluttered with junk and old food into a hallway leading to the back. We pass one closed door and Frank opens a second. Entering, she takes a box of matches from a drawer and lights a lantern on a table next to the door. A reddish glow spreads across the chamber.

Frank steps away from the doorway, gesturing for me and Barrett to go inside. "I'll just go and change," she says, going back towards the door we passed by.

I enter the room. It's a strange place. Two windows are boarded up from inside, and it has a peculiar scent, like a gym or a bathroom, with a sour undercurrent—I think maybe fear. More lanterns are scattered about on surfaces and hanging on the walls, waiting to be lit. A free-standing shelf holds at least a dozen different colored dildos, small, large, and painful. An array of multi-stranded whips, paddles, riding crops, and bamboo canes decorates one wall; another is adorned with leather straps and manacles with buckles, chains, several pairs of handcuffs, ball gags and leather hoods. A large X-shaped cross on wheels with restraints on the arms and legs is in a corner. A barber chair sits in front of the hanging lantern—it's also provided with arm and leg restraints, and a nearby black leather futon is similarly equipped. Disturbingly, an unlit charcoal grill containing several pokers sits in another corner. Various bars, chains and pulleys dangle overhead.

A paradise for a sick mind.

A woman kneels on a mat in the center of the chamber, beneath a hanging lantern. WTF, she was in here by herself in the dark? She's short, like me, and her closely clipped black hair is like a skullcap. She's wearing nothing but a leather collar around her neck with a leash hanging from it, and leather bands around her wrists and ankles. As she rises, I can see that she has tiny, pointy breasts and sharply defined muscles—an athlete, then. She brings her arms up chest high and clasps her hands with her thumbs to the back, holding them out to Barrett and nodding her head. *"Ni hao, Sifu."* she says. I know from my time with Ye-ye that *ni hao* is a Chinese greeting.

Barrett returns her salute and says, *"Ni hao, Vivian."*

Barrett takes a seat in the barber chair and reclines it back a little. About that time, Frank returns. She's wearing a suit of black leather straps in a diamond pattern that leaves her tits and bush bare and her fat belly and hips bulging around the leather. Gross! She goes to the hanging lantern and lights it, brightening the room considerably.

"Come here, ladies," says Barrett. "Not you, Miss Natalie." Frank and Vivian go to him, kneeling on either side of the barber chair.

"Now Natalie, go to the mat. You can show me what you've got."

"What about Lupe and Tommy Burke?"

"Tommy won't hurt her unless I tell him to." Can I trust him? I totally haven't got a choice.

I have taken my clothes off for men hundreds of times. Normally, stripping is all about control—you want to make them want you more than they want anything else in the world. They know that they can't have you, at least not in the club, so they hope that if they give you enough money, you'll go home with them. Sometimes that works; mostly, it doesn't. But this is different. Barrett can and will do anything he wants with me. My goal is simple-stay alive, stay whole. And get him to call his dog off Lupe.

I look at the two women. Vivian's eyes are dead, her expression totally impassive. She looks like she's on something. In contrast, Frank is wide awake, staring at me with a lascivious expression like she just can't wait for me to get started. I'm familiar with that from the strip club, too; sometimes the women were my biggest fans.

I gyrate my hips like a stripper, and cross my arms in front of me, gripping the bottom of my shirt. I begin to pull it upward to reveal my titties when Barret suddenly says, "Stop."

"I've got a better idea," he says. "Ladies, hook her up." The two women rise and come to me, grab my wrists and guide me across the room toward the cross. The realization of what's about to happen hits and I struggle to get away, but they're both way stronger than me. They push my wrists upwards into the leather straps on the arm of the cross and snug them tight. I'm standing on tiptoes. The wheel me to the center of the room, then set brakes on the wheels to hold the cross in position.

Frank goes to a cabinet and opens a drawer, taking out a large pair of scissors, then looks at Barrett. He arches his back in the barber chair and slides off his pants and his undershorts, then sits straddle–legged.

"Get her out of those," he says to Frank as he begins to play with himself. Surprisingly, his dick is a tiny nub. I expected more from him.

I fight against the restraints as Frank inserts the scissors under the bottom of my shirt and starts to cut. But they're too strong. I just have to hang there and let it happen. Goose flesh springs up on my arms as chill air hits my sweaty belly; in a few seconds she's cut completely through the shirt and has removed it. I'm not wearing a bra—it got destroyed with the rest of my clothes, so I can I feel my nipples tightening. My scrub pants are more difficult, but those scissors are sharp! Frank cuts down both legs so the pants simply fall away from my body. I'm not wearing any panties either, so I'm now naked to Barrett's gaze. Frank hands the scissors to Vivian, who puts them back in the drawer, and then gathers up my ruined scrubs and throws them in the corner. All the while, Barrett just sits there, rubbing himself and smirking.

He orders, "Francine. Service me."

Frank kneels in front of him and goes to work on that pitiful little dick of his with her hands and mouth.

"Play with her, Vivian," Barrett says. "Get her ready for me."

Vivian walks up to me, places her hands on my shoulders, looks into my eyes with her brown ones. Is that a hint of sadness I see? She leans forward so her nose touches mine, then nips at my lips, once, twice. She puts her mouth full on mine and her tongue creeps inside. After a sec, I return the kiss and feel my nipples tighten some more, and a tingle in my loins.

Her hands leave my shoulders and run down my body, over my nipples, my belly and into my bush, which I can't help thrusting forward to meet her. She kneels in front of me. Her tongue twirls inside me, causing little shocks; my eyes drift to Barrett; Frank has increased the intensity of her ministrations, but he still doesn't seem to be hard. Pressure builds within me—I close my eyes and give myself over to it, rotating my hips into Vivian's eager mouth.

"Enough, Vivian," Barrett says. My eyes snap open in time to see him push Frank away and get up from the barber chair. He goes to the low commode where the scissors were. He opens a drawer and comes out with a small bottle of clear liquid and a syringe. He makes a show of filling it, puts the bottle on top of the commode and taps the syringe with his fingers to remove the air bubbles, then lays it next to the bottle. He goes back into the drawer and retrieves a length of surgical tubing. Holding it, he approaches me.

"No..." I croak. "No drugs! Please." I don't have a prayer if I'm drugged!

He wraps the tubing around my right forearm and pulls it tight, then undoes my right wrist before going to get the syringe. I struggle to reach my other wrist but it's impossible, then I shake my right arm to dislodge the tubing—also futile. I flail at him as he approaches again but he just smiles and catches my wrist in his hand, pulling my arm out straight so hard that it hurts. Smiling wickedly, he says, "If y'all make me blow this injection, I'll just keep trying until it takes." I stop struggling. I yelp at the quick pinch as the needle goes into my vein, then the world spins and fire explodes in my head.

He reattaches my wrist to the restraint and says to Vivian, "Finish her.", then goes back to his chair to enjoy the show. Frank again assumes her position in front of him.

Vivian goes down on me again, and the sensations from her tongue erupt all over my body. My heart pounds and the sweat runs off me in a river; I'm burning up inside but my skin is freezing. My breaths come quicker and quicker and I close my eyes as lights go off behind my eyelids. My whole body seizes up as every muscle contracts and excruciating pain overwhelms me.

I must have passed out, because the next thing I hear is Vivian screaming, "*Sifu*! What are you doing? No!"

My eyes snap open. Barrett is advancing, a fillet knife in his hand. He grabs my breast and presses the point ever so gently next to the nipple. I let out a ragged scream. He pushes a little harder and I feel a warm stream on my skin. He steps back, holding the tip of the knife so the light glints off my blood. He's now grinning broadly and has a rampant hard-on. I scream again and so does Vivian as he assaults my other breast. She flails at him, but he brings a hand up under her chin, sending her tumbling across the room.

He reaches for my chin, holding my head immobile as the sharp point of the knife creeps toward my eye! My mouth flies open and I scream and scream and scream...

A loud THUMP! comes from the door, followed by a crashing sound as it explodes inward. A naked man rushes in, making for me and Barrett. I'm still screaming as Barrett spins to meet him. OMG, it's Ye-ye! But something's wrong! He's naked! And wielding the headpiece of a brass bed? OMG! OMG! His eyes! What's wrong with his eyes?

Chapter 38

Icy terror swells in Lupe's bowels as she sees Tommy Burke on the floor, a dark stain spreading into an irregular ellipse on the expensive Oriental carpet. A fecal stench reaches her nostrils—she's not sure if it's coming from her or the corpse. Her fear is not for herself, it's for Eduardo. Her little boy just killed a man!

Lupe immediately runs to Sykes and places two fingers on her neck—she nods to Judy; the detective's still alive.

Judy says, "Lupe! Get the gun from Eduardo, then cut me loose."

Lupe gets the revolver and puts it on the kitchen counter, then picks up the Burke's knife and frees Judy. Judy runs over to Sykes, moving the detective's hands from the wound in her belly, replacing them with her own. Her shoulders tighten as she applies pressure to slow the bleeding.

"What are we gonna do?" Lupe moans.

"Call 911. Lupe! Do it now!"

"My phone. It is in the car..."

"Use the land line!" Judy says.

Lupe calls and gives the details to the 911 operator.

"We're sending someone right now," he says.

She hangs up, thinks a sec, picks up the receiver again and dials a number from memory.

It rings. Again. Once more, then, "This is Nattie. Thanks for calling. I promise I won't ghost you, so hang tight till I can clap you back."

Shit. She depresses the plungers on the receiver rest and punches in another number.

More rings, then. "Hello. You've reached Daniel Merkel. I'm sorry I missed your call..."

God damn it! She hangs up again, hesitates, then punches the keypad once more. It rings. Again. Come on, pick up, pick up...

A sleepy voice. "Hello?"

"Leon! This is Lupe!"

"Lupe?" his sleepy voice says. "Shit girl, do you know what time it is?"

"Leon, we need you! We just killed Tommy Burke..."

"Who? What! Are you OK?"

"Yes, we are fine."

"Where are you?"

"Home. In the guest house."

"Stay there. I'll be right over." The phone goes silent.

By this time, Eduardo is clinging to his Mama's leg, crying. Heedless of her nudity, she picks him up, shushes him, sits on the couch and kisses him on top of his head.

A few minutes later, there's a pounding on the door. "Paramedics! Open up!"

Lupe slides Eduardo on to the sofa, then runs over to open the door. The first guy through does a double take when he sees she's naked, but he hurries on in.

"Over here!" Judy McMasters cries.

The first paramedic heads her way while the second one, pushing a gurney through the doorway, spots Tommy Burke and hurries to him. A moment later, "This one's dead."

"She isn't," says the medic with Sykes. "Help me here."

"Is she going to live?" Judy asks.

I don't know, lady," the medic says. He looks Judy up and down, notices the blood on her belly that ran from beneath her breast. "Are you OK?"

"Yes," Judy says, looking down and noticing her nakedness. "I'll just get some clothes on."

She goes upstairs and comes down in a minute wearing a robe, tosses another to Lupe.

As the medics are loading Sykes onto the gurney, the front door opens again and Leon Kidd rushes in. Both Lupe and Judy run to hug him. As the medics hurry Sykes out, the ladies tell Kidd what's happened.

"Where the hell did Eduardo get a gun?" is Kidd's response.

"I found it in a box like the one I found in the big house," Eduardo says. "I didn't touch the gun, Mama Lupe. You said to never touch a gun! I didn't touch it until the bad man was gonna hurt you."

"Where did you find the box?" asks Kidd.

"Like in the other house, I said. It was in a safe in the pantry."

"How did you get the safe open?" Judy asks.

Killers!

"I use that same word that Mama Nattie used," says Eduardo. "I din't remember how to spell it, so I had to try a few times."

"Where is the box now, " asks Kidd.

"In my room. I get it." He suits action to words, returning in a moment with a steel box. He hands it to Lupe.

Lupe works the latches and throws back the lid. Inside lies a black, leather-bound book. Before she can turn back the cover, there's another knock on the door. Kidd goes to open it. Two cops, a white man and a black woman, enter.

Lupe turns her back to the door as if to hide her nakedness under the partly open robe from the new arrivals, slides the book inside and belts it tightly around her waist, then turns back to the officers.

"I'm Officer Reales and this is Officer Smyth," the woman says. Noticing Burke's body on the floor, she asks, "What's happened here?"

"Home invasion," says Kidd. "This man assaulted this family, and he was shot and killed."

"Who shot him?" Officer Smyth asks.

Lupe, Judy, and Eduardo say simultaneously "I did!"

Officer Reales glowers at them. "Okay people, this isn't going to work..."

"Don't say anything to them without a lawyer present," Kidd interrupts.

"Who the hell are you?" Reales asks.

"Lieutenant Leon Kidd. I used to be on the Job with CCPD."

"You got some ID?"

Kidd shows her his gold detective lieutenant's badge, with the word *retired* embossed on the front.

Officer Smyth, who has gone over to examine Burke's body, pipes up, "Hey Reales, you know who this vic is? It's Tommy Burke!"

Reales sounds incredulous. "The guy that killed all them women?"

"That's him."

She gives Kidd his ID back. She addresses the group. "Okay, if nobody's talking, we'll have to take everybody in and wait for the lawyers."

"A typical intimidation tactic," Kidd says to Lupe and Judy, like the cops aren't even there. "Dare to exercise your Constitutional rights, and we'll just make everyone as uncomfortable as possible."

"Hey, were you even here when this happened?" Officer Smyth asks.

"No, but I'm here now, and I'm not going to let you run roughshod over this family. Seems to me somebody deserves a medal here."

Both cops look as if they want to run Kidd in, but in addition to being a former cop, he was also a lieutenant in the Marines. His presence is not something easily ignored. Reales asks, somewhat snottily. "What do you suggest?"

"Let the CSIs secure the scene. Let this family get cleaned up and get some sleep. I promise I'll bring them down later with their lawyer and we can clear all of this up."

"No way," says Reales. "My watch commander would have my ass if I let two witnesses have a chance to collude."

"Who's your watch commander?"

"Sergeant Stebbins."

"I know her. Get her on the horn and let me talk to her."

Reales and Smyth look at each other. "Okay," Reales says.

Kidd has a discussion with Stebbins, promising that he'll take responsibility that Lupe and Judy won't discuss the evening's events with each other until detectives have a chance to question them. "It's either that or I'm calling the hospital to come and get them to treat them for severe emotional distress," Kidd threatens. "Then it will be days before you can talk to them. Maybe the press will even get there first"

Stebbins apparently sees the wisdom in Kidd's approach. "Put Reales on the line," she says.

After talking to Stebbins, Reales hangs up and says, "OK. They can get cleaned up and get some sleep. The detectives will talk to them tomorrow."

"We'll be up in the main house if you need us." Kidd says. "C'mon, ladies."

Lupe, Judy Eduardo and Kidd head outside, across the wide lawn to Hyacinth House. Kidd, walking next to Lupe, says, "Okay. Who shot Tommy Burke?"

Lupe and Judy look at each other. "Eduardo did," Judy says.

Kidd digests this information. "Nope," he responds. "It was one of you."

"Burke had Judy taped to the stairs," Lupe says. "So it would have to be me."

Once inside Hyacinth House, Kidd spends twenty minutes with Judy and Lupe getting their story straight. "Judy, you can say you don't know much because you passed out when Burke cut you. That way we don't have two people telling the same story, which would be a huge red flag." He helps Lupe concoct a simple tale about how she got to the hidden box while Tommy was dealing with Sykes, grabbed the revolver and shot him. "That kind of revolver provides a lousy surface for fingerprints, so it won't be surprising if they don't find yours. And we'll have to get some GSR on your hands before tomorrow, in case they check." Some gunpowder from one of Kidd's bullets would do the trick.

"Go to bed, ladies, and sleep if you can. Why don't you let me have that book you found, Lupe. I'll read it while you're sleeping to see if there's anything important in it."

Lupe is reluctant, but she knows that she is shot from being awake all day and threatened by Burke. She gives the journal to Kidd.

***

After the ladies and Eduardo have retired, Kidd finds a comfortable seat in the living room and opens the book.

On the first page, he reads:

The Journal of Rebecca Feiner

Holy shit! Kidd turns the page.

May 28, 20___
I have been a nervous wreck ever since I received that letter from Barrett...

Some hours later, when he's finished reading, Kidd closes the book and rubs his eyes. Then he picks up the phone and punches in a number he remembers all too well.

"Federal Bureau of Investigation, Quantico office. How may I direct your call?"

"Give me the HRT, please..."

Chapter 39

Darkness.

Cold sweat coats my body. My skin's on fire, and the reek of swampmud is strong in my nose. Ye-ye's face dances in my mind. The two bloody pits in the center of his face. OMG! Did Barrett take my eyes too? Is that why I can't see?

My arms are pinned underneath my body—I roll over to free them. They tingle all over and they hurt to move. My back, my legs and my face are burning, itching. Somehow I get my hands to my face. I close my eyes, feel my eyelids, the orbs beneath them. Relief wells up inside me like a strong tide. My eyes are still where they belong! But why is it so dark?

The world brightens, coming gradually into focus. Black columns rising from the earth, sharp dark fingers springing up around them. Splashes of purple light illuminate a web of interlaced thick cables above me, hung with scraps of cloth fluttering in the breeze. The music of the swamp surrounds me; continuous chirping, water splashing, a low rumbling almost like a dull roar. I rub my eyes again; the pain in my arms is still there, but the tingling is going away, to be replaced with the same itchy fire consuming the rest of me.

I sit up. A breeze blows and my skin chills. I'm naked! I run my hands over my hot itchy hide—it feels like coarse leather, slick with slime. I clench my fingers so my nails dig in and little pustules pop, intensifying the wetness. My head spins and acid rises from my stomach into my throat; I turn my head to the side so I don't throw up on myself, saturating the earth instead.

In the woods, sitting on muddy ground, I'm suddenly aware of another sound; a high-pitched whining, seeming to surround me, little bodies tickling my skin as they light. Mosquitoes! I'm immersed in a cloud of them and they're biting, biting, biting...

I flail my arms all around, but I can't get them off; there are way too many. I start to stand, get halfway up, then my head spins again and I fall down in the muck. Now I realize that I'm covered with it. Somewhere I read

Killers!

that mud will keep mosquitoes away; I roll around in it and rub my body with my hands to get a uniform coating. It doesn't seem to help much.

Where the fuck am I, and how did I get here? An image flashes before me—hanging from a cross in Barret's house, Vivian making love to me with her mouth. Barrett approaches with a syringe held high—he drugged me! Is that why I'm so sick? A much more disturbing image materializes—he's coming at me with a knife, to take my eyes. Vivian screams, Ye-ye bursts in, rushes Barrett and lays him low with a blow from the head bars of a brass bed. Oh God Ye-ye's blind! The motherfucker blinded him!

Ye-ye and Barrett go down in a heap and the two of them are struggling on the floor. Vivian's trying to undo the buckles that hold me, Frank is trying to stop her. Vivian turns on Frank with a flurry of blows that end with the sheriff flying across the room, slamming into the wall and collapsing in a heap. Vivian finishes releasing my bonds. I move toward Ye-ye to help him, but Vivian stops me. I try to fight her but she's too strong. She hustles me out.

A movie of us slogging through an area knee-deep in water plays in my head, it's surface coated with a mass of lime green algae. The water is pee-warm and my feet sink into black mud beneath it; the reek of sulfur rises to my face. I'm scared there's snakes. I don't want to go, but Vivian has me by the hand, pulling me forward. She makes a joke—"At least we're not leaving tracks." Ha ha.

Eventually we get out of the water. Vivian keeps pulling me forward. "Where are we going," I ask her. "Away," she says. "Away from him."

I remember no more. I must have passed out from the drugs or the trauma. I still don't know where I am, but I remember that Barret brought us to an island. Unless Vivian took me on a boat, I'm prolly still there. But where the fuck is Vivian?

My heart jumps into my throat as the sound of splashing and branches snapping drowns out the nightnoise. His roaring voice fills my soul with dread.

"Natalie! God damn you! I will find you!"

Barrett!

Chapter 40

When she awoke in the hospital earlier that evening, M.B. was unsurprised to find Nattie gone. The plan they'd agreed to was for Nattie to retrieve their stuff from Tybee Island, then get a room in Savannah to wait until M.B. and Danny were released from the hospital. She glanced at the table next to her bed and spotted her cell phone; she retrieved it and called Nattie. It rang four times and cut to voicemail. "Nattie. Call me when you get this." She hung up, then saw the icon at the bottom of the screen that indicated she had received a voicemail. She brought it up.

The speaker murmured. Was that Nattie's voice? Why so faint? M.B. played the voicemail again, holding the phone to her ear.

She could barely hear the words, "How far is Tilghman's Landing?" an unintelligible mutter followed, then, "Whatever. I hope you're planning on bringing me back here, Sheriff." Another interval during which someone else was speaking, but M.B. couldn't make out what they said. Nattie again: "So can you tell me what's happened to Ye-ye?" Bad country music filled her ear, then the voicemail cut off.

Calling Quantico, she was surprised to hear that an assault on Tilghman's Landing by the FBI's Hostage Response Team was already in the works due to a tip from an informant. However, the fact that Nattie might be there was new info. "Put the SAIC on the line," M.B. ordered.

Presently, M.B. sits in an uncomfortable metal chair in a Sikorsky UH-60 helicopter; she had to call in almost every favor anyone ever owed her to get sprung from the hospital to go along on the raid. She feels rather than hears the thrumming rotors because the headphones she's wearing close her off from the world. She's in full battle dress, including a Kelvar vest under her OCP jacket, her helmet and goggles in her lap, even though the HRT leader told her he expects her to remain a non-combatant. She hasn't been equipped with an H&K MP5 sub-machine gun like the other agents in the chopper, but she is packing her service weapon—a Glock M19.

Because of the open door, it's cool in the chopper but M.B. expects it to be stifling as soon as they land, even though it's nighttime.

Killers!

Her stomach goes out from under her like she's on a roller-coaster ride as the helo suddenly swoops towards the settlement below. As a green light on the wall flashes, two agents clip on to a line hanging in the doorway and lean backwards outside, their feet firmly braced on the doorsill. A monitor standing nearby gives them a thumbs-up and they fall backwards out of the chopper, gliding smoothly to the ground thirty feet below. Two more agents rise from their seats to follow them. M.B. sighs; since she's been strictly forbidden to exit the chopper, she hasn't been equipped with rappelling gear.

***

A nearly full moon bathes the village in sallow light. People peer out of windows, alerted to the invasion by the helicopter noise above. It's the worst possible situation for an urban assault—the agents have absolutely no idea who is a combatant and who isn't until they're fired upon. Their orders are to restrain everyone until they can sort them out, but to fire on no one except in response to an attack.

Half the agents spread out to hit the individual trailers and cottages while the other half mount a direct assault on the general store. One pulls the screen door open and pushes the wooden door inward while a second flips a flash-bang inside. Both look away and cover their ears. After the explosion, the agents thrust the door wide open and all four rush in, only to meet a fusillade of brass-jacketed lead.

Terry Atwater is crouched behind the bar peering over the sights of an AK-47. He's wearing shooter's earplugs that close off at loud explosions and, recognizing the flash bang when it bounced off the floor, he looked away and closed his eyes. Now he sprays half a mag of 7.62s at the doorway. The assaulting officers wear level III body armor, which is constructed to stop anything less than an armor-piercing round, but the impact of the heavy bullets takes two of the agents down. Atwater's gun stops chattering as the mag is spent; he ducks down to eject and reload, but an expertly trained agent jumps up onto the bar, levels his MP5 at Atwater and releases a two-round burst. The child molester's head pops like a melon. The agent shouts "Clear!".

182

Thomas A. Burns, Jr.

***

Those dreaded words crackle in M.B.'s headphones—"Agent down!". The chopper settles on the packed earth in front of the general store, where four agents mill around in front of it like ants from a hill that's been kicked. M.B. briefly recalls the SAICs orders and thinks, *Screw that!*, before undoing her harness and tumbling out of the chopper, Glock in hand. The general store's windows shatter as rounds from Atwater's AK buzz through the air and she dives into the dirt, slithering like a snake the rest of the way to the front door.

She hears "Clear!" from inside and enters the room. Two agents crouch over a third who is prostrate on the floor–it's the squad leader, who took two 7.62s to the chest. They did not penetrate her vest, but the impact did effectively put her out of action for the duration. M.B. realizes with a start that she is now the ranking agent.

The agents rapidly clear the rest of the general store easily, since it's unoccupied. Her question, "No sign of Natalie McMasters?" is answered by shaking heads.

"Find her!" M.B. orders.

After about ten minutes, the HRT agents have the entire population of Tilghman's Landing—twenty-three souls—lined up in the parking area in front of the general store. Most are poor Gullah folk, scared out of their minds, as any sane person would be when guarded by masked people in battle dress holding automatic weapons.

M.B. spots a white face in the crowd and her brow wrinkles. "Hook up the white guy and bring him in here," she says to one of the agents. "And watch him very carefully." She turns and goes into the general store.

By the time the agent enters with his charge, M.B. is sitting at a table in the dining area, with an empty chair across from her. The agent marches him up. M.B. looks at the prisoner, recognizes him, and says, "Hello, Lester. Have a seat."

Lester Wollenz's turns pale on hearing his name. The woman who addressed him reminds him of his grandmother, whom he dispatched with a carving knife many years ago.

Killers!

"I'll make this short, Lester," M.B. says. "A young, blonde woman showed up here a few hours ago. Her name is Natalie McMasters. You are going to tell me what happened to her."

Lester summons his courage and replies, "Why should I help you? What's in it for me?"

M.B. looks at the agent standing at Lester Wollenz's side. "Agent Evers. Please wait outside."

"Yes ma'am." Evers crosses the room and disappears.

M.B. takes her Glock from her holster and lays it on the table, her finger on the trigger. She stares into Lester Wollenz's rheumy brown eyes with her pale blue ones. "If you tell me what I want to know, I won't blow your pervert ass away right now. Do you believe me, Lester?"

Lester looks into her eyes and sees death. He swallows, then nods.

"Larry took her into the swamp," he says. "On his boat."

"Where in the swamp?"

"To an island out there. I don't know where it is. I ain't never been."

M.B. picks up the Glock and trains it on the center of Lester's chest. A bright red beam leaps from the muzzle, and she makes little circles over his heart with it.

"I swear! I heard him talk about the place, but I ain't never been there!"

The sharp smell of urine convinces M.B. he's telling the truth.

Chapter 41

A **full moon shines through cottony clouds. I dive into the brush,** behind a large tree. I'm kneeling in bloodwarm water, my hands on the tree, when black ants covering the trunk swarm on to my arms. My mouth opens to scream but I stop myself—if he hears me, I'm dead. I hunker down as Barrett breaks into the clearing. Wearing only a pair of ragged cut-offs, the muscles on his torso and his legs shine in the moonlight. It's just my imagination that his feral eyes glow red—right?

He brandishes a large knife with a curved blade at the sky.

"Natalie!" he roars again. "Vivian! God damn you, I'm going to chop the two of you into dog food when I find you!"

I lower myself as close to the water as I can, peering at him through the grass so the whiteness of my face doesn't give me away. My bowels cramp as he turns and stares right at me. OMG, he sees me!

But he doesn't. Maybe it's the mud I smeared on. He turns away, tearing into the underbrush again. "I'm going to fucking find you," he grates, all traces of the Southern gentleman gone.

I have got to get the holy fuck out of here! But where is here? As far as I know, Vivian didn't get me off the island. And Barrett hasn't found her yet—he wouldn't be cursing her name if he had. Think, Nattie, think!

OK, I'm on an island. Water on all sides. If I keep going in the same direction, I'll find the shoreline.

Then what? I'm a good swimmer, but I remember those fucking gators. I know there's a boat at the house, but I have no idea where it is.

I suddenly notice the ants on my arms and shoulders, crawling all over my bloody mosquito bites. I push away from the tree trunk, scoop up murky water with my hands to wash them off, trying not to think about what else might be in that stinking water that I'm rubbing into open wounds.

In the direction opposite where Barret disappeared, I spot a large tree about twenty feet away. I head for it, staying low and moving as quietly as I can. The swamp noises help drown out the sounds of my passage. Reaching my goal, I look for another landmark in the same direction. They taught me in Campfire Girls that this will stop me from going in circles.

Killers!

My name drifts to my ears in the humid air, further away this time. Thanks for letting me know where you are, asshole.

I count thirty-four trees before I see the glint of the river. I made it! But now what? Poking my head through the rushes on the riverbank, I can see the opposite shore at least a hundred yards away. The surface of the river is still and dark, but an alligator could be five feet away and I'd never know it until it seized me in its jaws and pulled me under.

I know the house is on the shore. If I circle the island, I'll find it eventually. I have no idea whether to go left or right, but does it matter? I either have the time or I don't. More troubling is what I'll do when I get there. Even if I find the boat, I have no idea how to run it, and I don't know if I can even figure it out. And if Barrett doesn't find me first, he'll turn up there again eventually.

I didn't see any guns in the house, and I can't take him down with anything less.

Turning right, I begin moving along the shoreline, when I hear a new, faint sound. A low, pulsating throb. A helicopter?

I freeze in my tracks and wait. It's getting louder, I think. Who the fuck would be here with a helicopter? Shit, does it matter? I look upward. Even this close to the riverbank, there's way too much canopy for anyone to find me, especially at night. The only place where I have any hope of being spotted is in the river. Where the gators are.

The humming is getting louder. The chopper is heading this way! A white beam cuts through the air, moving back and forth, penetrating the canopy so the tree branches look like a giant spider web, and lighting up the forest more brightly than day, but I know that I still won't be seen even if it's right over me.

"There you are, you little bitch!" I wheel and see him charging through the undergrowth, his knife held high, gleaming in the light. I don't even think—I just turn and do a racing dive into the canal.

The water feels excellent on my mosquito bites, belying the danger from the gators. I swim with strong strokes for the opposite shore—no sense trying to signal the chopper unless the spotlight's right on me. A splash behind me tells me that something big has entered. Barrett or alligator, same difference.

A white glare bathes me. They found me! I roll on my back, waving frantically at the hovering chopper, shouting, "Here, here!" even though they can't hear me. Fuck, I can't hear me!

My spider sense tingles and I look to my right. It's Barrett, five feet away, his knife clasped in his teeth like a movie pirate. He removes it with one hand, reaching for me with the other.

The surface of the water heaves and something impossibly large rises between us. Barrett's eyes widen as huge jaws gape, wrapping themselves around his torso. The gator rolls, and blood spurts from Barrett's mouth as he's pulled under. I can't hear my own scream as I wheel and begin swimming for shore. Where there's one, there's more...

Killers!

Chapter 42

I t's Thanksgiving Day and a light rain is falling outside; a wintry chill is in the air. We're all back at Hyacinth House; me, Danny, Lupe, Eduardo, Mom and Uncle Amos. Leon Kidd is with his fam, as he should be, but M.B. has joined us for the long weekend. And we all have so much to be thankful for.

Poor Danny nearly died from his wounds. By the time I returned from Tilghman's Landing, sepsis from peritonitis due to the gut shot had set in. They kept him in an induced coma on heavy antibiotics. Lupe flew down to Savannah and the two of us virtually lived at the hospital until last week, when he was pronounced well enough to come home. The doctor told me the only thing that saved him was that he was in such fine physical condition. He totally isn't now though. He lost nearly thirty pounds and is still weak as a kitten.

I was in agony for a couple of those weeks because it seemed that I had one mosquito bite on every square inch of my body (yes, I mean EVERY damn square inch!). The fuckin' things suppurated so my skin was all slimy and sticky for another week, and when they finally began to heal, they itched some more and left my hide feeling like indoor-outdoor carpet. Between that and the busted teeth I looked like something out of a Wes Craven flick.

Lupe is subdued; it seems like an underlying anger constantly simmers inside of her. She and Mom cooked the fine meal on the table today, but it seemed that her heart wasn't in it. She says she doesn't blame me for what happened because I was a victim too, but deep inside, I think she does. Eduardo is not doing well in school; he fights a lot and doesn't pay attention to his teachers. He's still living with Mom in the guest house, but I've got Gary McDougall working on getting him back in the big house with us.

Lupe won't talk about that night with Tommy Burke, but Mom has told me most of it, including that Eduardo shot and killed Burke. I suspect that's what's behind Eduardo's recent bad behavior. I wanted to get him to a shrink right away, but Lupe said no. She's afraid if anyone finds out what he's done, he'll be taken away from us again. Both Mom and me told her

188

that a doctor must keep such things confidential, but Lupe really doesn't trust many people. God knows, she has good reason not to. But Mom and me will keep working on her.

And then there are those of us who are not here.

Ye-ye's alive, no thanks to the Marquis. Barrett took his eyes the night he was captured, but kept him alive because of some insane loyalty to his *sifu*. Blind and handcuffed to a brass bed, he strained at his bonds repeatedly during his captivity, until the bed was weakened. Recognizing my voice when he heard me screaming in the next room, he broke free with one mighty heave. He had seen the lay of the place before Barrett blinded him, so he had a good idea where I was. He lost the fight with Barrett and was knocked unconscious, but the Marquis was so frantic to be after Vivian and me that he didn't bother to give Ye-ye a *coup de grace*.

We had a fight after we returned home. I told him he couldn't live at Green Lake Pavilion anymore. Naturally, he can't drive, so it would be next to impossible for him to manage his own needs so far out of town. He does seem to have an uncanny sixth sense that allows him to navigate nearly as well as many sighted people, and he's still very formidable at Tai Chi Chaun. But some things he just can't do. So with Danny's and Lupe's consent, I offered him a place with us at Hyacinth House. But then Vivian came along.

Like many other women, Vivian had fallen under Barrett's spell. By the time that Ye-ye met her, she had been initiated into his BDSM clique, but she had no idea that he was into anything but kinky sex. All she saw the night that she brought Ye-ye down with the taser was that the old man was assaulting her *sifu* and her lover. She remained unaware of Barrett's true nature until she saw Ye-ye blinded and her *sifu* coming at me with a knife— that's when she decided that she had to get us both the fuck out of there. After getting me away from the house, she went back to steal the boat so we could escape from Tilghman's Island, but she had to continually hide from Barrett and never succeeded. She was detained by the FBI along with the rest of the people of Tilghman's Landing after the raid, but they released her when me and Ye-ye vouched for her.

Feeling guilty and responsible for Ye-ye's blinding, she asked him to become her *sifu*, and offered to live with him at Green Lake Pavilion to do those things for him that he could no longer do. I have to confess that I felt more than a twinge of jealously when he told me he had accepted her offer.

Killers!

Former Sheriff Frank and Lester Wollenz are in Federal custody awaiting trial. With all the charges against them, it's unlikely they'll ever get out of prison.

The FBI never did find Barrett's body. Because of the feeding, there were so many gators around that island that it was impossible to do more than a cursory search. He never floated to the surface, so it was assumed he was in an alligator's belly. I totally hope the poor thing didn't get indigestion.

M.B. has her old job back with the Behavioral Analysis Unit in Quantico and was made SAIC of her own group as a reward for closing so many serial killer cases at once. She came to visit one weekend, and I invited her to spend Thanksgiving with us since with Chipper gone, she has no family of her own. Uncle Amos seems to have taken a shine to her; he had no prob agreeing to come today when he heard she was going to be here.

I miss Rebecca so! I finally did read her journal, which Kidd told me had a great deal to do with my rescue from Tilghman's Island. I was way shook that the last words we spoke to each other were in anger, but after reading about her experiences with the Marquis, I totally get where that anger came from. And of course, I have her to thank for this beautiful new home where me and everyone I love can live together as a family.

We've also made another new friend—Julia Sykes. She also had a rough go of it after Tommy Burke shot her, and she and Danny both ended up in the same support group for trauma victims.

Now I wonder where I'm going from here. For a good while I really thought I wanted to join Uncle Amos at 3M, but this last affair has totally given me a bellyful of crime and criminals. I'm going to finish my degree at State, but it's an open question whether I'll apply to law school or not. I won't move away from my fam and Hyacinth House, so I'll have to get accepted to a local school or I won't be going at all. And even if I did become a lawyer, I think I'd want to stick to something like real estate closings and stay far away from criminal law.

Uncle Amos speaks up. "Now, before we dig into this wonderful dinner that Judy and Lupe made, I'd like to ask Nattie to say grace for us."

When I asked Uncle to be here, I knew this might happen. And there's no way I'm going to do that. I open my mouth to tell him so, but M.B. interrupts.

"Nattie, I'd like to say grace, if you don't mind me upstaging you."

A wave of relief washes over me. "Totally. Go ahead.

"Please bow your heads." She waits for compliance. "Heavenly Father, we thank you for bringing all of us safely here today to enjoy this wonderful meal together. We ask your blessings on all of us, and especially for this loving family that hosts us here today. Please let your light shine upon them, and keep them safe and healthy in your care. Bless this food and the hands that prepared it for the nourishment of our bodies and give us your grace for the nourishment of our souls. This we ask in Jesus' name. Amen."

"Amen," I respond, along with everyone else. I don't believe in God, or if there is one, choose to worship it if it will tolerate someone like the Marquis in this world. But I can agree with her sentiment.

Uncle is looking at M.B. with a silly grin. She notices, and smiles back at him.

Maybe something's just getting started...

---The End---

Did you enjoy Killers!? Have you read the other Natalie McMasters Mysteries? If not, get your copy of the first book, Stripper! from Amazon now by visiting the link below:

https://www.amazon.com/gp/product/B07C87Y2FH?notRedirectToSDP=1&ref_=dbs_mng_calw_0&storeType=ebooks

And be sure to sign up for my email list at:

https://www.3mdetectiveagency.com/contact/

Follow me on:

Facebook:
https://www.facebook.com/groups/541595279667727

Twitter: @3Mdetective

Blog:
https://www.3mdetectiveagency.com/blog/

Instagram: 3mdetective

Goodreads:
https://www.goodreads.com/author/show/17956517.Thomas_A_Burns_Jr_

Bookbub
https://www.bookbub.com/profile/thomas-a-burns-jr

Tumblr
https://www.tumblr.com/blog/nataliemcmasters

About the Author

Thomas A. Burns Jr. writes the Natalie McMasters Mysteries from the small town of Wendell, North Carolina, where he lives with his wife and son, four cats and a Cardigan Welsh Corgi. He was born and grew up in New Jersey, attended Xavier High School in Manhattan, earned B.S degrees in Zoology and Microbiology at Michigan State University and a M.S. in Microbiology at North Carolina State University. As a kid, Tom started reading mysteries with the Hardy Boys, Ken Holt and Rick Brant, then graduated to the classic stories by authors such as A. Conan Doyle, Dorothy Sayers, John Dickson Carr, Erle Stanley Gardner and Rex Stout, to name a few. Tom has written fiction as a hobby all of his life, starting with Man from U.N.C.L.E. stories in marble-backed copybooks in grade school. He built a career as technical, science and medical writer and editor for nearly thirty years in industry and government. Now that he's a full time novelist, he's excited to publish his own mystery series, as well as to write stories about his second most favorite detective, Sherlock Holmes. His Holmes story, *The Camberwell Poisoner*, recently appeared in the March – June issue of *The Strand Magazine*. Tom has also written a Lovecraftian horror novel, *The Legacy of the Unborn*, under the pen name of Silas K. Henderson–a sequel to H.P. Lovecraft's masterpiece *At the Mountains of Madness*.

Made in the USA
Columbia, SC
01 April 2022

58287829R00121